Barsteadworth College

How Workplace Bullies Get Away With It

I0563763

Dr Stephen Riley

chipmunkapublishing
the mental health publisher

Dr Stephen Riley

Published by
Chipmunkapublishing
PO Box 6872
Brentwood
Essex CM13 1ZT
United Kingdom

http://www.chipmunkapublishing.com

Edited by Regine Pilling

Chipmunkapublishing gratefully acknowledge the support of Arts Council England.

Barsteadworth College

This novel is a work of fiction. Names and characters are products of the author's imagination. Any resemblance to actual persons is entirely coincidental.

Dr Stephen Riley

Dedicated with love to the memory of my
mum and dad, Olive and Reginald.

Dr Stephen Riley

Barsteadworth College

Author Biography

Stephen Riley, born in 1955, is an artist, lecturer and writer. He grew up in a former cotton mill town on the eastern fringes of Greater Manchester, where the conurbation meets the Pennines. He left school at 16 and worked for several years as an engineer in Manchester and Bristol, before returning to education as a mature student to study fine art. He studied in Manchester, Exeter and Canterbury before completing a doctorate at Leeds University.

Convinced of the liberating qualities of both art and education, he wanted to share his knowledge and enthusiasm with others: young people and others who, like himself, had rediscovered education as mature students. In consequence, as well as working as a practicing, exhibiting artist, he became a fine art lecturer.

He taught in colleges/university colleges in Kent, Greater Manchester and Yorkshire, before taking a post at a provincial art school in the south of England. Here he was a well respected employee and colleague, and a highly regarded Lecturer, Acting Course Director and Senior Lecturer, until the arrival of a new manager brought about a change in his fortunes. Ultimately, facing stress-related mental health problems, he had to resign his post in circumstances that he is not, for contractual reasons, allowed to disclose. However, as therapy, as support for others who have undergone/are undergoing workplace experiences similar to his, and to reveal how workplace bullies operate and are tolerated by their managers, he wrote Barsteadworth College – Workplace Bullying and How to Get Away With It.

Due to the contract that prohibits Stephen Riley from speaking about the college at which his experiences took place, the book describes the experiences of the fictional character Daniel Ripley at the fictional art school Barsteadworth College.

Stephen Riley lives in Dorset in the south of England.

Dr Stephen Riley

Barsteadworth College

Chapter One
Author's Notes

1.1

Workplace bullying is a hot contemporary topic. It crops up in conversations between friends and colleagues and not infrequently in the television, radio and print media. The television programme 'The Apprentice' highlighted, for those who have not previously seen it, not only the deviousness and spite that exists within certain individuals who make it into management positions, but also the fact that those traits can be desirable in the eyes of senior managers seeking to make appointments. However, cases where a victim of workplace bullying has taken on the system and won are few and, because of this, are big news when they happen. 'Gagging clauses' in 'compromise agreements', which bring to a close the one-sided battles that take place between bullied employees and their employers/managers, ensure that the extent of the kind of abuses described below remain hidden and that one of the routine social sicknesses of our time and the knock-on actual sicknesses that result stay largely invisible. What follows is a story about the experiences of just one individual, but the events and manoeuvres described may go some way to explaining the disparity between the apparent frequency of workplace bullying and the number of successful cases against it, which seems to be exceedingly small.

1.2

What follows is a story: an account of the exchanges between various fictional characters in fictional settings. There are those who may think that this is in fact an account of my experiences thinly disguised through changes of names and locations. They may think that; I could not possibly comment.

Chapter Two
8 Years Ago

Daniel Ripley pulled back the net curtains and looked out onto Bessemer Street, which sloped away steeply into the valley. It was teatime on May Day Bank Holiday. He gazed over the rooftops of his home town. Dashley Dyke was one of a cluster of former cotton mill towns in that damp strip of land where Manchester meets the Pennines. He looked at the familiar redbrick terraces, grey slate roofs, buckled chimney stacks and the maze of TV aerials and satellite dishes. Beyond were the soot-blackened sandstone tower of St. Peter's, the tall stainless steel chemical tanks and low corrugated warehouses of Dashley Dyke Industrial Estate and, wrapped around the lot, the grey-green mass of Whitlock's Moor. It had rained for most of the day, but had now stopped. The roofs were beginning to dry and there was even a hint of blue between the pigeon-grey clouds. The sun, breaking through here and there, picked out the red and yellow sign on the front of new Aldi store and the multi-coloured carapaces of distant cars climbing up the steep incline of Sheffield Road. Early evening with that bit of heat just making itself felt. It would be quite pleasant to sit outside with a beer or two.

"Nice now, isn't it? Fancy nipping out for one?" said Dan.

"Yes, sure. Give me a few minutes to get ready", came the reply.

Dan jogged up the narrow staircase and into the bedroom, opened the faux mahogany wardrobe door, took a short-sleeved check shirt from its hanger, yanked down his faded 501s from the top shelf and finished the job with a splash of Calvin Klein Escape. He caught himself in the mirror. Not bad for 44. The barnet was long gone, the grey bits at the back and sides being routinely shorn down to a number 1 to match – almost. And that was OK. A man who'd grown up with images of Bobby Charlton, sparse blond flag flapping behind his head every time he broke into a sprint, knew the full horror of the comb-over, and it could not be countenanced. Beneath was a pair of small, wire-rimmed glasses. John Lennon glasses. Thinking man's glasses. He was no muscle-man, but a few hours each week in the gym and a good walk on Sunday afternoons kept him in reasonable shape. Best of all, he still fitted comfortably into his size 32" Levis. How many blokes of his age could say that?

Sophie came out of the bathroom in a gorgeous, seductive haze of perfume, flowery dress, long dark hair, made-up and looking lovely. She wrapped a black woollen shawl around her shoulders. It wasn't *that* warm yet.

They strolled down the old flagstones of Bessemer Street to where it levelled out by Junkie Towers, a maze of deck-access flats, real name 'Belgravia House'. The bypass was surprisingly busy for a bank holiday. They waited for the green man and took the short cut between the bookies and Superdrug into the town centre. The Miners Arms. No. The beer garden consists of two rotted bench-table sets, and people let their dogs shit on the verge by the car park. It stinks. The Friendship. No. There are always fights in there. The Dashleigh Arms hasn't got a beer garden. Neither has the Tipperary.

They settled on the Railway Arms. There was an Astroturf strip at the side, next to the lean-to that contained the gents. A few wooden-topped, cast iron tables had been set out on the dark green plastic grass. They were of that Victorian or faux Victorian design familiar from so many British pubs: Britannia in relief at the top of each leg holding a Union Jack shield in front of her belly, painted black. Each table had two or three white plastic garden chairs scattered around it. Window boxes containing half-dead daffodils had been strategically placed to screen-off the fuzzy silhouettes in the toilets. The Liverpool-Leeds trains that thundered overhead on the massive sandstone viaduct periodically drowned-out the conversation, but there were worse problems to have and you were right next to Market Street, so you could do a bit of people watching and daydreaming as you sipped your drink and chatted.

It was six-thirty and the town was beginning to warm up. A steady stream of new arrivals joined the hardcore all-day drinkers and packed the streets. With the footpaths filled to overflowing, the whole area was now an unofficial pedestrian zone. Cars honked and picked their way through the mass: lads in T-shirts with gelled, spiky hair; girls in pelmet mini-shirts with corned-beef legs; older blokes with beer bellies and nicotine fingers; older women with peroxide hair and catalogue tops. There were angry exchanges between frustrated drivers who clicked down door locks and mimed abuse at the drunks, who in turn responded with v-signs, 'fuck off' and 'wanker'. A beer can hit the windscreen of a silver Mondeo, spraying thick, beige foam over the car and passers-by. The wipers flicked to and fro, spreading the sticky liquid over the glass. The engine revved loudly as the car forced its way through the crowd with greater urgency to the sound of half-hearted jeering.

Market Street was now a zombie flick. The undead bellowed and screeched their way from pub to pub, sucking the life out of successive pints of psycho-strength lager. The atmosphere was mostly just boisterous, but now and then things broke down and, for no discernable reason other than the circumstances seemed to demand it, there was a punch-up. The police in their podgy stab vests watched from the edges and allowed the combatants to finish their business before wading in and dragging off the dazed, defeated ones to the armoured vans.

Dan was Dashley Dyke born and bred, and he had not been an infrequent visitor in the years he'd spent working in London, so the scene being played out before him was nothing that he had not witnessed a hundred times before. It was little different from any ordinary Saturday night, except that the Bank Holiday and the first bit of decent weather for ages had increased the numbers somewhat. Sophie, on the other hand, had only moved to Dashley Dyke when they got married six months earlier. Dan watched her usual serene expression fall away as the debacle unfolded before her.

*****

On Thursday the Dashley Dyke Gazette arrived. Dan leant against the marble-effect kitchen worktop and flicked through, absentmindedly. *Sick thugs burn pet rabbits alive. Hospital has worst mortality rate in UK – it's official. Man stabbed outside nightclub fights for life.* And then a face he recognised – or rather, he recognised some of it. *Man needs thirty-five stitches after unprovoked bottle attack.* That's Ryan Flint. *Poor little Ryan. Poor little* slow *Ryan. He'd never hurt anybody.*

*****

On the following Monday morning, Sophie left the house shortly before Dan. Within seconds she was back at the door, eyes filled with tears. She had gone to put her key in the car door, only to find a hole where the lock should be. Dan yanked open the door of the blue Peugeot hatchback. The contents of the glove box were strewed over the seats, the dashboard had been disembowelled and the radio was gone. More wires hung down below the steering column. Evidently they'd tried to hotwire it and failed. Interrupted by people walking back from the pub, probably.

Dan knocked at neighbours' doors to see if anybody had seen anything. It had presumably happened overnight. Colin, the Hell's Angel, said he'd seen nothing, but he'd had similar things happen to him in the past. The seat had been nicked off his Yamaha, right from under his fucking front room window. If he caught them he'd fucking kill them. Lee, on the other side, wouldn't come to the door. He'd been weird ever since his mum and auntie were murdered in what the Gazette had called a 'frenzied knife attack' in their flat in Ashton-under-Lyne.

Since moving back to Dashley Dyke two years earlier, Dan had devoted quite some time and energy to trying to persuade himself that it was not a mistake. But it was. The romantic vision of his old home town that his imagination had gradually constructed for him in his time away – a kind of misty Lowry-land with solid working-class values and brass tacks wisdom – was a fantasy. As for Sophie, her home turf in leafy Didsbury might only have been a 20-odd minute drive away, now the new motorway was open, but it was a different world. She had never been cut out for Dashley Dyke life. Dan *had* been, once – a long time ago – but wasn't any longer. They had reached the tipping point.

*****

On Saturday afternoon they sat down purposefully at the round white kitchen table to make plans. A mug of tea each and some chocolate digestives would aid the process. Dan was a PhD student at the University of Leeds. He also did bits of ad hoc fine art lecturing there. This didn't bring in very much money, and it was his wife's pay that kept them going. They agreed that Sophie would look for another job, elsewhere, and Dan would come to some sort of arrangement with the University. Sophie's job as a Project Manager carrying out short/medium-term contracts for the Health Service meant that she could be offered work anywhere in the country. Previously, there had been no reason to seek contracts outside of the North West, but now this arrangement presented the opportunities they needed. And since both of Sophie's daughters now worked in London, and Dan's first marriage had ended in his twenties without kids, when it came down to it there was no reason other than habit to be where they were.

*****

It was June, and Sophie had an interview for a 12-month contract as a Logistics and Procurement Manager at Basingstoke General Hospital. Dan drove the freshly repaired Peugeot whilst she prepared her presentation. The interview went pretty well, and afterwards they took the opportunity to explore. Basingstoke wasn't a place they knew much about beyond some vague awareness that it was one of those 'new towns', like Swindon or Milton Keynes. And so it was: all identical roundabouts and verges with fragments of suburb screened from the road by poplars, leylandii and manmade embankments, as though they had some kind of guilty secret.

No visible landmarks and confusing as hell to an outsider. On the other hand, it was in the middle of Hampshire and surrounded by some of the most beautiful villages Dan had ever seen. It looked like a very good place to start their new life.

*****

The postman delivered the good news and Sophie handed in her notice. Dan worked out a deal with his PhD supervisor. With his project so close to its write-up period they agreed that he could do the remaining work at home. His teaching commitments would be altered to fit into one day or two consecutive days each week, and the termly supervisory meetings fitted in around the teaching.

In September, Dan and Sophie moved into a former tied cottage; one of just five on Pigeon Farm, halfway between Andover and Basingstoke. Ivy grew up the walls and a soft coating of warm green moss covered the tiled roof. There was a small duck pond at the end of the row, and just past the garden fence a dense green forest began. They got regular visits from pheasants and grouse, and rarer ones from foxes and roe deer. Alice, the cat, struck up a brittle friendship with Wesley, next door, and the two set about clearing the area of mice and shrews, periodically bringing in tragic little samples of their handiwork to show their humans. Neighbours grew fruit and vegetables in their gardens, and when a new batch of jam or pickle was made, everyone in the row got a jar.

Dan lay on his new red and yellow Argos sun lounger in the warm afternoon sun. It was late September, but everything was still a lush, enthusiastic green. A light breeze lazily moved the leaves in the forest and the birds sang. Sophie dozed under her half-read John Grisham paperback. Dan glanced at his chilled Becks. *This place was always here. We could have lived out our lives in Dashley Dyke and never seen it.*

Chapter Three
7 Years Ago

On a January Tuesday, at about seven in the morning, the engine in Dan's 13 year-old Vauxhall Cavalier stopped. He was on the A34 northbound near Newbury and until that moment had been travelling at about 70 miles an hour. Rain hammered down onto the winding dual carriageway like stair rods from heaven, and the rush-hour traffic blasted by at full-tilt. He climbed out of the lifeless Vauxhall into a terrifying confusion of high-speed engine roars, screaming airbrakes, honking horns, flashing headlights and blinding spray, and somehow managed to push the enormous weight onto the verge. He skidded and clambered down the embankment, picked his way through a muddy field and found a lane. Ten minutes later, saturated, he reached a village and amidst all the wet green and grey saw the comforting red glow of a call box. It was the third such incident in as many months.

He trudged back through the sodden field to wait for the AA. Even if he could sustain the weekly 600-mile Leeds trip indefinitely, and that was by no means certain, his car could not. And he could not afford to replace it. The teaching at Leeds had to go. Buying a mobile phone might be a good idea, as well.

*****

Dan plundered the internet for details of art schools closer to home. Every fine art department within fifty miles of Pigeon Farm received a Daniel Ripley CV and covering letter. A week later he got a call from Frank Fuller, Director of the School of Art at Barsteadworth Academy of the Arts; 'Barts' to its friends. Dan's letter had been timely. They needed some additional visiting lecturing on the Arts Foundation Diploma. They also ran degrees. Would he like to pop down for an informal interview?

Barsteadworth was an hour away, traffic permitting. Certainly doable for someone who needed a job. Dan knew of

Barsteadworth College

Barsteadworth but had never been there. It was a reasonably sized southern town without a reputation for anything much more than being a reasonably sized southern town.

Dan backed the Vauxhall carefully into one of the few remaining parking spaces. A neat, well-spoken receptionist offered him a seat and paged Frank Fuller. A few minutes later Frank arrived, wearing a black suit and proffering a handshake. Dan guessed his age at about mid-50s. He was perhaps a fraction over both average height and weight, with a bit of a gut, though nothing exceptional for a man of his age. His face carried a little suntan and did not look like it was stranger to smiling. On top, his black hair had thinned almost to nothing and when he put on his close-work glasses, which he did at regular intervals, he bore at least a passing resemblance to Sergeant Bilko.

Frank showed Dan round the place. Quite a pleasant little college, really. 1980s post-modern architecture. Mostly single or two-storey with pitched roofs and big overhangs, like a series of interconnected pagodas, with cheerful red gutters and little Japanese-style quadrangles that contained bamboo, white stones and the occasional bench.

Dan had not known until his internet search that Barsteadworth even had an art school, let alone one that was able to offer degree-level study. And in fact, as Frank explained, it had until recently only been a local further education and adult evening class kind of place. The original Barts had been there a hundred years. The new building was put up in its place in 1986 – a foundation stone carrying the vaguely familiar name of the Education Minister of the day testified to that – but little else changed. Barts had plodded on with the same old low to mid-level courses. That was until the late-1990s, when the old Principal retired and a new one took his place: Silas Beasley. Silas was a whirlwind. He had massive ambitions for the place and the energy to match. He blasted through the dusty, complacent corridors of the old Barts and remade it on his own terms. By the end of the millennium the more well-regarded HNDs – most prominently Animation, Photography and Graphic Design – had been successfully upgraded to bachelor degree level, and in September last year a BA in Fine Art had been launched. Fine Art – Dan's subject.

The following day Dan got a call from Frank Fuller. He was delighted to offer Dan a day a week teaching on the Foundation Diploma.

*****

During the summer, a new full-time lectureship was advertised for the BA Fine Art course. Dan was interviewed in July and got it.

*****

Dan started his new job on 1st September; a few weeks before the students returned. Ronnie Foulkes, whom Dan had already met at the interview, was the Course Director. Dan waited in the vinyl-floored studio whilst Ronnie brought in two coffees in white plastic cups in those brown frame-and-handle contraptions that stop you burning your fingers. Ronnie handed one to Dan and opened the red plywood door into the windowless storeroom that doubled as the office. Shoving heavy rolls of paper and unopened cardboard boxes to one side, they extricated two chairs: Ronnie's venerable beige hessian one, which looked like a 1970s throwback, and a neat blue secretary chair for Dan. They chatted a bit about their backgrounds. Ronnie was 53, and had worked for many years on the Foundation Diploma. He cycled in every day to keep fit and save the planet, and he was careful about what he ate. Low cholesterol and all that. He seemed in decent shape: broad, medium build and height, with still a reasonable amount of salt and pepper hair. He looked a bit tired, though, especially considering the academic year hadn't yet started.

Ronnie explained the set-up. There were two other people teaching on the course: Barry Vicar and Mervin Botwinch, who shared a half-time lecturer's hours. Ronnie, who was full-time, ran the course and did most of the teaching. The other two were about the same age as Ronnie, and all three been dragged kicking and screaming to work on the BA from the Foundation Diploma, where they had been teaching happily for decades. Mervin had been Course Director of the BA for the first few months, but had then refused to carry on, on the grounds that he was suffering from stress and insomnia. Barry then refused the job point blank because of the damage it had done to Mervin. Finally, Ronnie – clearly too nice a guy and too loyal an employee to refuse – was lumbered with it.

Later in the day, Dan met Barry and Mervin. Justifying it partly by their minimal teaching hours – effectively one day a week each – Barry and Mervin made it clear that they were working on the BA in as distanced a way as possible. They would do their teaching and nothing else. Planning, administration, the whole running of a degree course was something they had no experience of, no training for and did not want to get drawn into. And, given that they still had teaching commitments back on the Foundation Diploma and the GNVQ, there was always a reason to be elsewhere, if required. Barry went on to give Dan a bit of advice on how to survive at Barts. Adopt his approach: keep a low profile, do only what you need to do, they will think no more of you if you bust a gut. If you want to kill yourself working for this place, they will be only too pleased to let you.

There was notionally another member of staff too: Terry Mortice, the technician. Ronnie took Dan over to the workshop to meet him. Terry broke off from the set of shelves he was making and shook hands. He looked late-30s, maybe early 40s; slim, wiry build and sun-tanned, outdoor face. Like the others, Terry had worked at Barts for most of his adult life. After a brief exchange of niceties, Ronnie and Dan left the building. Ronnie described Terry's working method: because he worked in so many departments – at least 3, as far as Ronnie knew – Terry's attendance in the Fine Art department did not seem to be for any fixed amount of time, and when it would happen could not be predicted.

With Dan still listening intently to Ronnie's briefing, the two made their way back over to the main building, skirting the edge of the packed car park. A large area had been cordoned off with high mesh fencing. Building materials – bricks, timber, pre-formed concrete shapes and double-glazed panels – were stacked inside. The occasional white safety helmet could be glimpsed momentarily above and between the various obstacles. A big yellow JCB digger scratched away noisily at the embankment, whilst a man in a check shirt and hi-vis slipover mouthed inaudible instructions to the driver.

"The new Genesis Centre", explained Ronnie. "One of Beasley's pet projects. All EC money. It'll be for new graduates. They'll be able to apply for subsidised workspaces for a year, to get them started. I think it means we're going places".

*****

During Dan's second week a morale-boosting staff meeting was to take place in the Conference Centre. He arrived in the large, low room to see the caretakers setting out the last few trendy, retro-style, Christine Keeler chairs. A few early arrivals had taken their places amongst the long, curved rows. Paintings from the Arts Council's Loan Scheme adorned the white-emulsioned breeze-block walls: a green and orange stripy one by Tim Head and another, anonymous one, with a blob of Blu-Tac where the label should have been. At the front were an overhead projector, a pull-down screen, a plain institutional table with chrome legs and smooth white top, and hanging from the ceiling, a smart new digital projector. Two technicians fiddled with a laptop, connected it to a flap they had opened in the floor and pointed a remote at the digital projector. Dan sat next to a woman with long, black crimped hair and large, over-engineered glasses. She was looking at the front and smiling. Dan couldn't work out what was amusing her. Some technicians were wiring up audio-visual equipment; that was it. She broke off momentarily and turned towards Dan. The lenses were huge and her eyes were tiny, like two dots in two freshly switched-off old-style telly screens. She acknowledged Dan with a nod and a smile and then turned back, still smiling, towards the technicians. As the room filled an older guy with a mop of grey hair and a beige acrylic v-neck with a geometric pattern on the front took the seat on Dan's other side. He smiled too.

"New, then?" said the man.

"Yes. My second week. And yourself?" replied Dan.

"Oh, me. I'm a lifer". The man grinned at his own well-honed joke.

With the room now packed, a thin, dark-haired man with angular features, sunken cheeks and a wispy black beard appeared at the front and started proceedings.

"James Ledlock. Vice Principal. Beasley's fixer" confided the man in the v-neck.

James Ledlock welcomed the audience back from their summer recess and made a couple of dry, witty remarks about workload, stress and such, and got the odd guffaw and wise crack in return. He then introduced Silas Beasley.

The Principal's 90-minute briefing necessarily included topics and terms of reference that Dan as yet knew nothing about... and lots of acronyms. Silas was delighted to report that the Academy was now a member not only of 'Colleges and Universities South Industrial Design Directorate', but also of the 'Southern Arts Group'. CUSIDD and SAG. Brilliant. Dan drifted periodically. The scores of perspiring, exhaling bodies in the low-ceilinged room didn't help. This Silas guy was impressive, though. He was small – probably no more than 5' 4" – but you would bet that no one had ever bothered to mention that to him. He had the natural authority of a man who expected to be at the top and to be obeyed; someone conditioned from the start to be a member of the officer class. And to give the guy his due, what he had achieved at Barts in just a few years was pretty special. On the other hand, he bore a troubling resemblance to Donald Pleasence in his most brooding Ernst Blofeld mode. In a moment of mental abstraction, brought on by a withering volley of mysterious acronyms and impenetrable statistics, Dan pictured Silas suddenly losing control, tossing an alarmed white cat to the floor and screaming 'kill Bond!'.

At break time relieved staff got off their rock-hard chairs, drew coffees from the stainless steel urn and fought politely for the chocolate digestives. The tobacco-addicted went outside for a smoke. Dan, the new boy, was introduced to Silas Beasley by Frank Fuller. There was an exchange of platitudes and Silas smiled with just the bottom third of his face. The meeting then resumed.

One thing that Silas said that did stick with Dan was that the Academy *punched above its weight*. It was meant to be both congratulatory and challenging. But Dan also found something ominous in it. Everyone knows what can happen to the protagonist-pugilist when this term is applied in its non-metaphorical sense.

*****

Back in the claustrophobic storeroom/office, Dan got down to work with his new boss. Ronnie explained more about Barts and the course set-up. It had been devised by James Ledlock, whose specialist area was mathematics, and Frank Fuller, who had graduated with a Fine Art Degree 35 years ago. Ronnie took down a copy of the comb-bound blue course handbook from the bookshelf and took Dan through it. It was no more than a framework without content. The course layout was like none Dan had ever seen before, and each of the modules comprised little more than a title, some aims and objectives and its allocated study time. There were lots of them too. Ledlock and Fuller went to conferences and they knew that the current thing with degrees was that they had to have had lots of modules. What they were stuck on, however, was what to put in them. That task had fallen to Ronnie who was writing the content as he went along, but he was no better placed to fill in the gaps than the other two.

Ronnie showed Dan the first year programme that they were about to launch: the same one that Ronnie had been obliged to operate last year. It was hopeless: the layout had anything up to four modules running at any given time, some of which were virtually identical. How should the art work produced for 'Seeing and Interpreting' (75 hours), differ from 'Recording and Development' (75 hours)? And because the modules all ran at the same time, they all reached assessment point at the same time. The students had been confused, as had Ronnie and the other lecturers, and neither group had been able to cope with the workload at assessment time. Ronnie had tried to get this changed. But it could not be changed. The Academy's embryonic degrees were validated by Waterhead University and, within the agreement, changes could only be considered once a year: in the summer. But even that tiresome procedure could not be used yet because the degree was new and it would be embarrassing for Barts' managers to ask for such fundamental changes so soon. It might look like they didn't know what they were doing. So here they were: Dan and Ronnie were about to deliver to the second cohort a programme that had already proved itself all but unworkable when delivered to the first.

Ronnie went on to describe the Academy's curious, cost-saving method of teaching cultural and historical studies. Students on all of the higher education courses would all attend the same programme of lectures: the Core Theory Programme. Thus, Fine Art students might find out about the revolutionising effects of injection-moulding on dashboard design, students of 3-Dimensional Design could become authorities on Renaissance painting, and Graphic Design students, if pressed, could probably speak with some conviction on the bronze casting techniques associated with Henry Moore's sculptures.

The student intake when the course started hadn't been the greatest, either. Course validation had come late in the year, few people knew of Barsteadworth Academy of the Arts, at all, and still less knew that it had started to run a BA in Fine Art. There hadn't been a lot of choice at recruitment time, explained Ronnie.

As Ronnie described the numerous problems he'd encountered, his tone was wistful rather than whingeing. He didn't blame anybody. He just saw these as issues that needed to be addressed as the course developed. However, things had already been like this for a year and change seemed unlikely, and from the sound of it some of the students had been close to rioting.

The two men weighed up the studio, wondering how they could fit thirty-odd additional students into it in a few weeks' time. It was a low-ceilinged, L-shaped space with rows of blue plastic tables and chairs set out neatly on its spotless, grey vinyl floor (which Silas Beasley had insisted must not be soiled). Red window frames provided views of the car park on two sides and the Japanese-style courtyard on the other. The red door in the plain white wall at the far end led, via the print room, into the main building. The one near Ronnie's 'store-cum-office' opened out onto the courtyard, giving handy access to the refectory and workshop. The fine art studios Dan was used to were large, messy, factory-like spaces, which encouraged students to explore paint, clay, wood, dead animals, anything... without inhibition. This looked like a graphic design office or a school room set ready for exams. At one side was a huge pile of pristine painting easels, which had hardly ever been used because the room was already jam-packed with desks. In the store were sugar paper, pencils, coloured tissue and large tubs of cheap acrylic paint: school art materials.

*****

October. The new first years, excited and noisy, had settled down happily to their first projects. The second years, surly and hacked-off after a year of dubious education, were a very different proposition. On their first day back Dan was introduced to them, before heading back to work with the first years. It was a couple of weeks later that he had his first proper encounter with the second years. On Monday mornings Ronnie would hold a meeting with them. This had been his way of dealing with their many grievances and keeping them informed on how things were developing. Three weeks into term Ronnie took Dan along to his first such first meeting.

Barsteadworth College

These events took place in the seminar *area*. There was no seminar *room*. A section of studio space had been cordoned off by Terry Mortice with 8' x 4' white-painted MDF boards, held together with metal clips and Allen screws which left 2" gaps in between. The whole structure was zigzagged so as to be precariously self-supporting. Noise spilling over from the still-chirpy first years on the other side seemed likely to disrupt the meeting. Dan and Ronnie took seats at the front, facing the class. The body language wasn't promising. The group – about thirty mostly mature students, mostly women – sat in silence; pouty faces, folded arms, legs stuck out rigidly under fold-down writing boards. They laid into Ronnie from the start. This seemed to be the point of the meeting. There were endless complaints. Some fair, some unfair, some absurd. The tirade was rude and at some times personal. The students clearly had no respect for Ronnie. They told him in no uncertain terms that he wasn't up to the job. The noise level on this side of the boards had now drowned out the first years, who had either shut up to listen in, or got fed up of it and gone elsewhere. Ronnie sat and took it all – made no attempt to defend himself. Dan was amazed and appalled at the spectacle. Ronnie seemed to have been reduced to the status of emotional punch bag.

*****

A week later Dan went to the Monday meeting once again. It was the same. Ronnie had taken the students' issues to Fuller and Ledlock and been sent back with the message that he was Course Director and it was for him to things sort out. But of course he couldn't, because these were things that were beyond his control and authority. He couldn't get proper fine art studios. He wouldn't make the existing ones bigger. He couldn't change the course structure. He couldn't change the Core Theory Programme. He couldn't get a proper full-time technician. And so on. He told the students this, and the show kicked off again. This had, apparently, happened to more or less the same pattern every Monday since the course began.

The next day Dan wandered nonchalantly into the second years' studio space to sound them out in an informal way. And certainly they wanted to speak to him. The key spokespersons were a tall, extremely thin local woman called Glynys Kerley, the year-group's official student representative, and a bespectacled Belgian woman called Collette Fondue, who never smiled. There were then several seconds-in-command, including Alice Furtle and Myra Biggs. They confided in him. They spoke as if Ronnie was an oaf and as though Dan would agree with them on that. *How dare they. This guy is busting a gut for them. Do they not see that he's stuck in the middle of something he never asked for and can't change? I guess they can't. They're all wrapped up in their own miseries.* Dan kept quiet and listened. They had little or nothing to say about their own work or art in general. Life seemed to revolve around preparing for the Monday morning meetings. They set up sub-meetings, prepared long lists of painstakingly considered and embellished complaints, they delegated tasks to each other, typed up lists, got things photocopied and held meetings with other people. They ran ideas past each other, decided who was going to say what, rehearsed and got themselves ever more wound-up in the process. Although there were most definitely issues that need to be addressed, there was still an education to be had for those who were interested in it, but complaining had become the core activity and an easy displacement. Studying and making art seemed to have been largely sidelined. Interestingly, the younger ones kept out of it. Rosalind Harris, Bart Doggitt and Tracey Bunn were producing some interesting stuff, and there were two sullen skateboard lads with fashionably ill-fitting trousers, who were less pissed-off with the degree's structural problems than they were with that bunch of moaning middle-aged women who seemed to think they ran the bloody place and never let anything drop.

*****

A couple of months into term. Dan and Ronnie took seats in the refectory. It was even newer than the main building and it looked pretty good, but it had been cheaply constructed and everything in it was hard: tiled floors, aluminium chairs and tables, two glass walls and two hard white plaster ones, dotted with clip-framed student etchings and photographs. There was nothing to absorb the lunchtime chatter, the clatter of cutlery and the relentless dragging and pushing of chairs. Everyone trying to make themselves heard over the din only upped the ante. The two men joined in with the cacophony and held a semi-shouted conversation as they extricated pre-packed sandwiches from moulded triangular casings and sipped coffee from cardboard beakers.

Dan wanted to tackle the issue of those Monday meetings. What was happening to Ronnie just wasn't fair, and the meetings were in any case totally unproductive. But Ronnie wouldn't have it. He didn't mind and it was a good way of letting the students blow themselves down. Besides, he had other problems. That Barts was only just emerging from further education level and had little understanding of how degrees were structured was obvious, but as Ronnie explained, there was another issue which on a practical, day-to-day basis was even more serious, as far as he was concerned. Barts didn't have the funding that established degree teaching institutions had, so a lecturer teaching on a degree here would be expected to teach roughly double the number of hours that a university lecturer would, leaving just a few hours per week for all the other work: researching and writing new teaching, pastoral duties, attending meetings, report-writing, updating records, planning study visits, ordering materials, taking part in committees and so on. Dan had noticed that he had a much larger teaching load than he'd had at Leeds, but had just seen it as a temporary thing – getting the new course going, getting the new first years started. But it wasn't. It was always like this. In fact it was worse. Ronnie was protecting him from a lot of things because there was too much to take on all at once. In addition, although the notion of real academic research of a kind that would be recognised in a university, had yet to arrive at Barts, it was expected that each individual would be an active researcher or practitioner within their own subject area and would periodically produce something, though no time was allowed for this. There was the 'Research Forum', at which a tiny number of die-hard lecturers would periodically give talks about their work, like enthusiastic hobbyists sharing their private passions with the like-minded. Course Directors, like Ronnie, were allowed an extra hour per week of admin time to cover the additional duties that came with course management. In many higher education establishments the running of the course is considered a full-time job in its own right and the Course Director does little or no teaching. Ronnie got an hour a week to do what others got a whole week to do.

Dan looked at Ronnie. There were dark rings under his eyes and he drooped at the shoulders. He seemed to have a kind of haunted look. His pre-term freshness, such as it was, had gone.

Dan told Ronnie that he would do all he could to take some of the burden from him. He had brought a lot of exciting new teaching from Leeds, and the few sessions he had done with the second years seemed to have lightened their mood. On the other hand, Dan was new to Barts and its procedures, and he was aware that Ronnie was devoting a substantial amount of time to mentoring him. For the time being, this probably cancelled out any respite his teaching input provided.

The Christmas holiday came as a relief to both men.

*****

When the phone rang on the morning of New Year's Eve, Dan expected it to be a member of his or Sophie's family, ringing for a chat or to say 'Happy New Year'. So he was quite shocked to hear Frank Fuller's voice. Ronnie had collapsed and was in hospital. All Frank knew was that Ronnie was seriously ill and would be off for some time. The immediate problem was that the course needed a stand-in leader, and in spite of the fact that he had been at Barts for a few months and didn't even know his way around the building properly, Dan was natural choice for the job... on account of the fact that he was the only choice.

Chapter Four
6 Years Ago

As term started in January, the students on the BA Fine Art degree at Barsteadworth Academy of the Arts found themselves with a new Acting Course Director.

Dan held a meeting with the students and told them what had happened. He then got them started with their new post-Christmas projects, grabbed a coffee and assessed his new circumstances: Ronnie's office – now *his* office, for the time being. He was surrounded by art materials, overhead projectors, plan chests and Ronnie's state-of-the-Ark desk and computer. The room was a 12 feet by 6 feet fibreboard box, with studios on three sides and the Students' Union office on the fourth. It had no outside walls and therefore no windows, just an extractor fan which, when it was on, blew the smell of Dan's sandwiches into one part of the studio and sucked in oil paint fumes round the door from another, but in any case in that confined space was too noisy to use except in the most desperately skanky of circumstances.

*****

Dan asked Glynys Kerley into the office. He told her that the Monday meetings were now finished. Instead there would be 'surgeries' in his office at fixed times each week, to which students as individuals, or in small groups, could bring their problems. Glynys acquiesced without comment. Dan put up a notice next to a list of dates and times. He then asked Frank Fuller for a meeting to discuss the changes he would like to make to the course.

Frank's was a lovely office. Situated on the first floor, it had windows all down one side overlooking a planted area and was the size of a mini conference centre. A funky black and chrome computer with an ergonomic keyboard was perched on a curved, light wood desk that fitted into and around a corner. There was a large rectangular table finished in the same light veneer as the desk, surrounded by a dozen or so generously padded chairs. Brightly coloured abstract paintings and flyers from exhibitions adorned the white-painted walls and in the far corner was a well-stocked bookshelf. It contained mostly course documents, handbooks and regulations, but also a few large, richly illustrated art books. Dan set out his vision for amending the course's unworkable structure. There would never be more than two modules running at any one time; one that set out the studio work and another that set out the written work: clarity of structure, so that the students could declutter their minds and let their creativity run free. Frank re-explained the once-a-year rule, but after a short time they both agreed that it would be as well to start canvassing straight away in order to get things onto agendas. It was also clear to Dan that his appointment as Acting Course Director would be used to create a face-saving loophole for Barts' management. Everything could be blamed on Ronnie. This new guy has been able to see through the mess he was making of things.

*****

Dan arrived at work at 7.30am. This was now routine. There was huge workload and this was the only way to deal with it. He could get 2 hours of paperwork done before he started teaching. On some days there would be gaps in the teaching and he could nip back into the office to write reports, update student evaluation records, order materials... Now and then he would have a whole half-day with no teaching and could really get stuck into things. Today was such a day. He lifted the pile from the in tray and started to work out priorities. This is overdue. This is overdue. This is due by tomorrow. I'm a member of *what* committee?

Glynys Kerley was first student to arrive. She usually was. At 8.15 she knocked on the office door. She wanted a tube of cadmium red oil paint from the store. Dan gave it to her and logged it in the book. He went back to his paperwork. Where was he? Two minutes later she was back. Come to think of it, she might as well have a tube of titanium white whilst she was at it. She used loads of that. And some stand oil. A short time later there was another knock: Ben Pogson. Could he have

30

some canvas? Two metres ought to do it. And would Dan come and show him how to stretch it. There had been a canvas-stretching workshop, but he'd missed it because his dog had died. Dan cut the canvas and logged it in the book. Where was the canvas stapler? They'd need the canvas stapler. As he was about to leave with Ben, Vikki Membrane arrived. She shoved a grubby piece of paper towards him. Could she just have this list of stuff before he went and helped Ben? He'd be at least half an hour doing that, and she would be stuck and wouldn't be able to get started. Ben huffed. Dan went back into the store and started to work through Vikki's list. Pliers, soldering iron, extension lead, rubber gloves... A first year, whose name eluded Dan, stood in the doorway in hooped pink and back tights and black Doctor Marten's boots. She wanted to know what they were doing today. She'd missed the module intro yesterday because there'd been a party the night before and she couldn't get her shit together to come into college. Wasn't Barry Vicar supposed to be looking after them today? Asked Dan. She thought he probably was, but she hadn't seen him and no one knew where he was. Dan told her to check out the workshop. Barry might be in there... or the Foundation studio. If she couldn't find him, she should come back and he'd deal with it later. He could do nothing for her right now.

He had all this other stuff going on. The phone went. Shirley from Academy Statistical Services. Where were the figures for that last round of assessments? He had no idea. He said he'd get onto it right away. Ben paced about impatiently behind Vikki. Three more first years hovered behind Ben, looking for an opportunity to pounce. They muttered indistinctly when hooped tights girl sulked off in the direction of the refectory, kicking the door open, partly to demonstrate her anger, partly because both hands were in use assembling a roll-up. They muttered even more when a second year, Judi Baynes, barged to the front to pass on the message that Irene Klaxon wouldn't be in today because her son was ill. Wasn't there a form to fill in? Could Dan give her a copy? She'd drop it in with Irene on her way home tonight. Dan took down the fat blue ring-binder that contained all of the standard forms. He unclipped the permission-to-be-off-because-your-son's-ill form and gave it to Judi. Thing was, it was his only copy – would she get it photocopied and bring him the original back. She said she would, but she wasn't going to use *her* copy card. It cost ten pee a copy with that, and she was a mature student with responsibilities and couldn't afford to be paying the Academy's administration costs on top of her own, not with her massive debts. No. He'd have to give her the departmental code so she could use the staff photocopier in reception. She was doing him a favour anyway. He should be doing this. Dan couldn't remember the code. He took down the slim red ring-binder that contained the code numbers, found the one for the photocopier, jotted it on a yellow post-it note and gave it to Judi. The phone went. It was Frank. Would Dan pop up and run through some budget figures with him? It was pretty urgent. He needed to get this stuff polished off this morning. Dan said he just had a few things to finish, but would be there as soon as he could. Vikki's eyes rolled to the ceiling. The phone rang again. Dan ignored it, but could hear the message going onto the voicemail. Student Travel Services. Had he reached a decision on where they wanted to go? And how many were going? *Shit. The trip*. He'd done nothing about it. And it was February. And the trip had to happen before the end of February.

He finished off Vikki's order and set off to help Ben, only to be engulfed by three anxious first years. The roof was leaking into their space. There was water everywhere. They had waited long enough whilst he was handing out those materials. He had to sort this out. There were health and safety issues. The floor was wet. Someone could slip and crack their head open. Dan looked at Ben, who nodded silent resignation to the fact that this was an emergency that took precedence over his canvas-stretching tuition. Dan rang the caretakers' office. No reply. He rang reception and asked for the caretakers to be radioed. He beckoned the first years into the storeroom, whilst he dug around in the mass of tools, equipment and art materials for suitable receptacles. He found a plaster-mixing bowl and the two wax-melting pans. That ought to do it. Dan and the students wove around the maze of tall, white, clipped-together MDF boards that defined the studio spaces and set out the receptacles under the dripping water. This would have to do until the caretakers could sort it out properly. Dan remembered Ben and walked back to the office-storeroom. Grant Rathbone was waiting by the door. Ben had got fed up of waiting and had gone for a fag and a coffee, Grant told him. And could he have a wax-melting pan?

It was lunchtime. Dan retreated into his office-storeroom and locked the door. He picked up his old leather briefcase and took out the aluminium foil package that contained his tuna mayonnaise sandwiches. He waggled the mouse. The screen saver vanished. There wasn't time to do anything worthwhile with that paperwork he'd started earlier, but at least he could catch up with his email... and telephone messages. *That bloody trip. Shit.* He picked up the first of his sandwiches. Radio One was blaring through the acoustically transparent walls. He couldn't think. He'd have to say something. He put the sandwich down and swung out of his door to the identical one that led to the Students' Union office. Kirsti Nottle, the SU President, broke off from the telephone conversation she was somehow having above the din and sullenly turned the radio down.

Dan went back to his office, locked the door again and picked up the sandwich. There was a knock at the door. He ignored it. Someone tried the handle. More knocks. He put down the sandwich, switched on the extractor fan to disguise any noise he might make, and picked up his sandwich again. The fan wowed and droned overhead. The strip light flickered. Radio One was marginally quieter, but still as audible as it would have been if the radio had been in the room with him. The knocking at the door stopped. He thought he heard some footsteps trail away. He took a bite of the sandwich and laid it down on the opened foil as he looked at his Barts email account. 44 new messages. Not to worry. A lot of them would be junk: of the 'has anyone seen my mug', or 'I've lost my keys – they've got a World's Greatest Dad key fob on them' sort. He heard muffled conversations from the SU office. Doors opened and closed, and Radio One went up to even louder than it had been before. He got out of his chair to complain again. Kirsti had gone to lunch. It was Toby

Mandela, the SU Vice President. He sneered from under his blond dreadlocks and turned the radio off. Dan went back to his sandwiches. There were more knocks on the door; more yanks on the handle. He could hear voices. "I'm sure he's in there". "I saw him go in". And then a shout: "Can we have some paint?" Dan maintained his silence. The voices gave up. He looked at his watch. 1.25. Shit. I'm teaching in 5 minutes. The little Lexmark printer flopped the names of the afternoon's tutees into its tray. First years. He grabbed the clipboard that held his blank tutorial forms and opened the door. He was ambushed by 2 second years wanting tools and materials. Others picked up on the noise and emerged from their studio spaces. Within seconds he had 7 students around him. He went back into his office and dug out what they wanted as quickly as he could. He didn't bother to log anything in the book. That would fuck up the records and the ordering, but what could he do? He was fifteen minutes late for his first tutee, Miranda Frost. Dan picked his way through the labyrinth that was the studio and apologised for his lateness. They settled in front of her paintings – dramatic alpine mountains with tiny skiers whizzing down them – and started the session.

His third tutee was James Diggle. James had made a mould of a 2" high toy soldier lunging forward with a rifle-cum-bayonet, cast lots of replicas and painted them in bright primary colours. He also had lots of pictures of dead people he'd downloaded from the net. Before Dan was able to speak, he was interrupted by second year student Elvira Gabicci. He'd seen Elvira once or twice before, but she was not a great attender and they had scarcely spoken until now. She wanted him to update her on what had been happening in second year lectures and such. She was a mother and a busy person, she explained, and it wasn't easy for her to find time to come into college. Dan told her that it was up to her to be in college for tuition when it happened. He did not have time to repeat lessons. Elvira was indignant. She certainly could not guarantee to be available for teaching events just because he had timetabled them. He would have to drop what he was doing and attend to her needs. Ronnie used to reprise missed teaching for her, she reckoned. Dan could almost believe that this was true. When Dan pointed out that he was busy teaching the first years, Elvira got even huffier. She was a second year. She had rank over those kiddies in the first year. Besides, if Dan wasn't teaching her group, who was? She hadn't seen any lecturers. Dan told her nobody was. That was it: Elvira was outraged. Did he mean to tell her that her class did not have a lecturer assigned to it all day, every day? Dan told her that it was precisely what he meant. Elvira was dumbstruck. She stomped off to Frank Fuller to complain.

It was five-thirty in the evening. Most of the students had gone. Dan went back to his one-room sick-building syndrome. He hadn't dealt with his emails or his telephone messages. He looked down at the paperwork he had started ten hours earlier and tried to make sense of it. He couldn't. And there was no time anyway. Tomorrow's classes had to be prepared for. There was teaching material to write, and when it was done it would all have to be photocopied so that there would be handouts for everybody in the morning. He concluded his teaching prep and tramped off to reception to run off the copies. At the desk was one of the evening receptionists. They started at five and worked 'til nine, covering the night school classes. They always seemed fresh and cheerful compared to those who'd been there all day. Dan picked up the departmental post, which was still addressed mostly to Ronnie Foulkes. He locked the store-office door at 7.30pm and trudged out into the car park, trying to remember where he'd left the Vauxhall. He took the post with him, so he could read it after dinner.

*****

Frank called Dan up to his office and offered him a coffee. Frank poked and prodded at the Krups percolator, and a few moments later they each had a small cup of strong black liquid that smelt better than it tasted. Dan weighed-up Frank's outfit. He was wearing black, head to toe. He always wore black. In fact, fine art lecturers in all the places Dan had ever worked usually wore black. It was partly a practical thing. Fine art studios are dirty places, full of paint, charcoal, clay and mess. Anything you sit on or brush past is likely to mark your clothes. It wasn't so much that black clothing didn't show marks – it did – it was just that after you'd washed it any remaining stains were usually invisible. Black made sense. But it was also a bit of a statement, a tiny fragment of residual artists' rebellion, the last trace of a lost bohemian spirit. Black was Goth, Punk, Beatnik… Every generation had a use for it and ascribed a meaning to it. Frank wore black jeans and black t-shirt on casual days, and a black suit with black formal shirt for meetings. But since he hadn't been a lecturer for years – decades, probably – the practical thing didn't count. There was only the 'statement' part left. Dan had a certain admiration for Frank's resilience in this and his refusal to tow the tweed-suit line suggested by Silas Beasley's example, even if it was only tokenistic. The t-shirt was of reasonable quality. The pants were OK – probably Marks and Sparks version of the 501. The shoes, however, were those shapeless, rubber-soled blobs you find at fifteen quid a time in those poxy shoe chain-stores with names like 'Shoe Deal' or 'Shoes R Us' on the High Street of every hard-up English town, all knocked-up in some lousy, Godforsaken sweatshop in China. Frank's style statement crumbled away at the feet.

Frank spread his hands on the table. He'd had a call from Ronnie's wife, Audrey. Ronnie had cancer of the bowel. He was undergoing chemotherapy and radiotherapy, and if he was ever going to come back to work – and that seemed pretty unlikely – it wouldn't be for a very long time.

As Dan absorbed the news, Frank sat back in his high-backed swivel chair and related a tale about a bloke called Gerry Frisby. He'd been there long before Dan's time. Part of the 'Old School'. He'd run one of the art courses – an HND, if Frank's memory served him correctly – but he'd become outmoded in his thinking and it had become necessary to relieve him of some responsibility. Soon afterwards he took early retirement. And soon after that, he died of cancer. But what Frank couldn't get over was that Gerry's wife, Betty, held him responsible for Gerry's death. She made out that it was what Barts' management in general, and Frank in particular, had put Gerry through that had killed him.

Barsteadworth College

"Me?! She says I killed him!" protested Frank, with a pained grin.

Dan shook his head and rolled his eyes upwards in assent. *As if.* Frank was a nice guy. *How could anyone think that of him?*

They got back to business. Dan was going to need some new staff. Frank said he'd had a think about this. For the time being they could switch Linda Froggatt over from the GNVQ and get some input from Phil Flanagan, who had been doing some visiting work on the Foundation Diploma and the Photography Degree. Both were in their early 30s, had lots of energy and enthusiasm and were trying to make it as higher education tutors. Linda had been working with 16 to 18 year-olds and would be very much at home with the younger students. Phil had emerged as a highly successful artist in the mid-90s – one of Saatchi's darlings, indeed – and was now making use of his knowledge in teaching. It would be Phil's experience as a practicing, exhibiting professional that would be the biggest benefit to the students. They could start after Easter. He could have a day a week from Linda and the odd session from Phil, as negotiated with the other Course Directors he was working for. He'd have to give up Barry Vicar, though.

Dan did a quick mental calculation. He wouldn't have many more teaching hours to use, but at least with these new, young lecturers there would be some input for the students that had a bit of currency, edge and variety to it. Ronnie, Barry and Mervin were all abstract landscape painters. Between them, Linda and Phil covered sculpture, performance, photography and video.

*****

"You're tired. I'm tired. We're all tired", yelled Sophie, making an angry silhouette in the lounge window. "You're doing eleven-twelve hour days all week and your PhD on Saturdays. I want to go out today; do something. It's Sunday. We should have *leisure*, like other people".

"But I have to get tomorrow's teaching ready", protested Dan.

"You can do that tonight. I want to go out at least for a walk or something".

"But if I work on Sunday nights I don't sleep. My mind races. I can't wind down. You know that".

"All right. Let's go out now. You can do your prep this afternoon. And then tonight you can relax. Have some red wine to knock you out or something."

Dan assented.

They took a stroll around the picturesque Hampshire town of Stockbridge. There was an old petrol station, which didn't seem to have changed since the days of hampers, headscarves and the open-topped tourer. They bought fudge from the newsagents and gazed at the well-fed trout in the shallow waters of the River Test, which were facing upstream and manoeuvring for position as kids threw in bits of bread for them. There was a small art gallery. It was closed, but you could see in through the window. The building was old – Georgian, probably – but it had been carefully refurbished. The bow window frame had been scrupulously painted with fresh white gloss. Neat, hand-painted black letters proclaimed 'Stockbridge Contemporary Art Gallery'. The inside was a pristine white space. On a wall hung a large, dramatic painting of frenzied white horses splashing through blue and white water; in the window was a group of serene flamingos carved out of driftwood with steel poles for legs; and on the floor was a bigger-than-life-size hare made from grey chicken-wire, rearing up on its hind legs, boxing. It wasn't the most challenging work he'd ever seen, but at least these guys were doing something. Dan hadn't made any art for over a year.

*****

It was the beginning of the summer recess, the first Monday after the students had gone home. Dan unlocked the office door and sat at his/Ronnie's desk, enjoying the silence. All

Ronnie's stuff was still in the drawer. Endless half-dead felt-tips, a small Aurora calculator, some foreign currency left over from a field trip – massive denominations, worth nothing – a device for supporting the wrist so you didn't get repetitive strain syndrome from moving your mouse and a squashy, oversized red button that you were supposed to press to relieve stress. Dan thought about Ronnie. He wondered how he was doing. Over the months he'd sent Ronnie a couple of 'get well soon' cards and had little notes in return. Ronnie wrote about what he called "this evil disease", apologised to Dan for all the crap that had now been dropped on him and joked about the chemotherapy: "it might be stressful", he reckoned, "but nowhere near as stressful as working at Barts".

It wasn't that bad, was it? Maybe it was. The arrival of Phil and Linda had been a help, but just as he had been when he had first started, they were in reality apprentices who needed to be shown everything. Any benefit they'd brought to Dan in terms of reducing his workload was more than matched by the time and effort needed to guide them.

He had a meeting scheduled with Frank Fuller for 8.30am. The end of year shows had taken over everybody's time for a few weeks. With those concluded there was a backlog of information to be passed in both directions. Dan climbed the open-plan staircase to Frank's office, knocked and was welcomed in. Each man placed a heap of A4 papers on the large light-wood table and settled into a chair.

"How's it going with Phil and Linda?" asked Frank.

"Good. Very good. They're settling in. I was surprised to see that no one was doing student-led seminars. I've introduced those for the second years and I've had Phil do one or two. We did them all the time at Leeds. It's a good way of keeping the students involved and focused. It's really brought them on. Linda is working mostly with the first years. I just love the way she teaches. I guess she's using her GNVQ techniques; bosses them around like a school teacher. I don't think I'd dare do it, but the students don't seem to mind; in fact I think they rather like her. I could do with a few more hours though", said Dan.

"Well that's one of the things I wanted to talk to you about. Because you've got another year group starting in September, there will be money for another half-time lecturer. I've set it up with Personnel. The advert will be going out any time. You'll be getting another member of staff too. The Core Theory Programme is being scrapped. Praise be. And each department will get the theory lecturer closest to its subject. You'll be getting Patricia Kleb", announced Frank.

"Not before time, I think." said Dan. "Patricia Kleb. Yes, I've seen her about. Had the odd chat. Can't say I really know her, though."

"Oh, she's very good", Frank continued. "You'll like her. She started as a mature student as well, like you. She's doing a PhD on Barbara Hepworth. She used to be a typist. You'll have to watch out for her though. She's very efficient, but a little insecure."

"Really? She always seems confident and together, from what little I've seen of her. Always immaculately dressed."

"Well, appearances can be deceptive", continued Frank. "It was her father. He was a right bastard, apparently. I don't know what his problem was, but it seems he was always on her case, from right back into childhood and up into her adult life. Told her she would achieve nothing. Put her down at every turn. It was only after he'd died that she found the nerve to study. I think what she's done, how she's dragged herself up, has been amazing. But she's still... Well. You know..." Frank waved his hands in front of his face.

"What? Reticent?" Dan suggested.

"Yeah. Reticent. That's the word. Very insular. Keeps herself to herself. Doesn't have much confidence."

Barsteadworth College

"It's a shame, that. What a git. I wonder what makes a person treat their kid like that", Dan speculated.

"Anyway. Best of all – you're going to like this – contact hours are being reduced substantially for next year. Because of the number of degrees we've got up and running, we're now entitled to more funding. It'll still be probably one-and-a-half times what you're used to at Leeds, but it's progress. It'll take time, but we will eventually get it down to something like university level."

"That's great, Frank. Any actual figures?"

"No. Not yet. But I'll let you have them as soon as I have them"

"OK. Right. My turn. I've drafted the changes I want to make to the degree." Dan spread out his papers: a mixture of diagrams and notes. He then turned them through 180 degrees so they favoured Frank's viewpoint. "I want consecutive not concurrent modules. Like I said earlier in the year, I want a situation where at any given time there's only one practical module running and one theory module. It was at its worst in the first year set-up. I've changed that beyond recognition, I think. But I've applied similar thinking to the second and third year programmes. It makes practical sense. It's similar to all the BA programmes I've encountered elsewhere and it makes it possible for theory and practice to be integrated properly. What's being taught in the theory sessions can be tailored to work with what's going on in the studios. I've also moved the Professional Studies modules. They didn't make sense where they were. And I've redrafted the content of several of the modules. Well, in fact, I've got rid of some and drawn up some new ones. Quite a few were, essentially, duplicating each other, whilst there are some important subjects that aren't given nearly enough coverage and others that aren't even touched at all. See what you think."

"Right. Well. This looks good, but there's a lot of it", said Frank. "Leave it with me".

*****

In September, with much of the year's planning done and the students not yet back, Dan was able to attend a one-day symposium on 'Fine Art Practice as Research' at the University of Plymouth. He glanced round the auditorium. It wasn't as big and grand as he'd expected. It had dark wooden panels up to head height then, the rest of the way up, tall white walls containing tall part-leaded windows with hefty, rack-and-pinion opening devices that reminded him of school. A hundred or so padded, grey institutional chairs were fixed together in rows by little steel brackets that each was equipped with at its sides. The place was about half-filled, mostly by little groups of two or three middle-aged academics, who took papers, files and small plastic bottles of water from briefcases and chatted quietly amongst themselves. Dan picked a seat. He was on his own. He looked around to see if there was anyone there he knew. Just one familiar face: Debbie Greenwood. She saw Dan and came over.

"Hi. How are you Dan?" asked Debbie.

"Fine. Yeah. Fine. Sorry you didn't get the job", responded Dan.

"I've been meaning to ring for feedback, but haven't got around to it. I suppose one of the internals got it?" said Debbie.

"Yeah. You're right. Linda Froggatt got it", said Dan.

"Was I wasting my time? Was it always going to be her? Were the others just a formality?"

"No. Not exactly", said Dan. "Basically, for me anyway, it was a draw between you and Linda. You both had very good interviews. Frank and I couldn't separate you. But going round the table, it was the student rep who swung it Linda's way. She'd been working with them for the last couple of months and they like her. So, there wasn't bias in the way you mean it. She wasn't guaranteed anything. But she just had an advantage regardless, because of the work she'd been doing with us. In fact, Phil Flanagan was another interviewee and he'd been working with us too, but he's just that little bit less experienced and the consensus was that he wasn't quite ready. He'll still be doing VL work with us, though."

"If you say so", said Debbie, in a tone of good humoured irony. "I'll tell you what though, Dan. You need to watch that Linda. That is a very ambitious and manipulative young woman".

Debbie went back to her seat on the other side of the auditorium. Dan pondered. *Sour grapes, probably.*

*****

October. Dan helped Linda set up the Kodak carousel slide projector at the back of the lecture theatre. Bloody unreliable things that they are. They also readied the video player and primed the overhead digital projector. It was Linda's turn to give a lecture on her own artistic practice to the students. Dan thought it would be useful for the students to see the range of input they now had. He had done a session himself, Mervin and Phil had each done one and even Frank had been persuaded to join in, talking lovingly of his days at the Royal College and showing old slides of his geometric abstract paintings. Linda was a sculptor and performance artist. She had stills to show and also videos of her performances.

Linda paced nervously at the front of the auditorium. She was fairly petite with an attractive, young looking face, surrounded by neat blond hair arranged in a bob. Students filed into the semi-darkened room, filling the back rows first, then begrudgingly taking more forward ones as space was taken up. With everyone settled, Dan turned the lights down and took a seat in the largely empty front row.

Linda clicked on her first slide – a giant sculpted penis that had been chopped in half – and began to talk about her work and its influences. She instantly forgot her nerves and warmed to her subject. She had gone to Blodbury Private

School for Girls and then on to the big city to study art. Filchester School of Art and Design, like lots of universities and art colleges in the 1980s, had been a hotbed of radical feminism. Dan remembered that time well. He'd been at college too: as a mature student at Manchester Poly. Finally, moves to address one of society's greatest, longest standing idiocies and injustices were making themselves felt. It was a liberating moment for everyone: men as well as women. Injustice within a society diminishes everyone. *People* began to step out of their social straightjackets and live in ways that society's demands had previously precluded. What a moment this was, and how much more it might have been? But how often had humankind's best ideas – movements and religions based on peace, understanding and equality – been hijacked by fools and zealots?

On the one hand, there was a group of serious, intelligent women, working for equality and justice, and seeking alternatives to frequently destructive male philosophies. On the other, there were the likes of those who had graffiti'd 'CASTRATE, MUTILATE, ANNIHILATE' next to the Venus circle-cross symbol on the sandstone facade of the Grosvenor Building at the Poly. All men were rapists. All men were misogynists. All men stereotyped women. All men were guilty of a new kind of original sin, simply by dint of being men; and all women were exalted by a new kind of original virtue; that of not being men. Radical feminists debated who were the right sorts of people to run the world. They decided that they were, and that men should be exterminated. Women who disagreed would not suffer quite the same fate, but might at least expect a long, intense stint of cultural reprogramming. Had Linda sided with the intellectuals or the nutters? The answer played itself out before them in words and images. Linda explained that she had been spurred on by male lecturers at Filchester. Some of them didn't like her work – clear evidence of their misogyny. Valerie Solanas had set the right sort of example for aspiring radial feminist artists. She wrote the SCUM Manifesto – a diatribe of psychotic hatred against men – and shot Andy Warhol. A man who made screen-prints of pop stars and soup cans was clearly a threat to world peace and the ascent of women. He needed to be stopped. If you weren't actually up to shooting men yourself, the least you could do was try to work some sort of art voodoo by making effigies of their genitals and abusing them. "They were heady times", said Linda, looking dreamily into the middle distance and clicking on an image of male genitals bound tightly in curtain material. "Anything seemed possible". With her slides used up, she showed a video of one of her performances: the young Linda Froggatt in dungarees and steel toe-capped work boots, chucking a six-foot fibreglass penis out of the studio window.

Linda now switched to her postgraduate study. By the time she completed her bachelor degree she had spotted that she was not at all bad looking. It was also at this time that she fell in love with fellow student and future husband, Sky Gelding. The extermination of men was going to have to be reconsidered. Her work and her look softened and became more seductive. Gone was the foundry worker image. Her videos now featured a sultry, sophisticated Linda with ball gown, bleached blond hair and deep red lipstick, pouting and blowing at dangling objects set swinging by her breath. By the time she received her postgraduate diploma, she was already achieving a significant level of success in London art galleries. It was short-lived, but an important lesson had been learned: transform your aggression into seduction and you make far more progress.

*****

It was 8.30 sharp, as Dan looked up from his desk and Patricia Kleb walked into the office. She was never late.

"Morning", said Dan.

"Morning", said Patricia.

The SU people had been moved to a place in the main building and Fine Art had inherited their old room. The old store-office was now just a store. Patricia was the only other full-timer, though she would still be doing some work on the Foundation Diploma. She and Dan had been working together for a couple of months, now. They had desks facing each other. Old 1970s teak veneered ones, with recessed chrome handles. There was a third one side-on to theirs, used as-and-when by the part-timers and visiting lecturers. There were three four-drawer grey filing cabinets and a tall bookshelf that had been taken from the store-office. Other shelving, left behind by the SU people, was fixed to the wall by cream-coloured slotted steel bars that ran floor to ceiling. The inside walls were made of the same dowdy grey-brown cardboard panelling that the old room was, and the outside one was concrete block-work, painted to match the same murky colour, though Dan and Patricia had brightened the place up a bit with posters and flyers from art exhibitions. The main thing, though, was that the room had a window. Even though the yellow, linen-effect vertical blinds were dirty and the operating mechanism was broken, this was still a boon.

Patricia wore an immaculate bottle-green trouser suit with a red brooch, necklace and earrings which all matched. She was about 40, at a guess. She had a broad, pale, flat face with very thin, very straight lips, painted in the same red as her accessories. There were deep vertical lines either side of her mouth that gave her a 'marionette' sort of look. Her hair was straight and black, with a neat, level fringe that finished halfway down her forehead and ran parallel with hers lips. It was a glum face. Philip Larkin's words ran through Dan's mind: *They fuck you up, your mum and dad.*

Patricia took her seat before her numerous neat box files, which were stacked on the shelves behind her. They were colour-coded to indicate to which course and year group they referred. A sub-section for each module was then identified by serial number and shelf position. She reached across her desk and pulled a heap of A4 files towards her. There were documents held in neat clear plastic folders with brightly coloured spines, papers clipped together simply with staples and a couple of old, battered ring-binders, one blue, one red, which, with their shallow slopes and smooth surfaces, destabilised the rest of the pile: Patricia's marking pile. She took off the top one and began to read; silently at first, then "sheesh", "pfoow", and "have you seen this crap?"

Barsteadworth College

"What is it?" Dan replied.

She shuffled round to Dan's desk and laid a couple of stapled-together pages in front of him. "First year essays", she said. "Listen to this." Her finger followed the words as she read out loud. "*Modernism was an art movment invented in the late 1800's by Piccaso, Monet and Dali alot* (yep 'alot' all one word) *of modernism was sureallism which is about dreams and that and is very weird with melting clocks and that and its about Freud to who sed evrythings about sex.* It's utter bollocks and there's no punctuation", spat Patricia.

"Aye. It's not exactly Shakespeare, is it? Whose is it?" asked Dan.

"Trevor Fink. The Goth", said Patricia.

"Oh yeah, Trevor. Not our most illustrious scholar. I think he was a clearing student", said Dan.

"I dare say", said Patricia. "I think the entry qualification by then must have been the ability to fog a mirror".

"I dare say. And I think he's dyslexic", said Dan.

"Everybody's dyslexic", said Patricia. "I've had the forms back. I think there's only five out of the forty-odd of them that don't claim to be dyslexic."

"Well, even so, you better send him across to see Ulrike in Support Services."

"I will", said Patricia.

They went back to their work. Dan quite liked Patricia. He felt they had something in common. He admired the way she'd kicked off her miserable background and done something with her life. Her carefully assembled outfits, setting her apart as an Art History tutor, were an interesting contrast to the usual paint-spattered, charcoal-dusted look of the studio lecturers. On the other hand, she had this maddening habit of, whenever she was describing how someone had failed to notice something obvious, saying, loudly "HELLO-O", like they did in American sitcoms. And the fear induced by all those years of undermining by her father was palpable; she went out of her way to prevent anyone but the students from seeing her teach or knowing the content of her teaching material. Most of it was a mystery even to Dan. Efforts to talk to her on the subject had an attritional quality: polite evasion would be followed by begrudging cooperation, then by the provision of something peripheral and superficial, and then the repetition of the whole process, until Dan, with a million other things to think about and, in any case, trust in her competence, gave up. But she did have a sense of humour, though the subject was always the same: the daft things that students had said or written. You could imagine her father picking holes in her in the same way all those years ago. *Man hands on misery to Man*... and woman.

*****

Dan had had it up to about *here* with Terry, the incredible vanishing technician. It was well into November and he'd scarcely been seen all term. Dan stomped off to the workshop. Terry was in the office, drinking tea.

"Terry, I need a word", said Dan, curtly. Morty, the other technician smirked and looked at them both. This was evidently a scene he'd seen played out many times before.

"Yeah?" said Terry.

"I've got a load of things that need doing and nothing seems to be happening."

"I know. I've got the list". Terry pulled a grubby, misshapen piece of paper from his pocket with some bits of writing on it in pencil. "I'm on it. I'll get to it as soon as I can".

"You said that last week, and the week before".

"There were emergencies in Foundation", reasoned Terry.

Barsteadworth College

"There are always bloody emergencies in Foundation. It's a room full of kids painting shells and twigs with System 3. How can there be 'emergencies'? It's November. I've been waiting for some of these jobs since August. Have there been emergencies every day since August? Look I want these jobs doing and I want them starting today". Dan could feel the heat beneath his collar.

"Well I can't promise that", said Terry.

"Why not?" asked Dan.

"I just can't, that's all", said Terry.

"Look. This is ridiculous. I need boards installing. I need stretcher-making workshops. The students need help with their work. We're grinding to a halt in there."

"Well, you'll have to speak to Frank", said Terry. "I answer to him, not you. And I can't be in two places at once."

Dan turned on his heels, smacked the door open with the heel of his hand and crossed the courtyard. He trotted up the familiar stairs to Frank's office. Dan knocked and poked his head round the door. Frank was in. Dan was steaming. He laid on Frank all of the problems he was having with Terry, relating all of the futile conversations he had with him – all of them very much like today's – and the chaos this was causing in the studios. Frank was very sympathetic. He shared Dan's outrage. This was totally unacceptable. He'd deal with it. Not to worry.

Dan came out of Frank's office, relieved at having got this off his chest and feeling that things would now be OK. Coming the other way was Sue Stoke, Course Director for the GNVQ in Art and Design; another of Terry's customers. She could see Dan's still semi-agitated state. She smiled.
"What was that then?" asked Sue.

"Oh, I'd just about had it with that flamin' Terry Mortice. The bloke's a law unto himself. I can't get anything done. He works in 3 departments and plays everyone off against everyone else. Frank said he'd sort it", said Dan.

She laughed. "Frank'll sort it then, will he?" she posited, mysteriously. "He's likeable Frank, isn't he?"

"Yes. Seems like a genuine sort of a guy", agreed Dan.

"You'll get used to this", said Sue. "Frank agrees with everybody. Each time you go to him with a problem he'll sympathise, agree wholeheartedly with you and tell you it's as good as sorted. Trouble is, as soon as he gets the other guy's point of view he'll agree with that too. It's called a 'Fuller Fudge'. It's legendary here. Frank is that rare thing, a man who can produce an outcome designed to please all parties, even if there are diametrically opposed views."

"So it won't make a blind bit of difference, then?" said Dan.

"Not a bit", said Sue. "Are you coming for a drink on Friday? I'm leaving. Got a job at Edexcel".

*****

Dan sprawled on the sofa in his navy blue towelling dressing gown and gazed at the hefty Toshiba television. On the screen was an image of undergrowth, static but for an occasional flicker of movement in the middle. A narrator talked quietly and lovingly about some rare lizard that was in there somewhere, if you looked carefully. There were footsteps upstairs. Sophie stepped softly down the open-plan staircase.

"What are you doing?" she asked in a half-awake voice.

"Watching telly. Lizards. There's one in that undergrowth, apparently".
"It's half-two in the morning" said Sophie.

Barsteadworth College

"I couldn't sleep. They reckon you should do something if you can't sleep, not just roll around in bed. So I'm watching telly. I had it on quiet, so as not to wake you".

Sophie sat down beside him. "Why can't you sleep?" she asked.

"Because I didn't sleep last night or the night before and I'm so worried about not sleeping tonight that I can't sleep. That's how insomnia works, isn't it?"

"You never used to be like this. What's going on? It's work isn't it? I thought now we'd moved here and now you've got those extra people things would be fine", said Sophie.

"It doesn't seem to have made much difference. It's great that we've moved – a twenty-minute drive to work instead of a one-hour plus one: that's fantastic – but at work it's the same. Patricia's takes care of what she always took care of, but now I'm her manager, instead of someone else. So that's more work. There's Linda and occasionally Phil. They're good but they're new and only part-time. They know nothing of the admin and systems. I'm spending loads of time mentoring them or getting things ready for them. They've cut my teaching hours, a bit, but there's actually more to do than there was before. There's Mervin who does what Mervin does, and we've scarcely got a technician. I'm the manager, storeman, secretary, technician, therapist and the bloke who bandages cut fingers. And we've got half again more students than we had last year. I'm writing the third year programme as we go along. And I'm the only full-time member of staff. Most of the time I'm the only one around, and I've got a hundred and twenty-odd students bending my ear. At the end of the day there's more to do than at the start. There's not enough time between getting home and bedtime. I can't wind down. I'm just knackered. I'm exhausted. And I've got my PhD to finish."

"Look. We'll talk about this tomorrow. I'll make you some warm milk. Take a Nytol", said Sophie.

"I hate taking them. They make me drowsy in the morning" said Dan.

"Take one, just to get you through," said Sophie, "you can have a Red Bull in the morning when you get to work. And it'll be Christmas in a few weeks. You'll be off."

*****

There was an end-of-term feeling at the last tri-annual Staff Development Day of the year. The students had finished and gone home, and the lecturers and admin staff were all in a relaxed mood, chatting happily amongst themselves as they filed into the Conference Centre.

James Ledlock, dark suit as always, started the proceedings. Silas Beasley was away in London, 'batting for the Academy'. Then it was Aileen Dimley's turn to do a session on the Academy Resource Strategy (ARS, for short). Aileen was well known to the audience, and to Dan by now, who had seen several of her performances. Aileen was Director of Infrastructure Services. It seemed that nearly everyone at Barts was a Director. Every employee above Senior Lecturer and below Vice Principal was a Director of Something. Course leaders were Course *Directors*, who then answered to *Directors* of School. All administrative managers were also called Directors. Although many Directorships were responsible posts with large budgets and significant numbers of staff to manage, and might well have warranted the title 'Director', Aileen Dimley's role of 'Director of Infrastructure Services' was something rather different. She managed four caretakers, a couple of administrators and a maintenance guy called Keith. Aileen was one of the people who had been around at Barts since long before Silas Beasley's time and had been rewarded for her long service and loyalty with a Directorship, even though her role would be more recognisable to most as something along the lines of 'Building Services Manager', and she often gave the impression that she had something to make up for. Aileen's contributions at the Staff Development Days were always something of a joke, though she could never see it. In spite of that, or maybe partly because of it, Dan quite liked her. They had occasionally stopped for a chat in a corridor or in the queue in the canteen, and he thought she was a good egg: 'Salt of the Earth' type, and a fellow Northerner. In her late-50s, she reminded him of the kind of women who had been around him when he was a child; not so much his mum, who was younger then and had been of fairly slight build, but of her friends and workmates on the school dinners. And she had a son, Royston, who was studying painting in Bristol, and she was interested to hear Dan's thoughts on what he was doing.

Aileen thanked James Ledlock for his introduction and walked to the front. She was of a physique which, if she had been a man, would be called 'stocky'. She wore a plain grey skirt, no discernable make-up and one of those shiny, knitted polyester tops that were popular in the 1960s, with a fine ribbed pattern down the front and short, tight sleeves which exposed her podgy white arms. She prodded the laptop, and on the pull-down screen behind her the Barsteadworth Academy of the Arts logo gave way to some large columns of small figures.

Dan knew what was coming, but hoped for Aileen's sake that it wasn't. For reasons he had never understood, Aileen always seemed to assume her audience was made up of idiots who needed her patience and valued her condescension. She kicked off, speaking to her audience of highly trained and highly experienced lecturers, managers and administrators as though they were kids struggling to take in what she was saying. She threw in long words that were slightly mispronounced or not quite appropriate to the meaning she was seeking and then waited a little while for things to sink in, or asked if everyone had understood what she had meant by this or that long, slightly incongruous expression. Given that this was in a northern accent that she continuously tried to tidy-up the effect was comical: East-Lancs mill-girl drawl punctuated sporadically with over-pronounced aitches and the Received-English long 'a'. Vera Duckworth meets the Queen. There were stifled sniggers and sideways glances in the audience. Aileen took all this as nervous discomfort at how difficult these concepts were to understand and patiently took things down another notch and simplified her mother-to-child delivery still further, as her listeners tried to keep a grip on their bladders. James Ledlock hid his face in his hands, pretending to be concentrating. Next to him Angela Tippex, Director of Corridors or something, pressed her hands into her lap and faced downwards. They looked like a couple silently sharing some profound thought or a moment of grief at a funeral. Giggling spread along rows. A noise like a bark went up somewhere near the back, as someone couldn't hold his laughter in any longer. A mixture of uncontrolled hilarity and embarrassment spread out in waves from the epicentre. It was all lost on Aileen. To make things worse, once order was restored, she went through her columns of figures – screen after tedious screen of them – in mind-warping pedantic detail. At break time the coffee urn and even the chocolate digestives were by-passed. There was a fight to get out, followed by shrieks of relief and laughter in the corridor and scrums trying to get into the toilet.

*****

It was the last Friday before Christmas; a cold morning and still dark outside. Dan clocked himself in the long mirror in the harsh fluorescent light of the downstairs gents. His eyes looked tired and puffy, and the fact that he'd become a stranger to exercise was apparent. He'd put on a few pounds, though the issue was less the amount of weight than how it was distributed: he had a sort of 'slumped' quality. A medium sized man, but out of shape. He slumped back to his office via the print room. Frank stood framed in the doorway.

"Thought I'd come down and see how you're doing."

"Fine, Frank, fine. Catching up on a few things now there's a bit of peace and quiet", replied Dan. "Pull up a pew. We don't often see you down here."

Frank pulled out the part-time lecturers' chair and sat down, glancing around the room at Dan's flyers and posters and Patricia's colour-keyed filing system. Dan hoped Frank would think it was his.

"No, you don't. I should get round the studios more than I do. But you know how it is... So you're settling in OK?" said Frank.

"The new office? Yes. It's a lot better. It's got a window."

"And Patricia? She's OK in here?" continued Frank.

"Er. Yes. Fine. Don't see much of her, really. It's the first term: she's been working mostly on Foundation. We'll see more of her in the spring", said Dan.

"Yes, yes, of course. Front-loaded, Foundation..." Frank looked out of the window, then back at Dan. "Look, it's about Ronnie," he said, at last. "You know he has cancer. Well it's cancer of the bowel... I think you knew that? Anyway, they've tried to keep it under control, but they can't. It's spread... to his liver. That's it. It's just a matter of time now. It's not survivable. All they can do is make him comfortable".

Chapter Five
5 Years Ago

Dan sat in the waiting room of Cherry Tree Group Practice. In front of him was a low table strewn with well-thumbed copies of Country Life, People's Friend and Woman's Own. Outside, the morning mist was clearing and the trees were showing a few shoots of green. Opposite was an old couple who sat very close together and spoke to each other in whispers. Next to them, a young woman struggled to keep control of a bored, over-energetic toddler. Behind all four was a print: one of Monet's Giverny water lily paintings with the Japanese bridge in the background. The little orange light came on next to Doctor Proctor's name and a disembodied female voice spoke from the grille underneath. "Mr Ripley? You can go through to the doctor's surgery now".

"We got your tests back. There's nothing much wrong with you, really, medically", said Doctor Proctor.

"Hum."

"Is everything OK at home?" asked the Doctor.

"Yeah. Well, no. I'm not sleeping and that's disturbing Sophie's sleep, and then we're both tired, and then we're both on each other's case", said Dan.

"And why aren't you sleeping?"

"I dunno. Stress, I suppose. That's what they say now, isn't it? It's all stress now. We all suffer from stress".

"And what's making you stressed?" the Doctor pursued.

"Well, I can't remember when I last felt well", said Dan. "I used to be the guy who never got colds. Until last week I hadn't been off sick since 1995. I remember it well. One of those really awful bouts of flu. You know; the ones where you think you're dying. Everyone at work had it. But as far as I can tell,

Barsteadworth College

I've had three lots of flu in the last six months, and in between I seem to have had constant colds. And as for my bowels, they're all over the place. But the worst thing is the tiredness. I'm just tired, tired, tired."

"And what about work?"

"I love what I do…"

"You work at the art college, don't you? It must be lovely."

"Yes it is", enthused Dan. "I love teaching, and it's great just being with the kids. They can be a real pain some times, but you're just endlessly amazed at the things that they come up with in the studios. All those young minds. They have – well most of them have – this moment when the penny drops; when they find the thing that interests them; and then they're off; they've got it; they're on their way to becoming artists. It's fantastic. It makes you feel so good".

"So what's the problem then?"

"It's everything else. We're under-funded, understaffed. The facilities are wrong. We've got three computers for 120-odd students. The students get hacked off with it all and they're on my back. I don't blame them. They know they're being sold short. But there's nothing I can do. The guy before me got ill and the one before him chucked it in because of insomnia. All sounds very familiar, really. The staff I *have* got are under-trained. Well, they're *not* trained. They're trained as artists, but don't have a clue about how a teaching organisation runs. I'm running them, I'm running me, I'm running everything. I'm there 12 hours a day. I'm a stranger to lunch breaks. And as for coffee breaks… forget it."

"So you work 12 hours without a break?" asked the Doctor.

"Yes. There's work to be done. I have my sandwiches and a kettle. And, in any case, senior managers often set up meetings for lunch times, so you can attend without interrupting your teaching", explained Dan.

"And this happens regularly?"

"Oh yes. At least once a week, often more than that", said Dan.

"And you don't complain?"

"Well, you can't. It's what everybody does. That's the norm. You can't *not* show up for the meeting. You can't tell the Vice Principal to reschedule it. They'd think you were mad. If you ever expect to be promoted you don't complain. And you don't show any sign of weakness. You drink more coffee and press on. Or Red Bull. We punch above our weight".

"And what about weekends?"

"At weekends I work on my PhD and prepare the next week's teaching."

"You're doing a PhD? On top of all this?" Doctor Proctor shook his head. "So do you take any time off?"

"We usually go for a walk on Sunday afternoons", said Dan.

"And exercise? What about exercise?"

"That would be the walk on Sunday afternoons."

"And you wonder why you're tired. Look. This can't continue. As far as I can tell you're drifting into Chronic Fatigue Syndrome, if you're not there already. You've got to take breaks. Lunch breaks exist for a reason and your managers have no right to make you work through them. And you've got to find time for exercise", stressed Doctor Proctor.

"But I can't", said Dan. "If I don't do the work it won't get done. There simply is no one else to do it. And if I fail, it will look like my fuck-up. It will be my failure. They won't blame themselves; they'll blame me."

Barsteadworth College

"Well, it's up to you", said the Doctor. "There are no pills for this one. It's a lifestyle thing. It's up to you. Your life. Your choice".

*****

Dan took his allocated seat at the back of Barsteadworth Minster. His place was amongst the other Course Directors, high above the altar on seating specially constructed from planks and scaffolding for the occasion. It was degree day. Barts didn't have enough space to host such an event, so they hired the biggest and most venerable building in town. Lecturers, students, admin staff and proud families all filed to their predetermined positions until the building started to look uncomfortably full. He looked at the massive ancient architecture; the bottom part Saxon; the upper part Norman. Hung along the sides of the nave at high level were regimental flags from this or that Victorian colonial campaign. Beneath were plaques commemorating young officers from wealthy local families who been killed in the Crimea, the Transvaal or at Jutland. At the far end was a magnificent stained glass window depicting some biblical tale or other. This place had been around long before they all existed and would still be around for a long time after they'd gone.

Five minutes earlier, Dan had been outside getting his excited graduates in order and giving them their final pep talk when he was interrupted by Frank Fuller, who wanted a quiet word. Audrey had phoned. Ronnie had passed away peacefully during the night. His family had all been with him.

The speeches started. Beasley was first. He said something profound and stirring – and long – about young people and the future. Then there were guest speakers. But Dan couldn't take anything in. He was struggling with heat and pressure in his tears ducts. He wanted to scream or shout or something. *Why are you all talking such shite when Ronnie's just died? You really don't give a fuck, do you?* The students – the ones Ronnie had recruited, the ones he'd busted a gut for, the ones who'd given him the emotional-punch-bag treatment every Monday morning – stepped up, smiling, and collected their degrees. *In another hour they'll all be pissed up, laughing and arsing about on the college lawn. None of them will even so much as think about Ronnie.*

*****

"Thanks for coming up, Dan. Take a seat". Frank spun round in his office chair to face Dan and studied him from over his reading glasses. Dan sat by the big light wood conferencing table and looked back at Frank.

"The Course Director's job will be advertised nationally. You realise that, don't you? We can't simply pass it on to you just because you've been doing it for the last couple of years. It has to be advertised. Rules and all that", said Frank.

"Oh, yeah. I understand that. I know it was a secondment and I know that the job itself is a different thing", replied Dan. "And I know I only got the secondment because I was there, in place. You had no opportunity to test the market".

"Quite. But you will be applying?" asked Frank.

"Yes. Of course," replied Dan, in an instant, in order to show enthusiasm, just in case he did want to apply, though he wasn't sure he did. His mind swept to that conversation with Doctor Proctor.

"And there won't be any favours. You'll have to compete for the job. Same as everyone else", emphasised Frank.

"I wouldn't *want* any favours", said Dan, surprised at the slight tone of indignation in his voice. "I'm happy to compete and be judged on my record".

*****

Sophie looked up from her dinner, glass of red wine in hand. "Whatever you want to do, I'll support you," she said.

Barsteadworth College

"I just can't make up my mind", said Dan, poking a fork half-heartedly into his chicken bhuna. "I'm not sure if I'm just applying because everyone expects me to, and I'm not sure it's not just pride: making sure I get it just to prove that I can."

"Well, that's no reason to apply for a job. You've got to want it."

"Part of me wants it. On many levels it's a very satisfying job. Helping young people get a start in life: what could be better? And being around art all the time: it's fantastic", said Dan. "But it's so full-on, so exhausting. I haven't seen the inside of my studio for nearly two years. I'm supposed to be an artist. I only went into education to support myself as an artist, but education has taken over. I'm not an artist anymore."

"So don't do it then."

"I don't know… Another thing is: I've done the hard bit. I've got the course set up, I've rewritten the whole bloody thing, and it works now. We've had a cohort go all the way through from induction to graduation. Phil's been taken on as a proper half-timer now. Linda and Patricia have been around for a year. Everyone's a lot more experienced and more effective now. The whole thing is tried and tested and has been made to work. And I'm the one who's made it work. I'm the one who's had all the crap and all the sleepless nights. Next year there will be more money. The teaching hours are coming down again. We'll be getting a proper technician. It'll almost be like a normal job. And now – right *now* - I should pass it on to someone else?"

"That's still not the right reason to take the job", said Sophie.

"No, it's not, is it?"

*****

Dan stirred his coffee and waited for his grubby old computer to spring to life. He knew he'd made the right decision. The sense of relief was enormous. He'd also asked to switch to a part-time lecturing role. This was granted, and he was now a Half-Time Senior Lecturer. He'd completed and passed his doctorate, too. 'Doctor Ripley'! Yes, that sounded pretty good. And he was now a regular in the gym once more and was getting back into shape. He'd even been back into his studio, though he couldn't quite remember what it was he did in there. Maybe this wasn't too bad a problem for an artist to have. It was a clean slate; a moment to start afresh after a long period in some kind of intense wilderness. Sure, with a new Course Director about to start he'd feel a twinge of jealousy over his old job. But it would be a bit like that situation when you see a dumped ex-girlfriend with a new bloke; though he would be the dump-*er*, not the dump-*ee*, and that is more or less OK. The overwhelming feeling was one of excitement at a new beginning; a situation in which he could enjoy his teaching whilst being involved in his own practice again, and feeling more relaxed and freer about it all. He felt pretty darned good!

A spring in his step, Dan trotted up the stairs to see Geoff in IT about completing the installation of the new Fine Art computer suite. Ten iMacs, with scanner, printer and specially made consoles. They wouldn't know themselves! As he turned on the half-landing he almost bumped into two people who were coming the other way. Frank and a woman. Dan looked at the woman. Cold blue-grey eyes. He felt a shudder.

"Ah, Dan", said Frank. "This is Stella Jobby, the new Course Director. We were just coming down to see you. Stella, this is Dan Ripley." The woman smiled but didn't speak. They shook hands.

"Hi. How are you? Welcome to Barts", said Dan.

Dan knew three things about Stella Jobby. Firstly, Linda and Phil had been on the interview panel and had learned that she had worked for many years at Twickendean School of Art. The story of why she was leaving, however, seemed vague and incongruous. It was due to the closing down of the MA in Fine Art – the kind of department that colleges did *not* tend to close down – and this in turn was due to a takeover of

Twickendean by Langsmead University that had not yet taken place and seemed unlikely to. She did have amazing references, though. Secondly, James Ledlock, in a quick out-of-the-corner-of-the-mouth conversation with Dan in a corridor, had made it clear that he would rather have appointed him than Stella. The third thing was that, according to Linda, she was quite attractive. For now there was no judgment Dan could make on the first two of these, though he could not see how it was that Linda thought Stella was attractive. To Dan, she just looked like a dressed-down Margaret Thatcher. Late-40s maybe, possibly 50, with brown cardigan, fawn cords and Shredded Wheat hair, though, of course, there were those who found even *her* attractive. But there was something else in the encounter that struck him far more fiercely than any of this: that shudder, involuntary and from somewhere that could not be identified. He felt like the dog obligatory in all Hammer Horror movies that barks and recoils, seemingly at nothing, because it has sensed something malevolent that no one else can see.

*****

With the start of the new academic year a couple of weeks away, the lecturers were finally allowed back into the main building from their exile in the library. Dan wandered through the new spaces. There had been frantic activity in the Fine Art department. Builders had erected new structures and modified old ones; electricians had fitted new lights, sockets and telephone points; caretakers had unpacked new furniture and decorators had coated just about everything with a fresh layer of white vinyl matt emulsion. Stella got the room previously used by Dan, Patricia and everyone else, though it had now been redecorated in brilliant white, had a new blind and was fitted-out with a new light wood corner desk, like Frank Fuller's, and a new computer. For Dan and the other lecturers a new office had been created by sectioning off part of the studio with plasterboard. It was equipped with new birch-effect desks and royal blue office chairs. Dan's ancient computer had been reinstalled on his new desk by the IT department. There was a whiff of freshly cut MDF in the air. A brand new factory-style north-light building had been erected on the other side of the car park to (more than) compensate for the lost studio space. All this change. All this money. All *now*. This must be what they had to do to get Stella. *Oh, the power of coming in new from outside.*

9.00am: the first ever post-Dan team meeting. Stella walked into the lecturers' new office, smiling, wearing another caramel/taupe ensemble and accompanied by a tall, slightly portly young man, who also smiled at the group. Stella had by now met everyone several times over, individually and in small groups, but this would be her first opportunity to address them all as a team. It was mostly small talk: a few platitudes about how pleased she was to be here, how she was looking forward to getting to know everybody and how great things were going to be. She then moved on to the only substantive business of the day: introducing a new appointee; the tall, slightly portly young man. This was the new Visiting Technician: Tim Small; her husband. Dan sensed a certain tension in himself and amongst his colleagues. There were a few sideways glances, but only with eyes. Heads didn't move. And then there was silence which, after a few embarrassing moments, Stella broke with a quiet laugh and a few more platitudes about how happy they were all going to be working together.

The meeting ended. Dan swung round in his chair to face his desk, and thought. What had he just witnessed? Dan had been Course Director until a couple of weeks ago. Had there been a vacancy advertised for a Part-Time or Visiting Technician he'd have known about it. Sure, there was a plan to appoint a Full-Time Technician this autumn. That was being advertised now, but this other post – the one Tim Small had just landed – didn't exist... did it? Dan rang Donna in Personnel and queried it. Donna wasn't clear what had happened. She was vaguely aware that someone called 'Tim' had been appointed, but how and in what capacity she didn't know. She said she'd get back to him.

*****

Barsteadworth College

Dan called into Stella's office for one of many mentoring meetings in which he would hand over the reins of the course. Tim concluded a conversation with his wife and left the room. At six foot and with that touch of excess weight, Tim Small was nothing like his name. He smiled a lot and although he didn't say very much, he was quiet and well-spoken when he did. You could imagine him as the nascent material for someone who, in his maturity, might be thought of as 'jolly'. A Dickens character out of his time.

Stella had this habit of switching the subject from the business of the day to something more personal. Today she wanted to talk about Tim and how they'd met. Though confused as to why Stella would want to tell him all this, Dan listened, politely. Tim's background was a wealthy and privileged one, but in spite of his expensive private education his reading and writing had always been very poor. This was put down to dyslexia and as a consequence of this difficulty, his parents decided that he should go to art school so that he could continue his education in a place where his more hands-on aptitudes could be developed. He landed a place at Twickendean. This was where he met Stella; she the tutor, he the student. Stella was 20 years Tim's senior, but that was just what they both needed. A match made in heaven. Stella had found a hot young lover and Tim had found someone with the motherly qualities that he craved. It had been good for Tim in other ways, too. From struggling with the course – especially those tricky written elements – he was revitalised. Suddenly he could write, and he knew what to write. And he got very good marks.

*****

Donna in Personnel had not phoned Dan back and had avoided his subsequent calls. However, it was a small college and sooner or later they had to bump into each other. In a brief, quiet conversation in the corridor by the photography studios, Donna told Dan what had happened: there had been no advert and no recruitment process. Stella had insisted that she needed some additional, part-time technical help and said she had found someone to do it. Frank Fuller had then rubber-stamped the transaction. Personnel had only been called in at the end, to do the paperwork on an already done deal.

*****

Dan was at lunch in the refectory with the rest of the Fine Art team, something he was beginning to find increasingly tiresome. Two circular stainless steel tables were pushed together to accommodate the group. Linda and Stella chatted excitedly. Tim sat quietly at Stella's side. Mervin gazed absent-mindedly around the room. Phil and Patricia followed the conversation and occasionally tried to a get a word in. Dan gave up and just watched and listened. Periodically Stella would turn away from Linda in order to try to involve others. "What do you think, Dan/Phil/Patricia/Mervin...?" But Linda was fixed on Stella. Previously, Linda had buddied-up with Mervin – used his age and authority to argue her case with Dan for various things she wanted in the department. Now Stella was here, this was something altogether better. They had become close friends. They'd discovered that they had lots of things in common. Not least was that they each had a young son called 'Jonte'; though Stella's Jonte was an adopted Peruvian orphan and Linda's was supplemented with a sister called Fifi. From today, though, they would have even more in common, as Linda's husband, Sky Gelding, had just been appointed as the new Full-Time Technician. Both Fine Art Lecturers, both with their Technician husbands under the same roof! It was perfect. This time it was an official appointment and there had been interviews, but since by now the Small-Jobbys and the Gelding-Froggatts were friends to the point of quasi-family, and since it was Stella's department, the outcome was never in doubt. Terry the old Technician had been made to reapply for what was essentially his own job, or would have been, had he ever done it. He had no chance and he knew it. Not only had his reputation preceded him, he was as aware as everyone else of the new filial regime that had taken grip of the department. He was found work elsewhere in the college.

Barsteadworth College

Dan already knew Sky. He had met him on several occasions before Stella's arrival, at parties at colleagues' houses and at student events in town centre pubs. He was a tall, thin man, mid-thirties like his wife, and although, with his sensible glasses and neat black hair he looked like a filing clerk or minor bank official, he was in fact a hippie and, as far as Dan was concerned, an excellent illustration of why those well known philosophers, the Sex Pistols, were right to say 'you should never trust a hippie'.

Sky had a value system that somehow mixed and matched Christianity, Taoism, Marxism, Hinduism, Buddhism, Islam, Gnosticism, Feminism and pragmatism. He was permanently on the moral high ground, regardless of whatever contradictions and absurdities needed to be clambered over to get there. And when that failed to work, he could always switch to what he liked to call 'the wisdom of silence', which boiled down, basically, to shutting-up because you know you are out of your depth and pretending that your silence is your way of keeping your own counsel because you know that what you would reveal, if you spoke, would be so profound that it would blow the minds of those present. When he did speak, his voice was quiet and his language mystical. Sentences almost always had the word 'energy' in them, and the few that didn't had 'spiritual' or 'aura' instead. Sometimes, when he was really on form, he could squeeze all three into one sentence. But, without ever seeing the contradiction, he would shift seamlessly from his New Age hyper-liberalism into the most reactionary form of political correctness, scrutinising those around him with his keenly-tuned probity antenna, ready to spot any unguarded non-pc comment, which would seldom be challenged then and there, but instead stored up for later use in more advantageous circumstances. Sky moved peacefully through his world in a state of moral wholesomeness, looking down on others... and down the blouses of colleagues' wives at parties. After a few drinks his persona would slip from that of The Pope's more high-minded brother to wanna-be sexual predator. Work-related house parties were ideal for him: there was no need for those awkward opening lines because barriers had already been broken down by circumstances and existing relationships and, for the same reasons, women who would not normally have given him the time of day were obliged to be polite and at least to exchange small-talk with him, thereby giving him the opening he was looking for. He'd once tried his luck with Phil Flanagan's wife, Kate: in the early hours of the morning at a party at the Gelding-Froggatt's own home he'd tried to persuade her into a bedroom. Kate had found herself all at once stunned at the sudden change in personality, horrified at the way he leered over her and reduced to laughter at the incompetence of the approach.

The lunchtime refectory roar and clatter was at its peak. Phil came back from the counter with a round of foaming coffees on a brown plastic tray and placed it on the table. It was quickly worked out whose was whose, there was the routine ritual of the offering and refusing of coins – *don't worry, get me one back next time* – and the conversation continued. Dan looked at his fawn cardboard cup. It had a stylised picture of a ceramic cup and saucer at a jaunty angle on the side, with a swirl of brown vapour rising above and the word 'Coffee' beneath. Stella and Linda were making plans for themselves and their families. They already shared babysitting duties and set the world right over red wine on Saturday nights. "You can't trust someone who doesn't drink red wine", joked Linda. The subject then moved on to a holiday the new extended family fancied making: to Corfu, next summer. Stella said that she *loved* Corfu. "Oh. It's the best", Linda concurred and launched into a story about an idyllic childhood trip to the island.

*****

Stella had set up a Saturday night party at her new house. She, Tom and Jonte had moved out of temporary rented accommodation into a dilapidated old house that they were now doing up. This was to be the house warming. Dan and Sophie walked up the gravel drive. It was a peculiar house of exciting and unusual design; a one-off built on a hillside by an eccentric architect in the 1930s. His intent, according to Stella, had been to combine aspects of Lutyens with a 'Lake Como' sort of feel. Approached from the drive, it looked like just yet another Barsteadworth suburban bungalow, but the plot it stood upon fell away sharply towards the rear. On the right hand side, reaching from front to back, was a large wooden balcony held up on poles at a dizzying height from the garden beneath, giving expansive views across the rooftops that trailed away in the valley below. At the back, the house became quite imposing. Here it was 3 storeys deep, each level having a prominent bow window. It could be seen for miles from anywhere on the council estate over which it majestically presided. The only drawback was that the deep, bowed aspect had an ominous feeling when seen from below, which, indeed, was the only way it could be seen properly and in its entirety. Grey in colour and towering over everything, it looked in daytime like a Normandy gun emplacement and, as the sun went down, like something that might stir Bram Stoker to pick up his quill. Still, it was cosy enough inside – a house of many faces.

It was clear that Stella was keen to develop a social circle with colleagues. Barry had left the department, but Mervin, Dan, Phil, Patricia and partners were all invited, along with a quite a few (mostly mature) students. Sophie and Kate messed about on the improvised dance floor. Phil tried to explain semiotics to Gloria Colon. Gloria Colon tried to flirt with Phil. Phil didn't notice, or pretended not to. Dan leant against the wall nursing a can of Fosters and wondering what he was doing there. He remembered he didn't like parties. You're in a house full of people who you wouldn't necessarily choose as friends, and you've got to make conversation with them. Why? *I'm an artist, not a fucking diplomat.* Because you work with people, it doesn't necessarily mean you'd want to be friends with them outside of work. This consideration did not seem to apply in Stella's thinking. Friends and colleagues were the same thing. The only thing to do was to get pissed. Make it more interesting. Dan tipped up the can and sucked warm, bitter fluid through the ring-pull hole.

Sky, also with beer can in hand, sidled up, leant on Dan's bit of wall and turned in towards him. "I see Mervin's had a few. What do you think of him?"

"Mervin? Oh, he's alright. He can be a bit of a pompous ass", said Dan with a bit of a laugh in his throat, "but you know where you stand with him. Speaks his mind. Yeah. He's alright".

"Yes. But what do you think about his work? It's a bit of a cliché, isn't it?" probed Sky.

"Well, yeah. I mean, I wouldn't want one. It's not exactly 'cutting edge'. But he knows that. He's quite open about it. He does his thing and that's it. He doesn't care; doesn't want to change the world. He likes to paint and that's it. *And people buy them.*"

Sky remembered an earlier appointment and sloped off into the gloom. Most of the house seemed to be open-plan, or it had double-doors left open so that each part seemed connected to all the other parts. People milled around, dancing, chatting, looking for other people. Dan found a big old sofa covered with a brown woollen blanket. He'd have to get up in a minute – the can of Fosters was nearly done – but for now he sat back, glad to take the weight from his feet. He faced an old marble fireplace and a pair of large, silver-coloured, plastic loudspeakers that seemed to have been modelled on a 1950s B-movie spaceship theme. Enya warbled her version of Celtic music. *Ocean of emotion. Motion motion motion. Motion lotion potion. Botion dotion wotion.* He wouldn't be rushing out to buy that one.

The room was pretty dark. Either side of the fireplace, above the speakers, two small art deco wall lamps with candle-style bulbs and no shades gave a pale orange glow, which was sucked in almost entirely by the dark 1930s wallpaper. Additional light, however, bled in from adjoining, more brightly lit rooms behind and to the side of where Dan was seated. The familiar evidence of a house only just moved into was everywhere: unopened boxes, random piles of books, clothes and LPs, and a shrink-wrapped washing machine with a Currys delivery note fixed to it. Someone flopped down next to him. He was made momentarily weightless by the sudden redistribution of air in the sofa. It was Linda.

"Have you seen the state of Mervin?" asked Linda. "He's pissed and dancing with one of the students."

"Well, of course he is. It's a party. That's what you're meant to do."

"Yeah, but it's a bit inappropriate, isn't it? He's old enough to be her dad", pressed Linda.

Dan looked round, past some concertina doors, to the dancers. "But he's only *dancing* with her. Besides, it's Lizzie. She's a *mature* student. She can take care of herself", he grunted. "Anyway, as far as I'm concerned, appropriateness is overrated". He was starting to get a feeling somewhere down in his bowels that he quickly identified as irritation. To think, he was missing Match of the Day for this nonsense.

*****

"Sit down", invited Stella in a polite and friendly tone. Dan chose one of the spare chairs. Stella faced him with her back to her desk and computer. "I wanted to get your views on Mervin".

"How do you mean?" Dan decided to play dumb over the things he'd heard at the party.

"Did you see his work at that Swot Gallery show? It's just so tired, boring and clichéd."

"Well, yes. You know. It is a bit last year's model."

"Last year's model?" humphed Stella. "It belongs in the middle of the last century. Look. I want rid of him. I've spoken to Frank, and what I can do is have him in for 'evaluation' and then set up various refresher courses that he has to do to bring him up to date. He'll refuse, of course, and then I'll be able to sack him. What do you think?"

Dan felt very uncomfortable. He had seen this campaign against Mervin grow in intensity. It wasn't just today and the sly comments at the party; Mervin's perceived inadequacies had become a routine topic at work, whenever he was not around. Stella, Linda, Sky and Tim made Mervin the butt of their jokes, usually looking at Patricia, Phil or Dan to see if they could draw any collusive comments or glances. They poked fun at Mervin's paintings: "wanna-be Rothkos that always end up looking like sunsets over the sea", Linda had called them, over coffee one day. Stella made it clear she did not like Mervin on a personal level either. He was too sure of himself, too opinionated.

"Mervin's paintings aren't exactly my cup of tea either", said Dan. "But that doesn't really matter, does it? That's outside of college. He's a good tutor, especially of printmaking. And we don't have another out-and-out painter, either. Whatever you think of his work, he knows about painting... and printmaking."

"Ah, well. I have something in mind for that. Do you remember that painter we had in as a guest lecturer the other week? Edward Bollinger?" asked Stella.

"The one who'd done his MA under you at Twickendean?" proffered Dan.

"Yes. Well he's looking for a job. He's doing some really interesting stuff, and he's a *lovely* man. Did you know he did his first degree at Oxford, in philosophy?"

There was a knock at the door. Two first year students flanked a middle one, who stuck out a bloodied right hand, wrapped in a mixture of sculptor's gauze and green paper towel.

"I'll get the first aid box", said Dan.

*****

Another Monday morning, another mentoring session in Stella's office. For once Stella was stood up, leant against the tall grey filing cabinet. "I don't know how to say this, Dan."

Barsteadworth College

She said "But I can't cope. There's just too much. I can't cope."

Strangely, although she was clearly suffering, Stella's facial expression – that customary almost-smile of hers – was as it always was. It seldom changed. It was her way of not giving anything away. Same with her voice: she only seemed to have one tone, whatever was going on.

Dan felt sorry for her. This was something he really could empathise with. "You'll be all right." He patted her shoulder with his left hand. "It's at its toughest in your first year. You're doing everything for the first time, finding out what you need to do, how to get things done, who you need to speak to. It *will* get better. You just need to stick with it. Mind you, I've noticed that you go home at five o'clock. I'd wondered how you were managing that. I was never able to."

"Five o'clock's when we finish. That's it isn't it?"

"Not here it isn't, especially for a Course Director. There's just too much to do. Ten hour days were pretty routine for me, and eleven or twelve hours wasn't unusual. You just get used to it. It's how it is. But it should be getting better. They've cut teaching hours considerably since I started."

"I'm not doing that", said Stella, angrily. "I'm not paid for that and I've got a young child to look after."

"Well that's what they expect here. Beasley has this saying: *we punch above our weight*. And that's how it works. Everyone works harder and longer than they're supposed to."

*****

"It's getting really horrible at work". Dan paired his knife and fork neatly on his finished dinner plate and fiddled with the stem of his wine glass. Half an inch of Jacob's Creek Merlot swirled satisfyingly around the bottom.

"Why? What's up? I thought you liked Stella", said Sophie.

"I did at first, but there's something really nasty going on. There's a sort of 'clique' started up. Stella and Tim, Linda and Sky; they're like a little private organisation within the department. Let me show you. It's like this." Dan grabbed a note pad form the sideboard and sketched out the departmental family tree. "The department's gone from being a group of individuals working together in the usual way, to this."

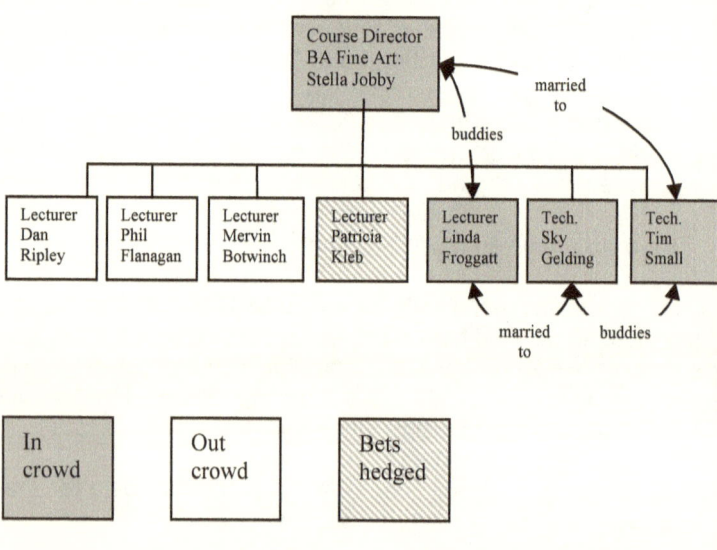

"And then there's the visiting lecturers", said Dan. "The criteria used to be: *do they have knowledge and skills that would be useful to the students and can we persuade them to come down to Barsteadworth?* The distinguishing characteristic of those that come now is that they're all close personal friends of Stella and Tim. They come down at weekend, party at Stella and Tim's for a couple of days, come in with a hangover on Monday morning, give a lecture and a few tutorials, and then set off back to Twickendean with hugs and kisses from their hosts and a substantial cheque from Barts. Cutting-edge stuff for the students, eh? What bullshit."

Dan ran his fingers over the drawing. "Look at this. Stella's married to Tim; Linda's married to Sky; and the four of them together behave like one big extended family. Patricia won't say boo to a goose, so she's kind of in with them too. It's horrible. You go into a meeting and they stop talking as you walk into the room. Or Linda whispers things behind her hand to Stella and they both smirk and glance at you. It makes you feel very uncomfortable."

"It sounds really childish", said Sophie.

"Well, it is, but it's very difficult to deal with. Two married couples, plus Patricia when it suits her, in a department of just 8 people. It's not just a stupid minority being hurtful and childish; they're in positions of power – well, Stella is, and Linda loves soaking that up – and they're damaging people. They've had the knife into Mervin for months. I think he's leaving. And now they've started on Phil. I keep getting these moments when I'm with Stella and/or the others and the conversation gets turned to Phil's faults. And they look at me, waiting for me to say something, and I don't."

"Shit. That's really awkward", said Sophie.

"It gets worse", said Dan. "Twice now – on top of all the cheap shots and anecdotes – Stella's had me in the office wanting to discuss the 'Phil problem'. I was in there with her today. I told her I wasn't aware of a 'Phil problem'. She'd told me I must have been. I must have seen the tense exchanges she'd had with Phil at Team Meetings. I said I had, but I just took that as part of the usual cut and thrust of debate. Phil is a very passionate man. He cares about what he does. It isn't personal; it's about the job. And the bottom line is, you *can* argue Phil down. He won't back a position just for its own sake; if you can counter his argument convincingly, he'll concede and he'll go along with you. I said to her 'you wouldn't want a bunch of yes-men and women would you?'"

"What did she say?"

"She didn't reply."

"Oh dear."

"Quite. But the thing is, I'm not just in there as 'me'. I'm supposed to be Stella's mentor until she gets used to the job, so I had to come up with some kind of objective managerial response; to advise her rather than saying what I really felt", said Dan.

"So what did you say?"

"Well, I kind of split the difference. I told her that I was starting to feel uncomfortable with having Phil picked apart in my presence, and then went on to say that if she had issues with Phil, then Phil was the person she should be speaking to."

Chapter Six
4 Years ago

It was a February Monday morning, 8.30. Dan was seated alone at his desk in the lecturers' office. He heard the door open and looked round. There was Phil Flanagan in trench coat and scarf, broad Irish face surrounded by a mop of unruly black hair, Buddy Holly glasses beginning to steam over at the unaccustomed heat and humidity. "Ah! So, how was 'the city that never sleeps' then?" said Dan, cheerfully.

"Humph". Phil hung his coat and scarf disconsolately on the rail in the recess behind the office door.

"Whaddya mean 'humph'? Didn't you have a good time? You can't go to New York and not have a good time".

"It was shit. I've just had a week where I felt like a complete outsider", said Phil.

"What are you talking about? You'd got Stella, Patricia and 50-odd students".

"Check this out". Phil produced a photo of a group of people dressed in winter clothes. "The team shot. This was in the hotel lobby on the last day." He pointed at the various faces. "Stella, Stella's husband, Stella's child, Stella's father-in-law, Stella's father-in-law's new wife. And that's me". Phil's finger went to a slightly uncomfortable looking figure at the back; same trench coat and scarf. "Patricia took the shot".

"Bloody hell. She took her whole family?" gasped Dan.

"Pretty much so, yeah."

"But she can't do that. There's only two people on that photo who're entitled to go... and the one behind the camera. Even Tim shouldn't be there. He's a casual employee. And as for her child and her fucking in-laws... what does she think she's doing? The students' fees subsidise the staff places on these trips, and she's using that to subsidise her family? That's *really* wrong", said Dan with a disbelieving laugh in his throat.

"Tell me about it. And not only that: they had almost bugger-all to do with the students once they were over there. They gave them a list of places they should see and then went off their own way, sightseeing and such. I think Macy's was the most favoured beneficiary of their intellectual input. I was taking whole troupes of students on my own around the museums. The worst bit was in the evenings, at dinner. I felt like a gatecrasher at a family party."

*****

It was the day of Dan's annual Staff Development Review. His private, one-to-one with his manager; the one clearly defined moment in the year when there could be a frank, confidential exchange between Lecturer and Course Director, where anxieties could be expressed and plans and remedies put in place. Dan entered Stella's office. She was all smiles. She didn't have much of an agenda: it was up to him, really. Was there anything he'd like to discuss? He didn't have much either. He was quite happy with his lot, but there was just one little thing – probably nothing – but he thought he should bring it up: he'd seen on the second year notice board details of a couple of seminar sessions that Patricia had planned, and they seemed remarkably close to the stuff he and Phil were doing with them. As far as he knew there was no available time in Patricia's modules for this and, from what he could see, there was a real danger of duplication. Stella said it was probably just a one-off; revision or something. She'd look into it. Dan asked her to be discreet. Patricia could be rather defensive

*****

There was a hint of spring in the air and enough warmth and light to last some way into the evening. Time for another Saturday night party at Stella and Tim's. Sophie and Dan caught the bus to the bottom of the hill and climbed up past the neat bungalows to the Lutyens-Como, gun-emplacement house. They stepped onto the gravel drive. Sky and Tim were seated outside of the front conservatory on white plastic garden chairs, glasses in hands. At the crunch of footsteps, the two men looked up from their drinks and, in a tone of heavy irony, Tim said "Oh great – Dan's here". Sky smirked and said nothing. Stella appeared from nowhere, rushing towards the new arrivals, arms outstretched, flustered and red-faced, saying "of course Dan's welcome – Tim's only joking".

Welcome? Dan could see the looks on their faces. He'd been taken by surprise. He felt awkward and pretended he'd not heard what had been said. He and Sophie went inside whilst Stella fussed and poured drinks. They left early.

*****

"…and it was clear I was about as welcome as a rash in a brothel. We left at about half ten. We were even able to catch the last bus back to the estate. Didn't need a taxi. Sophie didn't hear what was said, but she reckoned she could tell there was something wrong. She said there was an *atmosphere*", said Dan, his brow furrowed. The lunchtime canteen throng chatted and bustled around them. Trays edged noisily along the stainless steel rails in front of the counter, gathering up cod mornay, steak pie and chips or today's healthy option.

"It doesn't surprise me", said Phil.

"Why? What do you mean?" Dan looked up from his coffee.

"Oh. I didn't want to lay this on you." Phil looked back at Dan with a pained expression on his face. "But they've been slagging you off. And Mervin".

"So, what have they been saying?" pressed Dan.

"Well, it's not the only thing, but at the party Sky cornered me and wanted to know 'didn't I think you were a lazy bleeder?'", said Phil.

"WHAT? From that lazy little shit? If you can *find* him he's doing fuck all. I went to the store for something the other day and he was playing a computer game. He quickly closed it down. He was embarrassed and muttered something about downloading it for Jonte."

"I think that's what they were getting at with you: suggesting you waste time on the computer when you should be working. There've been sly little innuendos about computer games and such."

"Jesus. I don't even know how to play computer games. I've never played one in my life." Dan turned his palms towards his agitated face. "I don't even know what you do – how to work the bloody controls. Something else dawns on me, y'know. Way back when Stella first started – probably in her first week or so – I walked into her office and she was playing solitaire on the computer. My first thought at the time was *blimey, she must be good – I could never have found time to do that*. Not that I'd have wanted to. Then I realised: it hadn't hit her yet, you know, just how much work there is in the job. But I haven't thought about it since. It wasn't a big deal. But, thinking about this now: it's projection isn't it? I've seen *them* do it; so they invent a story about *me*. What else is there?"

"Well, that's the gist of it. You're lazy. That's what they're saying", replied Phil.

"Shit. I'm first in, last out – I think they resent me for that – and my half-day usually ends mid-afternoon. Stella doesn't even come to work on Fridays. And she's full-time; I'm half-time."

"Yeah, I know. For some sessions she's even hired Tim to come in whilst she's gone off to look after Jonte. Great isn't it – two lots of pay *and* a day off", said Phil. "That's what she sometimes has to do if she's got teaching on the Friday and can't get out of it: Tim covers her work and she goes home. If she hasn't, they're both at home."

Barsteadworth College

"That's corruption", said Dan.

"Yeah, well, whilst all that's going on, it's nice to be able to point the finger at someone else, isn't it?" said Phil.

"I thought there was something. They had this guest lecturer down the other week: Carina Crevice from Clapham. One of Stella's oldest friends, apparently. Still teaches at Twickendean. Stella introduced me to her on the Monday morning. Really off-hand and sarcastic with me, she was. I didn't know what I'd done wrong. I'd never met her before. I was there ready to be all nice and charming, but I scarcely got a word out before she started digging at me. I think it's pretty clear now that Stella and probably the others had been at work on her over the weekend and she was thoroughly briefed on what it was she was meant to think of me by Monday morning. Anyway, I went to her lecture, and I'm pleased to say that she's a lousy artist. All derivative, overblown, pretentious nonsense, and from what I could tell she's only made 3 pieces of work in the last 10 years. But you should have heard Stella's intro. You'd have thought it was the Second Coming."

"Yeah. I was there. Heard it all. Saw it all." said Phil, looking vaguely in the direction of the dessert counter. He brought his attention back to the table and looked at Dan. "They've had it in for Mervin, as well, you know. I think he's thinking of leaving".

"Yeah, I've had the Mervin stuff. Stella wants rid of him, but she knows Silas likes him and she has to tread carefully, so she's doing her best to make him feel uncomfortable – threatening to send him on refresher courses and such that are an insult to him and that she knows he won't go on – so he'll leave. I think it's working", said Dan. "What I have to tell you as well, Phil, is that just as they've been slagging me off to you, they've been slagging you off to me."

"Well, I don't suppose that should surprise me. What have they been saying?" asked Phil.

"Oh, I don't know. All sorts. Specifics are hard to come by. It's just that they reckon you're a recalcitrant fucker, really. Stella's actually had me in to discuss the 'Phil problem'."

"Fuck me. The 'Phil problem'? What's that, exactly?"

"Not sure, really. That you're a recalcitrant fucker, I guess", said Dan.

"Sounds a bit circular, doesn't it?" said Phil.

*****

One of the good things about getting in first was that you had a few moments of silence. You could gaze out of the window and think, and since work hadn't officially started yet, this apparent idleness was OK. Dan had known ever since he was seven, when he first found out that there was such a thing as dying, that the day his mother died would be the worst of his life. That was forty years ago, but he'd been right. And if coping comes easier with age, he could not have imagined how he might have felt if she had died earlier. He had loved and lost, he had been divorced, one of his best mates had died when he was a teenager, but he had never known pain like this. It had been a couple of weeks since he'd watched her die in Dashley Dyke General – complications around what should have been a routine operation – and one since the funeral. Even at the best of times words are crude tools for describing emotions, but for now they were all but useless. From friends and colleagues there seemed to be two sorts of response, both involving silence: those who'd gone through the same experience knew it was too awful for words. They just gave him a knowing look. Those who had yet to go through it knew it would be so awful that they wouldn't understand it until they'd experienced it, so they didn't feel qualified to say anything. They gave him a sympathetic look. It was a bit like the knowing look, but the eye-contact was much shorter.

He'd been trying his best to carry on as normal, but it was as though a huge hole had been bored through him. He'd tried to be his usual jokey self at work, but whether anyone else was fooled, to himself he sounded empty and unconvincing. He had accepted what had happened; he could deal with the fact that his mother had reached eighty and had had a better life than many. To that extent, he had dealt with it. It was just that it hurt so much, and in his enormous pain he felt raw and exposed.

*****

Friday lunchtime. Dan looked up out of the window to see Stella leaving the building. She seemed upset. Linda was tight to her side, arm around her shoulders, comforting her. The pair headed towards the car park. He looked back into the office. Phil proffered a typed A4 document.

"Have you seen this? This is what that's all about." Phil nodded in the direction of the car park.

Dan took the sheets from his hand. Two pages fixed with a staple in the top left corner. It was a detailed and savage complaint from the second years about the chaotic state the course had fallen into: the timetabling was confusing, rooms were double-booked, lectures had been cancelled without notice, they were being taught the same thing twice, there was too much theory…

*****

Friday night. Dan made three attempts to get Stella at home. On the third he decided to speak to the answering machine. "Hi Stella. I saw the complaint. I wanted to know if you're OK. What they said was well out of order; completely over the top. They get like that. End of term angst. They just get stressed and kick off at people. It'll be OK. Don't worry. Give us a call."

*****

Monday morning. The end-of-term team meeting was about to start in the lecturer's office. Dan was feeling pretty relaxed. The hard stuff was done, the degree show was over, the external examiners had been met and had gone away reasonably happy, and the holidays weren't far away. The main function of the meeting was to tie up the loose ends of the concluding academic year and start to plan for the next one. Dan helped carry in the bright blue plastic desks from the seminar room and assemble them into a large, eye-bothering conference table. It was just possible to squeeze himself and his chair between it and his desk. Phil, Patricia, Mervin, Sky and Tim did likewise. Stella and Linda strolled into the room last and sat together at the open end, near the door.

Stella announced that she hadn't had time to prepare an agenda, and glanced around the table.

"Dan, I've had a complaint from the students. The gist of it is that your teaching is all wrong."

What is she talking about? I saw the complaint. It was about her management failures. "What? What do you mean my teaching 'is all wrong'?"

"The students say it's too hard; they don't understand it; they don't like it; they feel overloaded; they're confused; they don't know whether they're coming or going. I've noticed this myself. Your teaching has stopped them working. Completely stopped them. And it drags everything back to the 1970s. Poststructuralism and all that: it's out of date. *Orientalism* by Edward Said: that is too. Why are you teaching this stuff? And it doesn't include anything on feminism."

This was all delivered with support from Linda, who was enthusiastically nodding and 'yes-yes'-ing like a sycophantic talking donkey, and who herself then took over the attack: "yes, and the students hate that first year module you devised too: *Understanding Materials*."

The two women sat back visibly revelling in their moment of triumph. It was clearly a well-rehearsed joint effort. Dan was flustered and embarrassed; completely taken aback. He'd had no inkling that this was coming. There had been no agenda; well, none that he'd known of.

Barsteadworth College

He had become slightly withdrawn since his mother's death. His grief had made him feel vulnerable and somehow diminished. His confidence had dipped. He was quieter. But work had become a form of refuge; a place where his mind could be quietly absorbed onto something he loved. Yet now, this exploded back into his face. He was being deliberately and unfairly humiliated in front of colleagues, most of whom he had been manager of until 9 months before. He was so shocked that he could hardly speak. In another time and place he would have acted differently, but here and now, that part of him that would have taken over and dealt with the situation seemed no longer to be available. He felt emptied, hopeless. They must have been aware, consciously or instinctively, of his weakened state, and chosen this moment to hurt him, when he was least able to fight back. The fact that it was women, not men, didn't help either. Most men know how to dish out an ass-kicking to another man, but are hardwired not to do such a thing to a woman, even if it was as richly deserved as it was at this moment. Dan was stymied and confused. He saw Linda and Stella steal a glance and grin at each other. Their plan had worked. He felt sick.

He did his best to clear his head and muster some form of defence, but at each turn Stella simply reprised her tirade as though she had heard nothing, with more nodding from Linda. He tried to keep his cool. He spoke calmly as he could.

"Post-structuralism emerged in the 70s, but it's still alive and kicking. People are still arguing and writing about it, and teaching it. And everything I use is from current anthologies. How can you say it's out of date? What better basis is there for critiquing postmodern art than poststructuralism? As for Said's *Orientalism*: it may well date from the 1970s, but it's an epoch-defining text. *And* it's in the current OU source book for arts undergraduates. And everything else I use is later than that, anyway. And I *do* include feminist texts. One I use by Griselda Pollock on Berthe Morisot comes to mind, and there are others."

Stella just repeated herself: these were old texts.

Dan regrouped. "And as for my lectures, there is no way the students don't like them or don't get them. I often find myself surrounded at the end by excited students who want to talk more about what they've heard."

"Lectures that students get excited about and want more of can still be bad teaching", said Stella.

Dan fell silent. How could you deal with logic like that?

Stella moved on: she was adamant: she was Course Director and that was that. Dan's teaching was rubbish.

OK, thought Dan. Maybe he shouldn't be defensive. He couldn't see what was wrong with his teaching, and the way the he'd been attacked wasn't right. But, like she said, she was Course Director. She was also supposed to be very experienced. Maybe she's got a whole load of new ideas and teaching material at her fingertips.

"OK. If you don't want me to use this stuff, what do you want in its place?"

Stella's face went even paler than usual and she stopped grinning. *Good grief! She's actually launched into all this crap without giving any thought to what it was she wanted.*

After a brief, flustered moment, Stella said: "I think we should be looking at existentialism and Franz Kafka."

Dan's head reeled again. *Am I really hearing this? She wants rid of stuff written over the last couple of decades, because it's out of date, and to replace it with the philosophy of the 1950s and the works of a novelist who died in the 1920s? That's what she would have been looking at when she was at college in the 70s. That's all she's got. This isn't an academic spat. It's not about the texts at all. It's about me.*

With Stella seemingly on the back foot, Linda intervened: "And anyway, we think you spend too much time on the computer. What do you do on it?"

"Yes", added Stella. "What do you do in all the time you're on the computer? I mean, it might be OK, but *we* don't know what it is you do."

Dan gasped in disbelief. If it wasn't that he was trapped in a corner and would have had to climb over colleagues or the desks to get out, he would have left the room. He shouldn't even dignify that sort of crap with an answer. As it was he felt compelled to stay and fight his ground. *But how do you defend that? How can you say what you do on the computer?*

"I do what you do, what everyone else does: I write lectures, check my email, file things...", he said, to which Linda ejected air from her nose and gave a wry grin.

Dan's explanation sounded lame. But that was all it ever could do. Not only was he trying to prove a negative – he wasn't doing anything wrong – there was no real shape to the allegation he was facing. It was just a wide-open accusation of some form of guilt, which in its vagary couldn't be answered. Stella looked triumphant. Linda smirked.

The meeting ended and the group made its way out of the room. As she neared the door, Linda said to Stella "Griselda Pollock: what a cliché", and glanced momentarily back at Dan, who was still trying to extricate himself from behind the blue desks.

He stood silently in the studio for a moment, gazing towards the car park, but seeing nothing, and then looped back to the office and picked out the file on the 'hated' module. The student feedback forms said that 89% were satisfied, happy or very happy with it.

It was lunchtime. He should eat.

*****

He avoided everybody and went over to Barsteadworth University's refectory. It was a five-minute walk from Barts and the thinking time was useful. Nothing they had said was actually true. It was always the case that some of the weaker students would resent anything that stretched them, particularly on Fine Art degrees, where there was always a bunch who wanted 'BA' after their names without having to work too hard for it. It wasn't unusual for that lot to grumble if they felt they were being overtaxed. But that wasn't what had been happening. For one thing, the teaching material in question was pretty standard BA stuff, drawn from the usual sources; and for another, it wasn't just the weaker students who were complaining. The signatories to the complaint included the stronger ones. They usually revelled in this teaching.

"Mind if I join you." Phil sat down.

Dan scarcely looked up from his plate. "How did you know I'd be over here?"

"Part guess; part I didn't want to be in our refectory with that bunch of twats, either. That was bullying. They were haranguing you."

Dan didn't want to admit, to himself or anybody else, that he had been bullied. He was a middle-aged man, highly experienced and not a school kid.

"You know what was really happening there, don't you?" asked Phil.

"I think I'm getting the picture. They don't like me. And that complaint, last week – she's trying to dump it on me."

"That's part of it. Since you've been half time there's a load of stuff you've missed. The timetable's gone to pot and she's been running around blaming you. She said it in front of Frank and Ledlock at the last School Board."

"What? The fucking cow. There's nothing wrong with the timetable. There were a few anomalies that needed to be sorted out towards the end of the year – rooming issues that couldn't be dealt with when I first drafted it last August – but she *knew* about that. I made it clear when I handed it over, and I've reminded her several times since. It's her responsibility now. I've not been Course Director for nearly a year."

"Well," said Phil, "she hasn't done anything about it, and the thing is falling to bits. Frankly, I don't think she understands it. Apparently students have been going to rooms that have other classes in."

"No wonder they're pissed off."

"Oh, that's just the start. You know Patricia's just supposed to running that little half-module with the second years?"

"Yes. Of course I do. I wrote the programme and went through it with her last summer. It's just a series of tutorials to prime them for next year's dissertation."

"Well, she's completely altered it without telling anybody. I only picked up on it a few days ago. I was about to do a session on that Anna C. Chave text, and they'd already done it. And from there I had a bit of a dig around. Seems she's now running a clone of the second year contextual studies programme we've been running. She's stolen our teaching."

Dan gasped. "I knew she'd done a couple of sessions, months ago. I had the same experience: I had to cancel some texts and find some new ones. But... let me get this right: she's copied our whole second year teaching programme and teaching it herself?"

"Well, a lot of it, yeah. She missed some because we've revised the programme as we've gone along, so some of what she's got is what we used last year. But there's no reason why we might not want to reuse that at some point, and she's keeping an eye on us and copying our new stuff when she can. She's also using the same format as us: student-led seminars."

"Her module doesn't have anything like enough time to accommodate that."

"I know. That's right. So to get round that she's expanded it from a half-module to something like a double-module. Theory's gone from being a day or so a week to virtually half the week."

"I don't believe it."

"It's true. She's expanded the second year programme massively and, of course, there isn't time for that. So on top of Stella's timetabling balls-ups, there are additional clashes because of Patricia's additional lessons. And like I said, she is actually teaching some of the same material as you and me. And the students are going nuts."

"How can... I've never seen anything like this. How can a fucking experienced, professional lecturer simply set up her own unilateral sub-course within a course and not tell anybody? Well, not just a sub-course, a duplicate of what her colleagues are doing. No wonder the students are confused. Does Stella know?"

"She must do. I tried to bring it up with her and she just shut me out. Wouldn't discuss it."

"So did I. You know, in a low-key way, ages ago. I thought whatever was going on was dealt with. But it isn't. And she's saying it's my fault? At least, according to that meeting it is."

"It looks that way: she'd rather blame you than Patricia."

"So, blame goes not with who did a thing, but with who she'd prefer to blame?"

"Could be. On the other hand, it could be that she's in on it, happy about it and blaming you is a bonus."

*****

Barsteadworth College

That evening was the annual staff get-together, organised by Silas Beasley's secretary in Barsteadworth Community Centre. It was a gloriously balmy summer's evening. The sun was beginning to set behind the allotments, the marking was done, the new graduates had gone home with their degrees and everyone could relax. Relieved lecturers, technicians and admin staff gathered outside in the gardens and drank beer and wine from plastic beakers. As a conversation with Tim Evans from Foundation came to its natural conclusion, Dan swung away and saw Linda coming towards him through the throng. She shoved her face into his and said "have you noticed how power is moving from you to us?", then smirked and walked away without waiting for an answer.

*****

Something was happening. Had there been any doubt about it before, there wasn't now. Dan started to keep a dossier. If he was going to be set up for something, he'd need evidence to defend himself. What follows is largely taken from Dan's dossier.

The first entry in the dossier was a summary of what had happened at the meeting along with the following email, which he had sent to Frank Fuller:

To: Frank Fuller
From: Dan Ripley
Subject: Confidential
2 July

Dear Frank

I wish to complain about the following. At a staff meeting on 1 July, I was subjected to the following assault on my professionalism by Stella Jobby.

1. I was told that my teaching 'dragged everything back to the 1970s'.
2. I was told that my teaching had 'stopped the students working'.

3. When I pointed out that some students had been very excited by my lectures and actually asked for more of them, I was told that 'lectures that students get excited about and want more of can still be bad teaching'.
4. I was told that I spend a lot of time in the office on the computer and Stella does not know what I am doing.

None of the above was in any real sense substantiated.

Regarding point 1: on the basis of Edward Said's 'Orientalism', which *does* date from the 70s, all of the texts I had used were denigrated, even though no other texts were mentioned. Texts are carefully chosen to form a contextualising framework for contemporary thought and practice. The Said text is epoch defining and still very relevant. It was abstracted from the *current* OU anthology of critical texts.

Point 2 was supported by vague reference to anecdote, and there was no balancing acknowledgment of the good that my teaching has done.

Point 3 is just bizarre.

Point 4 was accompanied by the proviso that what I do on the computer *might* well be fine, but Stella does not know what it is. The implication, however, is that I was doing something I should not or was wasting time, and I was put on the spot trying to account for a year in which *of course* I used the computer for many hours and *of course* I could not provide any specific account for what I had used it for – who can? I found myself trying to defend a nasty insinuation, which because it could not rationally be defended looked like it might have some basis in reason.

All of the above was delivered in front of other staff and I believe it was a deliberate attempt to embarrass and undermine me.

I should add as well that at this meeting, when I was challenged over the amount of time I spend on the computer, it was a joint effort between Linda and the Stella. Indeed, I gained the impression that the ambushes I was subjected to were a result of joint planning by Linda and Stella: one would say something and the other would back it up. Another attack was over a Year 1 module I had devised the previous year. They told me that 'the students hated it'. This being predicated on the basis of some conversation Linda had had with 'the students' (who were presented as being of one voice in this) meant that I could not challenge it. Afterwards, I looked in the module file: the student feedback forms gave it an 89% approval rating.

Regards
Dan

*****

Frank called Dan into his office and said he would deal with the situation discreetly, in order not to exacerbate things in the department. Dan, having now had a plenty of experience of Frank's ways of dealing with things, decided that this would probably not be enough and that he would keep on with the dossier.

*****

"Why didn't you tell me sooner? That was last week and you've been dwelling on it all this time", said Sophie, leaning back in the leather armchair, yellow coffee mug in both hands.

The test match burbled away quietly on the telly. Dan leant forward on the sofa and placed his green mug on the Ikea Lack coffee table, on a black coaster with a Mapplethorpe-like flower on it. "I don't know. I was embarrassed, I guess. I didn't want to admit to what had happened. But worse that that, I didn't deal with it. I didn't know how to. I'm as mad at me as I am at them. I should have been able to deal with it, but I couldn't. I've never been subjected to anything like that. I wasn't equipped. Maybe it's a class thing: cultural differences. I'm used to the working-class way of dealing with things: head-on, bluntly. I'm not used to all these manoeuvres and mind-games, all this underhand stuff. I can do rational argument and *fuck off you mealy-mouthed hag* – if I wanted the sack, of course – but I don't seem to have anything in-between."

"All four of them – Tim, Stella, Linda and Sky – they all went to private schools, you know", said Sophie. "They've had a life-time's training in this – negotiating alliances, vying for popularity and dumping crap on people without getting caught – all vital but unwritten parts of the curriculum."

"I think you're right. It does remind me of one of those American teen sorority movies, where it's all about trying to be popular and gather a clan to yourself and put other people down", said Dan. "It *has* been like that with this lot. I've had invitations to join the group, in the form of invitations to put other people down – Phil and Mervin, usually, Frank and Ledlock, less often – but I won't bite. That's why I've been shoved out. I won't join the clique. I've had my chance, and if I won't join, I'm the enemy too."

"It's all incredibly childish."

"Yeah, well I'm not going to play the game. I only go there to do a job. I'm not interested in being a member of anybody's juvenile gang. There's more to this, though. Patricia's always been envious of my programme. Well, I say mine; mine and Phil's, I mean. A lot of it I brought from Leeds, but Phil and I developed and updated it. When I was Course Director there was nothing she could do about it, but now she's trying it on, and I think she's got an ally in Stella: she's got her own reasons for attacking it. I'm increasingly getting the impression that Stella hasn't read anything since she graduated – *in the1970s!* – and she finds this unfamiliar material a threat, particularly all this nasty poststructuralism stuff, which, from what I can gather, she seems to see as both newfangled *and* outmoded."

"You're really saying she doesn't understand it? I mean, I don't either, but it's not my subject. She's Course Director. She should be on top of things like that."

"Well, I don't think she is. There's been no discussion about content. She doesn't say what's wrong with my stuff, apart from some vacuous nonsense about it being 'out of date'. She's just against it. And she won't say what she wants in its place. Well not in any detail and not in any way that makes sense. The only things she's been able to come up with are existentialism and fucking Kafka. They're more up to date! It's moronic. I've seen some of the tutorial sheets that she's given to students, left on desks. They nearly always refer the students to existentialism and Kafka. *Blah, blah, blah, experiment more and look at Kafka and existentialism*, over and over again. It's fucking ridiculous, but it's all she's got. I just wish other people could see. I can't imagine how some of her remarks would look to academics from another college, let alone a university. Do you know, there are no books in her office?"

A pigeon had landed on the batting track and refused to leave, much to the amusement of the commentators. Dan looked down into his empty mug and rotated it on its coaster. Sophie looked at him. "You know Harmony Morris?" she said.

"Yes, of course, one of the second years. A mature student. She's very good."

"Well, I was chatting with her at one of Stella's parties. She'd just dragged herself away from Tim. For some reason he thought Harmony had been to a private school, and he'd been trying ingratiate himself by saying that he thought *their* kind of education was something that set *their* sort of people apart, and he really didn't think much of people who'd been to state schools. Harmony had in fact been to a state school and didn't know why he thought otherwise. She also said she thought he was a prick."

*****

Stella and Dan scanned the timetable on Stella's office wall, the one Dan had drawn up a year earlier and that Stella had inherited. It was a large paper chart on which a grid represented the year, coloured boxes denoted the modules and initials showed who taught what, where and when. That year was over now, and Dan explained to Stella how to draw up a new one... *again*.

He waved his hands about, pointing to the different parts as he described them. "You start with the blank grid. You put your year groups along the horizontal axis, days down the vertical one. You then mark the modules on it: you know the order they go in and the amount of time devoted to each from the course handbook. And you know how many teaching hours each lecturer has: allocate their teaching hours as you see fit, attaching them to the modules they can best make a contribution to. It helps if you colour-code the modules and the lecturers' initials, so you can see at a glance where you are – you can use the same scheme as I've used here if you want. It's not as hard as it looks. It's just a case of getting started; then it just flows. It's just logic and common sense. You know you're done when all the lecturers' hours are allocated and all the modules are adequately covered."

"Yes. OK. I think I've got it. It's all pretty straightforward, really, isn't it?"

*****

"Can you come over to Portakabin 1 and help us with the timetabling?" said Linda, poking her head round the door into the lecturers' office. Dan was the only person in the room. She had to mean him. He looked round from his computer.

"I thought she'd sorted that last week. I went through it all with her."

Linda pulled her little-girl, pleading face.

Dan exhaled noisily. "OK, I'll be over in a minute. Just let me put this to bed." He clicked 'save' and shuffled a disorderly pile of papers into one neat stack.

All the desks in the portakabin had been pushed together to make one giant table. On top of the table was a huge chart: Dan's last-year's timetable, photocopied, blown-up and stuck together with Pritt Stick and Sellotape. On top of that were Stella and Sky on all fours, arses stuck up in the air. Indelible markers, bottles of Tippex and highlighting pens were strewn around them. They quibbled quietly about something. Stood around the tables were Tim, Patricia and Linda, hands on hips, looking seriously at whatever it was Sky and Stella were quibbling about.

"What are you doing", said Dan.

"We're making the new timetable by modifying your old one from last year", said Stella, with a certain smugness in her voice.

"That won't work. Days fall on different dates. Terms start on different dates. Easter'll be at a different time. Exam dates will be different", said Dan. "And we've altered some of the modules. And there are other things: reading w…"

"We've thought of all that", said Stella. "We're cutting and pasting the dates. We're cutting them out with a scalpel and moving them down to match up with this year's weeks."

Dan looked at what they were doing. There was a confusing mess of black and white lines, loose bits of cut-out text and letters, sticky things stuck to other sticky things. "Why don't you just start again with a blank chart? This is photocopied. You can't even see the colours anymore." No answer. "How long have you been doing this?"

"Look, if you've only come here to criticise… All morning", said Stella.

"I'm only trying to make sense of it, Stella."

"Well it's time we went for lunch, anyway. Will you help us after?"

*****

An hour into his rescue attempt, Dan was feeling increasingly frustrated. He was angry at himself for having got drawn onto it. It was an impossible task. He knew he'd only joined in to show willing, and the stupidity of it all was getting to him. Now he was the one on the large improvised desk, arse in the air, next to Stella, trying to make sense of it, but the more they did the more confusing it got. Sky and Tim, attention spans exhausted, stood by the window, chatting, joking about something. Linda and Patricia looked on, making irritating, futile suggestions now and then. They didn't believe in it either, but they wouldn't be seen to let Stella down.

This date moved and knocked that date on into a place where it shouldn't be. Reading week seemed to have got lost – had something stuck on top of it probably, but he couldn't be sure where, because several bits were stuck over several other bits and there was no telling which bit had reading week beneath it. And when was the trip going to be this year? And what would that do to the start of Content and Context? They needed to remove Barry's initials too. Whose initials were going to go there? And whose initials were going to go into the place where those initials had been taken from? Was this or that bit stuck where it was when all the photocopies were stuck together or afterwards? Did it still need to be moved, or not? Some bits that had been moved might have made sense *when* they were moved, but since something else had been moved they didn't make sense any more, so they were moved again, but then had a knock-on effect on something else. Some bits had got stuck in the wrong place because there was excess Pritt Stick everywhere and they'd been sat on. Other bits were then stuck down to correspond with them. And what had happened to Christmas? Christmas had gone. *Christmas had fucking gone.* He looked at the meaningless mess of letters and lines in front of him. *This must be what it's like to be dyslexic.* Nearly every member of staff was in this room. Umpteen man-hours on a farce, on something Stella should have done herself, like he'd done before her and like all the other Course Directors did without fuss every year.

"I've had enough Stella. This is pointless. It's just a waste of people's time. You know my view: it needs starting again and doing properly on a blank chart, so you can see what you're doing."

He went back to the office and resumed his lesson prep. The others stayed in the portakabin for the rest of the afternoon.

*****

9th September. The pre-term team meeting. Dan hadn't slept. The pre-summer one had started to go through his mind again. But then, Frank must have had that discreet conversation with Stella by now. *It would be OK.* What had happened before could not be repeated. They were all reasonable people. Professionals. It had been an aberration.

As was now routine for these events, the team dragged the blue Formica desks from the seminar room into the lecturers' office, shoved them together, worked chairs into the gulley created between them and the permanent furniture and squeezed into position. The gaps between each person were roughly equal, except for that between Linda and Stella, who were visibly sitting together.

As was also now routine, there was no agenda, though Stella had some hand-written notes and clearly there was business unfinished from the previous meeting. In order to start things off on a positive note and to show his willingness to address the key feature of that last meeting – his putatively outmoded teaching material – Dan announced that he had bought a copy of the latest Harrison and Wood *Art In Theory* anthology. He thought Stella would be pleased. An up-to-date theory book of the highest quality: just what she wanted. But to his dismay, she retorted that she "would like to burn that book", and dismissed it as "boring".

Boring? BORING? 1200 pages and scores of writers: Fried, Beuys, Krauss, Barthes, Habermas, Kristeva, Foster and the rest! Artists, critics, philosophers, curators – the most brilliant thinkers and writers on art and culture of the last 100 years – had all been brought to their knees by a mind so dazzling that it put them all in the shade, all humbled by one brilliant, incisive Stella Jobby insight: they were "boring". What was even more remarkable was that she had been able to make this devastating observation without even having read the book. Stella developed her discourse: "I don't understand why people don't buy other books", she added. Dan figured that he was probably the 'people' she had in mind and tried to explain that he'd bought other books too, but in the full flow of her tirade Stella was not for listening.

Patricia then interjected and said that she thought it was a useful compilation. And in a strange, instantaneous about-turn, Stella's tone changed completely, and she said they should buy a copy for the office.

After a brief, silent moment, which the team seemed to need to come to terms with the remarkable mental somersault it had just witnessed, Stella moved on and announced that she had "now read" the texts that she had criticised at the July meeting.

So she'd never read them? She'd delivered all that crap about how inappropriate Dan's teaching material was without ever having seen it. However, she now knew, since she'd now looked, that she'd been wrong in saying there were no feminist texts. Thus, it was necessary to change tack: picking on a Jo Spence article in particular, she accused Dan of using it simply "because it was by a woman". Dan was a poor lecturer and sexist if he did *not* include women's texts; and he was a poor lecturer and sexist – with a penchant for tokenism – if he *did*. How did he plead: guilty or culpable? He couldn't win… or was it that he could only lose? Dan again struggled to keep his cool, to pretend that this really was some kind of reasonable debate. He explained to Stella that all of his teaching material was carefully chosen on a range of bases: its relevance to what was going on in art at the moment, and to get a broad spread of standpoints, voices, methodologies and such… Stella had chosen badly in using the Jo Spence text as her target. She'd evidently only seen the name and not the content. It hadn't been the feminist associations that made this particular Spence text of interest to Dan. He explained to the meeting that he had decided to use it because Spence was working class and because she came to art education as a mature student and, as such, her battles with the system constituted a revealing and non-standard perspective on art education and this was valuable support for working-class and mature students who might find themselves in a state of culture-shock. At this Stella backed off and referred to her private agenda for another topic on which to attack Dan. Linda, close enough to read Stella's notes, grinned as she delivered.

In front of Patricia and the rest of the course team, Stella announced that Dan had accused Patricia of "stealing his teaching". Dan was mortified. He made some vague attempt to defend himself, but mixture of shock, embarrassment and the impossibility of proving a negative left him all but speechless. Stella revelled in her triumph and Linda shared the moment of glory. He'd never said "stealing" or "stolen" and he'd yet to have chance to bring up what he'd learned from Phil after the last meeting. All there had been was that low-key conversation back in February, and that was part of his Staff Development Review, which is supposed to be absolutely confidential. She was using his Staff Development Review as a weapon against him.

Whilst Dan tried to recover from his shock and embarrassment, Stella announced that she had invented a new post – Theory Co-ordinator – and had given it to Patricia, so that she could oversee the teaching of all art theory in the department. Senior Lecturer Dr Daniel Ripley would now have to submit all of his theory teaching to Lecturer Ms Patricia Kleb for her inspection and approval.

Once again Dan's head reeled with incredulity. Nevertheless, he knew he could not let the meeting end without clarity from Stella over what exactly she wanted from his seminar texts. All there had been were accusations, attacks and rhetoric. She had never actually said what she wanted. Kafka and existentialism, even if they could be taken seriously, which in this context they could not, were only two things. Lots of subjects needed to be taught. What did she want? He asked again:

"Stella, can you clear up something for me? Are you still adamant that post-structuralism is too hard and out of date, as you were in July? And if so, what do you want me to teach in its place?"

"I'm very happy to have poststructuralist theory in the teaching programme", said Stella, "and I have never said otherwise."

This time it wasn't only Dan who was astonished: the whole group – even her allies – fell silent.

The group extricated itself from the hot plastic chairs and filed out of the room. Dan, having been furthest from the door, was last to leave. Stella and Linda waited for him in the doorway and blocked his path. As he paused, Linda looked at Dan, smirked and said "I think you should have your penis injected with botox".

Dan was in a stunned state of disbelief. He looked at Stella. In spite of what he had just experienced, some part of him still expected her to see this remark as evidence that things had gone too far and to have something to say. But she did not. She just grinned. The two women then walked away.

*****

"Are you going to complain?" asked Sophie, propping herself up with an elbow on her pillow.

"I should, but I feel stymied by loads of reasons not to", said Dan, back leant against the headboard. "It's just like last time: I'm embarrassed by what's happened, but I'm also embarrassed that I don't know how to deal with it. And I don't want to admit to either to yet more people: either that it's happening or that I can't deal with it. I feel pathetic. I *am* pathetic."

"No you're not", said Sophie, angrily. "This is not your fault. It's their behaviour that's wrong, not yours. Your behaviour in the face of nasty provocation is impeccable. And you've avoided being goaded into saying or doing something that would get you into trouble. You're dealing with it in the only way you can: you're arguing your case. But you're up against irrationality. You can't win. The only thing you can do to get it resolved is complain, get it sorted out."

"I *have* complained: I complained to Stella about Patricia copying my teaching, and ended up having that used as a weapon against me; I complained to Frank about what Stella did at the last meeting, and exactly the same thing happened at this. And who would I complain to about being told I have should have my penis injected with botox? The person I should complain to – my line manager – was there, grinning. I could take it upstairs to Frank, but I'd find that too humiliating. Besides, with Frank's track record, do you really think anything would happen?"

Sophie leaned over and put an arm his shoulder. "Anyway, I think the 'botox' thing is more a swipe at me than you; at my new job, injecting the stuff. She obviously resents it. An affront to her feminist credentials! They don't stop her bleaching her hair and putting the slap on every day, though, do they?"

Dan shrugged. "No, but I'm not so sure it has much to do with feminism. More a case, I think, that you're making a fair amount of money at it and that pisses her off. And I don't think she'd have ever had a go at you about it, anyway. They're just trying to undermine me and she's trying to do her best to claim the moral high ground whilst she does it. I mean: my teaching's crap and my penis needs injecting with botox – it's an odd combination, ideologically speaking, don't you think?"

"Well, whatever the case, she has no right to say what she said. That really was unbelievable. What I think is an even bigger disgrace, though, is that her boss was quite happy for her to have said it."

"Yeah. And can you imagine if that had been the other way round; if I'd said to Linda she should have her vagina injected with botox? Not only would I lose my job, I'd never teach anywhere again."

"It's not only that is it? She couldn't even have said the equivalent to a woman. She's said it in the only circumstances she could: she's relying on your sense of chivalry in order to get away with it. And Stella backs her up. They really are poison, aren't they?"

"Yes, and they've poisoned the whole course team. The whole department's going to shit. Nobody trusts anybody anymore. I go in on edge now, just waiting for the next attack."

"What I can't make sense of", said Sophie, "was her telling you to stop what you were teaching because it was unsuitable, and *then* saying she was all in favour of it with no recollection of saying otherwise."

"I'm not sure 'sense' is that abundant a commodity in the department nowadays. Perhaps it's Stella's version of 'non-linear logic' again."

"What's that? 2 and 2 makes 5?"

"Yeah; or 6, or 27… or 153. Whatever you want on the day, really."

"You know, you really need to get something in writing. She's said one thing; then she's said the opposite *and* lied about what she'd said before. Whatever you do now, she can point to the occasion when she told you not to do it, and everyone else will have amnesia about the contradiction."

"Yes, I know. I'm going to email her for clarification tomorrow."

"That book-burning thing's a worry isn't it? You know what they say about people who burn books."

"I'm sure she'd like to burn me – and Phil – and I think she may have already frazzled Mervin. I don't think he's coming back. He's had enough."

"Poor Mervin."

"Quite."

"Look, love; there's no point in dwelling on it. They're just very unpleasant people. And you need to get some sleep now. It's very late."

"Fat chance. I'm just too wound up."

*****

Dan sent the following email and recorded it and his latest experiences in his dossier.

To: Stella Jobby
From: Dan Ripley
Subject: Yesterday's Meeting etc..
10 September

Stella
There seem to be some misapprehensions going around and I wanted to ask for, and give clarity on a couple of issues, not least because there are some that seem to call my competence into question on what I see as an unfair basis. I want to write this down to have these issues considered calmly, outside of the heated atmosphere of the meeting.

Timetabling
I gather you are unhappy with the timetable I handed over to you last summer. When I handed it over and in various meetings and conversations since I made it clear that we had not been well served by the computer rooming system and that there would be accommodation issues towards the end of the year that would need to be monitored and addressed. I am aware of how difficult the systems must appear and I am always happy to help in any way I can, but as a part-time lecturer I am no longer in a position to take an overview of things and I cannot continue to take responsibility for this up to a year after I have handed the job over to you.

Co-ordination with Patricia

Phil and I have tried very hard and over a long period to co-ordinate our teaching with Patricia's. As she teaches just 'theory' and Phil and I run two major modules in Year 2 that combine theory and practice, close co-ordination is vital. We need to see each other's teaching in order not to overlap. However, as you know, Patricia will not share things with other members of staff and we cannot find out what it is we are supposed to be co-ordinating with. By about the middle of last academic year, after months of asking and much too late to plan around, I had finally received some of Patricia's theory module handbooks. However, within a day she wanted them back – she needed them for something and insisted that these were the only available copies. I hadn't had chance to read them and I still, therefore, have no detailed knowledge of the content of the Patricia's modules. Phil and I have had to try to work with only the vaguest understanding of what her material is. We, on the other hand, have tried to have an open debate and have placed our information in the public areas of the department: we always pin copies of our teaching programmes and samples of each text to the noticeboard.

What happened between my 'Contemporary Practices' module and Patricia's 'Research Project Preparation' module is indicative. Contemporary Practices is supposed to be four times the size in study hours of Research Project Preparation. But Patricia expanded RPP massively and taught it off-syllabus: she effectively turned it into a clone of Contemporary Practices – whilst Contemporary Practices was running! No wonder the students were confused. But again – and I said this yesterday – this is not something I was party to (nor was Phil). It was a unilateral decision that affected us but that we had no knowledge of or control over.

It is, to say the least, rather galling to have to put up with these frustrations and then to be blamed for them. And I find myself bemused at the fact that it is Phil and I who have been repeatedly criticised when Patricia seems immune.

Seminar Texts

You were of the view, having spoken to some of the students, that some of the texts were too demanding and some of the subject matter was inappropriate. Would you let me have some clarification on this – which texts you want to get rid of and what you want to see in their place?

Regards,
Dan

*****

"Please… sit down". That now familiar invitation. Dan sat down and faced Stella across her office. Green zipper with white piping, fawn cords... "I thought we should talk… try to improve the situation."

Dan waited. Said nothing.

"The thing is, you were never a team, here", opened Stella. "I mentioned this to Frank. He agrees."

Of course we were a bloody team… til you arrived, that is. Should I tell her about the Fuller Fudge? She must know by now. She's got a bit of it and she's using it.

"I think we worked together quite well, actually, Stella."

"Yes, but you weren't a *team*", she stressed, "a *team*".

Oh I see. At least I think I do. 'Team' for her means we all go out together and pretend we like each other. Sod that. I don't have to socialise with people because I work with them.

Dan said nothing. Stella continued:

"Look. The away I see it, there has been a split in the department along gender lines and things have become ideological."

What is she talking about? Ideological? I've been harangued and abused and now I'm supposed to believe this is some kind of serious, intellectual controversy? They're pissing down my back and telling me it's raining. Dan wasn't sure if he was speechless, being enigmatic or just wasn't being drawn in to yet another absurd, frustrating exchange. Either way, he said nothing and just looked at her.

"As regards your email: I couldn't find words to reply to it…"

Couldn't find words? Couldn't find fucking words? What is she talking about?

"..but, you know, doing the best I can with it:" she glanced down at the piece of white A4 in her hand "I can tell you that I have never had any problems with the timetabling. It's all been absolutely fine…"

Dan glanced at the ceiling: panels, tiles sort of, white with a textured effect, held up by white metal strips that criss-crossed the room. He brought his head back level again and looked at Stella. *She's moaned to me about it – in roundabout terms, of course – and I know from Phil that she's moaned about it behind my back in the office and at the Academic Board in front of Fuller, Ledlock and the rest. What else has she got?*

".. but the thing is, because I never wrote it, I never really understood it, and I haven't been able to modify it or update it."

What? Who's been running the course for the last 12 months? Everyone else understands it.

"I offered to help you with it… several times", said Dan at last.

"Yes, but well, you know…"

He didn't know, but didn't imagine he was ever going to.

Stella picked up another piece of paper from the broad selection of possibilities on her cluttered desk. The gesture seemed to suggest it was a casual bit of picking up, as though any piece of paper would do, but her face took on that look that it had in meetings, when she was going to pull off one of her coups. This was something she'd been working on.

"I've had a good look at the handbook for Pauline's module. It says that she needs to cover 'relevant cultural contexts, theories and methodologies'. So she *had* to teach those subjects."

"I know what it says, Stella..." *Good grief. I don't believe it. She's scrutinised the thing, looking for loopholes. She's bending heaven and Earth to argue Patricia's corner.* "...I wrote the module. The thing is, it was supposed to be a series of tutorials to discuss each student's work. Of course it would need to take account of the relevant bits of theory. How could it not? But that doesn't give her carte blanche to expand it and turn it into something it was never designed to be."

"Yes, but look what it says here..."

"Stella. Listen: I wrote the flaming thing. You can't read additional secret intentions into the author, because I *am* the author. You can't argue this one. And, besides, there are just no circumstances that I know of where a lecturer can unilaterally, *privately*, change part of a degree, expand its allowed teaching time and to turn it into a clone of a module that's already running. It was bound to cause chaos, and it has. Why are you trying so hard to support her? It just can't be justified. What are you trying to do?"

Stella exhaled noisily. "I feel I have to support her."

"What?"

"Well, you know how insecure she is. And she finds you intimidating."

"What?! Me? Intimidating?"

"Yes. You know..."

"No, I don't. I'm just an ordinary guy. I'm not especially pushy or anything. I'm not aggressive. What's intimidating about me?"

"Your knowledge. Your ability."

Dan glanced again at the ceiling and around the room, and then back at Stella. "OK. So I'm more qualified than her, but I don't ram that down anybody's throat. I just get on with the job. And Patricia is a very able person. I am *not* intimidating."

"But you are. And it's not just that. It's the northern accent, the working-class thing, the way you dress, your glasses, the way you cut your hair."

What the fuck is she on? He tried to picture what she saw: bald head, FCUK zipper, Next jeans and shoes, narrow glasses from Specsavers' 'Fashion Eyes' range. The uniform of this week – what every other bloke in Barsteadworth was wearing. Not something that would keep John Galliano awake. He didn't know whether to be amused, embarrassed, flattered or just dismayed. He settled for a bit of each, but mostly the latter. *I come here to teach. I'm 48 years old. Why am I having this conversation?* He found himself squinting at Stella, as though there might be answers to be found in her powdery white face. "Look, as far as I'm concerned, Patricia is a very able lecturer. I'm sure she knows lots of things I don't. But I can't be responsible for her personal demons."

"Hmm". She looked at him briefly, then shuffled and scanned her pieces of A4. "As regards your seminar texts, I'm fine with them. Carry on as planned. I've just received Phil's texts from last year. I haven't seen yours yet. Would you let me have them?"

She lambasted my texts at the July meeting. At the one the other day she said she'd read them and was all in favour of them and had no recollection of ever saying otherwise. Today she hasn't read them – hasn't seen them yet, in fact, and therefore doesn't even know what they are – but she's in favour of them anyway!? But then, on the other hand, she'd cited the Said and the Spence ones specifically. So she's read some… or just seen them. Or maybe she's just seen the titles. Or maybe Linda's told her what they were and what she should think. What has she seen? What hasn't she seen?

"You've got them. They're all in the module file." Dan pointed. "It's one of the yellow ones, second shelf up, above your head".

"Oh yes. Of course. I'll have a look through, later." Stella tapped the bottom of her papers on the desk with both hands and made a small neat sheaf. The meeting was over.

*****

Dan rolled over in bed. 3.05am said the Alba radio-alarm with its indifferent red digits. Sophie had long since gone and got into bed in the spare room. One of them had to get some sleep. The team meetings, yesterday's meeting, the exchanges, frustrations and humiliations ran past his mind over and over like an endless loop of tape. Her latest position was that she was in favour of his teaching. *But she hadn't seen it!* She'd left herself a loophole. She could still change her mind. Not that she needed a loophole: she could retrospectively say that the conversation never took place. He knew she was capable of that. He'd seen it. He wanted something in writing. That would put his mind at rest. Or was he being driven to pedantry by the stress? First his mum, then those awful ritual humiliations at the meetings. He wasn't himself. He felt messed-up. Could he trust his judgment any more? Shouldn't he just be more relaxed about it? She *had* said go ahead. But everything she said was totally inconsistent, and she seemed to change her mind on a whim. What would her position be tomorrow? He hated pedants, but to act on anything she said was to go out on a limb, to set yourself up for a fall. She'd actively played the system in order to get rid of Mervin. She'd said she would, and she did. Had she said to the others about him what she'd said to him about Mervin, or was he just being paranoid? Paranoia and lack of sleep went together. Or was that the point? Were all these mind games part of the deal? Was he being hung out to dry? Was she just incompetent or was this all deliberate, skilful mind-fuck? The only answer was to get a clear, written instruction from her on what she wanted and what she didn't.

He'd email her tomorrow and demand it. Yes, that was the solution. Maybe now he could sleep.

*****

Back at the office desk Dan composed an email which politely thanked Stella for the meeting, said it had been useful but, as she had moved position with regard to his teaching, he still felt a little confused. Could he have her clear instructions on what subject matter she wanted him to teach and what she wanted him to exclude? He clicked on 'send' and turned his attention to a pile of fresh documents that had arrived on his desk. On top was a typed paper memo from Patricia Kleb, who was seated a few feet away at the next desk. It asked what his seminar texts would be for the coming year.

Dan held it up and looked at Patricia. "I've got your memo, Patricia. I can't tell you yet what texts I'll be using. Stella evidently has strong views on the content of my teaching, though I'm not sure what they are and I'm waiting for an email from her telling me what she wants me to teach. Also, the timetable only came out yesterday, so I don't know yet what sessions I'll be doing."

"OK. Would you email me with that so I know where I'm up to with things."

*****

Dan scanned his Barts email inbox. There had now been three weeks, two follow-up emails and a couple of spoken reminders (that had been met with silence) since he'd sent that email to Stella asking for clear instructions on what she wanted him to teach and not teach. It was evident that he would not be getting a reply.

"Patricia, it doesn't look like Stella's going to reply to my mail, but I need to get things moving. Those classes will be starting soon and I need to have something in place. So let's say I'll probably use most of last year's texts; maybe substitute a few with something new – where there's been duplication – but, yes, as long as Stella doesn't suddenly start hating them again there's no reason not to re-use them. You already have copies of them all from last year, so if you treat those as possibles/probables you won't be far wrong."

"Fine, but would you email me on that", said Patricia.

"Yes."

*****

Late September. For once Patricia had made it first into the office. She gave Dan a few moments to settle at his desk before speaking. "Dan, I've looked through your last year's texts. There's too great an emphasis on post-structuralism."

"Really? I wouldn't have thought so. Let's get them down and have a look." He took down his module box file and reached out the texts. Twelve of them: neat stapled photocopies abstracted from books and journals. "Hal Foster: that's not poststructuralist. Oh, mind you; you're doing that one now, aren't you? Griselda Pollock: that's not poststructuralist. Edward Said: that's not poststructuralist..." And on it went, and when they had run through them all only two texts out of twelve – the Barthes and the Baudrillard – could be regarded as poststructuralist. Patricia changed her mind and agreed.

*****

Another pristine Patricia memo lay squarely in the middle of Dan's desk. It asked for full details of the texts, videos and other teaching material he planned to use this year for Year 2, and reminded him that this was the second request for this information. In spite of the uncertain position he found himself in, he would have to commit himself to something. Those sessions would soon be upon him. He would simply have to take the risk of a public reprimand, or worse, for using something of which Stella might (retrospectively) disapprove.

A useful approach would be to look at Patricia's first year teaching and see how those 'possibles/probables' he'd told her about a few weeks earlier looked in that context; how well his proposed second year teaching would follow on from what was happening in the first year. He took Patricia's Year 1 module handbooks from their box files and started to read... and there was his list – different typeface, different document – but the same list. His Year 2 possibles/probables were now there before him: in Patricia's Year 1 programme. There were also other texts he used in previous years with Year 2 and would like to again, but these too were now in the Year 1 programme. In fact, looking at the overall content of Patricia's module handbooks, just about everything he would have taught to Year 2 and had taught in previous years was now going to be taught by Patricia in Year 1.

Patricia came back into the office and saw Dan with the open box file in front of him. She avoided eye contact and moved quickly.

"Patricia, we need to talk about this teaching material," said Dan. "I've just gone through your First Year module handbooks and..." He didn't get chance to finish. Patricia, head turned down, chin tucked onto her chest, muttered something incoherent followed by "yes, yes, look, I have to go; we can discuss it later," and vanished from the room.

*****

On 3 November Dan sent the following email and copied it into his dossier.

To: Patricia Kleb
From: Dan Ripley
Subject: Seminar Texts
3 November

Hi Patricia,
With reference to that memo you sent me – the one that asks for further planned teaching (texts, videos etc.). I note that the all of the texts I had planned to use (responding to your request for info on Year 2 texts) are in the Year 1 handbooks, as are others that I have previously used and might have liked to again. It is clear that much

of what I used to teach to Year 2 and indeed most of the topics I would expect to cover are in fact either taught or listed for reading in your Year 1 material. When Phil asked me to do a couple of Year 2 lectures recently, I found myself struggling for material. We thought maybe the thing to do was go deeper rather than wider, but in endeavouring to do this I found myself drawn towards what I think most would regard as MA teaching.

So I wondered what your thinking is regarding Year 2 theory? But I also think we need to look carefully at what we are asking of the Year 1. It looks like we are leaping into an examination of the historiography before we've done the history – deconstructing what they don't yet know anything about. Time for assimilation might well also be an issue. I think it would be good if we could all sit down together, debate this and work on it.

Best,
Dan

*****

Dan and Stella faced each other once again over the grey-brown carpet tiles of her slightly made-over office. "I'm aware of the problem", said Stella "but what can I do? I've been worried about it for some time, but she's so delicate. I feel I daren't say anything to her about it without bringing on a crisis."

"I don't know Stella, but I no longer have any authority. It's up to you. You're the manager. As it stands, she's teaching the second year programme to the first years, and as far as I know she did it last year as well, so I have no idea what I can teach to the second years because it will all be duplication."

"Well, as I've said before, it's too hard in any case, that material. You shouldn't be teaching it." said Stella.

Dan opened his mouth but nothing came out.

He wove between moving bodies in the busy corridors and crossed over Number 2 Car Park to the back door of the university's Mitchell Building. He found the quietest spot in the coffee bar and thought. *It's too hard again. In July it was too hard. In September it was OK. Now it's too hard again. But on the other hand, she won't intervene to stop Patricia teaching it…* to the first years! *It's too hard for the second years; but it's OK for the first years. Or rather, it's too hard for the second years if I teach it; it's OK for the first years if Patricia teaches it. And I have nothing left that I can teach because Patricia's teaching it all before me. Isn't this what they call mental cruelty?* Dan felt a strange sensation, as though a G-clamp had been placed over his head and was being slowly tightened into his temples.

*****

"Patricia, Patricia. We need talk about this teaching", said Dan to the figure that had darted in, picked something up from her desk and was now halfway back out of the door.

"Yes, yes. In the middle of something. Catch you later", echoed Patricia's voice from the corridor.

"I'm not sure if that's the third or the fourth time she's done that to me," said Dan.

Phil looked up from his paperwork. "The ideal person to coordinate theory: she doesn't speak to anyone. Actually, I've sort of spoken to her about it, in that roundabout way you have to with her. She says what she does in the first year is introductory, and you should be able to take things on to another level."

"How can I do that? She's put my *actual material* into her first year programme and onto the reading lists. It's not introductory; it's the same stuff. And what would this other level look like? And if Stella thinks it's already too hard for the second years, taking things upward would cause more problems. Besides, I'm not doing that. I know what Year 2 teaching looks like. I did it at Leeds with damned sight more experienced colleagues than these. I know what I should be teaching, and it's been taken from me. And you know what's even worse? Since she's now 'Theory Coordinator' I'll have to give her any new material I write, and she'll do the same again. I think, research and write, and she takes it over – with the Course Director's blessing. I am obliged to research and write Patricia Kleb's lectures for her. I feel physically sick with all this. I really do. I don't know what the fuck I'm supposed to do."

*****

Dossier – 5 November
As technician, Sky is the person responsible for setting up visual display equipment in the teaching areas. When Linda, Stella or Patricia request it, he sets it up nicely for them. The room will be set out with chairs neatly arranged and the projector or video switched on ready to go. This is what I'm used to technicians doing in the other places I've worked. Today I had a session to do in the seminar room. I'd booked a projector. When I went to the room nothing had happened. I went to the store and asked him what was going on, he didn't even look up from his computer; just pointed vaguely towards a shelf and said 'it's there'. Twat.

*****

Dan had two opened books on the desk in front of him and five more stacked at the side. With brow furrowed in concentration, he glared hard at the computer screen and typed as fast as his one-finger-from-each-hand style of typing would allow. The office door creaked open behind him. He turned. Stella's head and half of her body were in the room. "What are you doing Dan?"

"Preparing some new teaching material".

"You're supposed to be doing tutorials."

"I know", explained Dan, "I was. I gave a tutorial to Matthew Filbert, first thing. My subsequent tutees haven't shown up, so I'm taking advantage of the time to get on with some prep."

"Gemma Worble's in there."

"Yes. She's the only other one in there. But I gave her a tutorial day before yesterday. I've got nothing new to say to her."

"Yes, but you should be in there teaching."

"Who should I teach Stella? There's two students in there and they've both just had a tutorial. You know what it's like. The studios are like the Marie Celeste 'til lunchtime. And frankly, with having to rewrite all of my bloody teaching, I'm not short of things to do here."

"You have prep time for that. You should be in the studio."

"Doing what?"

Stella's head and body withdrew. Dan turned back to his desk. His whole body tensed. His sinuses were suddenly blocked and the G-clamp fastened itself back onto his temples and wound itself in half a turn.

*****

"I don't feel at all well, Sophe." Dan leant back on the sofa and rubbed his face and eyes with open hands. Sophie put an arm around his shoulders. Channel Four News was on but turned down. A neat newsreader mimed the important events of the day. "I'm just worn down by it all. I've had public humiliations, sexist abuse, been given endlessly contradictory instructions, and now she's on my case for spending time writing the new material she's made me write. And then I see the other ones being given special privileges. And there's all those other things that are hard to define. You know, a little conversation behind a hand followed by a snigger, or when they all stop talking as you come into the room. It's just horrible. Horrible. I feel all torn-up inside."

*****

Dan decided that 'bullying diary' was probably more accurate than 'dossier'. On 22 November he made the following note:

Barsteadworth College

Bullying Diary – Week ending 22 November

I have just had 2 weeks off with flu. In fact it's not just flu – it includes the effects of some pre-holiday injections, including one for diphtheria. And I've felt totally wiped out for a while anyway. This was the limit. I write this in a rare moment of lucidity.

When I first went sick – Monday 10 November – Sophie rang Personnel and told them and also left a message for Stella on her voicemail (at 9am). When it was apparent that I would be off for a second week Sophie rang and left Stella another voicemail message (on the Sunday night - 16 Nov).

Sophie then got a phone call on Tuesday 18 November from Personnel to say that they would like to know what was going on and when I was coming back. Sophie told them about the voicemail messages she'd left on Stella's voicemail. Personnel said they knew nothing about the messages. They looked into it and then rang us back: it turned out that Stella had not checked her voicemail. Instead she'd been running round college telling Personnel, other members of the Fine Art team, Frank Fuller and anyone else who'd listen that I had not phoned in and she didn't know where I was. All of this without ever having checked in the one place where the messages were likely to be: again making me look incompetent and unprofessional. And would anybody looking for a call from someone really not check their voicemail?

Chapter Seven
3 Years Ago

A freezing cold January morning. Dan sat opposite Stella in her office. Fawn skinny-rib zipper, fawn slacks, fawn shoes – those complicated, multi-panelled ones, engineered for extra comfort.

"Patricia's suffering from stress", said Stella.

"Yes, I know, clumps of her hair are missing. What's the matter with her?"

"Some of it's personal, but I hold you responsible for the rest of it."

"Excuse me?" This was becoming familiar. More shit was coming his way. He felt a rush of adrenaline; rage that he would have to control.

"It's a consequence you pressurising her over the teaching."

"What exactly am I supposed to do, Stella? She's taken away all of my teaching and left me with nothing to teach. I'm having to research and write a whole load of new teaching. And she's the *Theory Coordinator*, for goodness sake. She's the one who's supposed to be taking a grip on things. Instead, she keeps running away."

"You need to speak to her."

"I've been trying to speak to her. That would be the pressurising you're talking about. But she won't talk about it. She keeps avoiding me and evading the issue."

"That's what I mean: you're pressurising her."

"Hang on a minute. You're telling me off for *not* talking to her, and you're telling me off for trying to talk to her because that makes her feel pressurised? So let me get this right: I'm in the wrong if I talk to her; I'm in the wrong if I don't. Brilliant."

"You're not communicating with her."

"How can I communicate with someone who runs away every time I open my mouth? And, in any case, it's *you* that's not communicating with her. You said the other week that you couldn't bring up things up with her became she was so delicate. You're the manager."

"Oh you're just being impossible."

*****

Another day, another session in Stella's office.

"I'm not satisfied with the number of tutorials you're doing. You're not doing enough," said Stella.

"You write the timetable: you decide how much time I devote to tutorials. I do the tutorials you programme me for," replied Dan.

"You know that chart Linda and I devised to check that all the students got enough tutorials?"

"Yes."

"Well, of course, it also shows who's doing the most tutorials and who's not pulling their weight."

That feeling of outrage and adrenaline began again. *Not pulling my fucking weight?!* He had to keep control, not be provoked. "I do my share of tutorials. The thing is, I do loads of other kinds of teaching. I do lectures, seminars, the Professional Studies modules."

"Linda does far more tutorials than you."

"Haven't you heard what I just said? I do fewer tutorials because I do more of the other kinds of teaching. I can't be in two places at once. If you want me to do more tutorials I'll have to give up some of the other stuff. It's up to you – you timetable it."

Stella looked at the piece of paper in her hand. "Yes, Linda does more tutorials than you and so do I."

"Jesus. You're full-time and I'm half time. Linda spends most of her time with the first years. It's a classroom situation. She can get round all forty of them in a day, and she counts all of those conversations as tutorials."

"Well, they *are*. We get criticised every year on the Student Survey because we don't do enough tutorials. That's why I wanted this chart, to show just how many we do. As you well know, I gave the instruction at the last team meeting that every conversation we have with a student, however brief, must be followed-up with a tutorial form and recorded on the chart. You do know that, don't you?"

"Yes, of course I do."

"So why aren't you doing enough tutorials?"

"I *am* doing enough tutorials. I'm doing the amount that it's possible to do in the time I have."

"But Linda and I do more."

"I'm not getting through, am I? You're full time. I'm half time."

"Linda's half-time."

"Yes, I know. But Linda does the first years. I do the second and third years. It's totally different. The most I can do in a day is twelve, and that's if I give them half an hour each; but the further on they get, the more time I give them. I schedule them for three-quarters of an hour sometimes, often more with the third years. I'll sometimes spend hours with one student if they're really struggling. They get stressed in the third year, because of the degree show. They get mental blocks. I spent a whole morning with Miriam Figgis the other week. She's a good student, but she was going crazy, about to throw it all in. But we eventually worked something out. She's OK now. But it's often like that, so my numbers are necessarily lower. And another thing, as you well know, is that attendance is an issue: I can have a full day penned in, but only half of them will show up."

"Yes, and when they don't show up, you go back into the office, don't you."

"Yes, of course I do. It's a sensible use of time. And apart from anything else, I've got all that new teaching to write now."

"Well, I want you to stay in the studio and carry on giving tutorials."

"I *do* do that. If someone doesn't show up, I give a tutorial to whoever's there, but because attendance is so poor you soon reach the point where everyone has had a tutorial and there's no point in being in there. And it's not all that unusual for the place to be completely empty."

"Well, I want you to stay in the studios, giving tutorials."

"Even when there's no-one to give a tutorial to?"

"I want you to stay in the studios, giving tutorials."

Dan didn't respond. He had a headache… and this strange sensation that his eyes were about to bleed.

"Anyway, onto other things", said Stella "Did you decide what Level 2 seminar texts you'd be using this year?"

"Well, as you know, I'm having to start all over again with that, but from what I can see – just to get me started with the new term – I think I can safely use Roland Barthes' *Death of the Author* and Jean Baudrillard's *Precession of Simulacra."*

"I really want to get rid of that kind of teaching."

Dan looked at the ceiling. The tiles over the visitors' chairs were becoming familiar. He was starting to recognise individual cracks. *So this week's position on poststructuralism is that she'd like to ban it again.*

"You also said that because Patricia was now teaching much of your previous stuff that there was a danger that you might be forced upwards, towards MA level", continued Stella. "Can you *guarantee* that everything you'll use will be BA-level teaching?"

"Guarantee? What does that mean, Stella? As far as I know what I'm teaching is appropriate to BA level students, but I can't *guarantee* that someone, somewhere isn't teaching it to MA students."

"Hmm. Well. Be careful… Anyway, I was talking to Frank, and he was telling me that as far as he was concerned you are not a 'theory lecturer'; though he did say it was useful to have you teaching *some* theory because you've got specialist knowledge in certain areas."

"I've never said I was a 'theory lecturer'. I've always taught both theory and practice. In fact, when I was appointed here, it was because I was able to do both. We have second year modules that combine theory and practice. I teach on those… amongst other things."

The meeting was over. Dan made his way into the fresh air. He jammed his hands into his jeans pockets and pressed his arms against himself for warmth. A jacket would have been a good idea, but the refectory was only a short distance across the courtyard. So why was it necessary for Frank to make a case for his continuing to teach *some* theory? It was evident that Stella had been trying to get Frank to agree that he should stop teaching theory and should be confined only to teaching in the studio. Dan taught both theory and practice, and loved to do so. If Stella could take the teaching of theory away from him it would be a fatal blow; he would have to resign.

*****

Bullying Diary – 17 Jan
Got called in yet again to Stella's office. More pressure. She said that she couldn't understand what I had needed prep time for. (What does a lecturer need prep time for!?) I told her that the Professional Studies 2 module, which I am currently preparing, requires a large amount of admin time. Apart from anything else, you have to book in multiple specialist speakers, which isn't straightforward: you've got to track them down and find ways of making everybody's different availability fit into the timetable. Just catching some people is hard enough, and you may have to do it several times over to make it all work. It's like a human Rubik Cube. She disputed this, suggested I had spent too much time on it, but did not give any account of what the correct amount of time was, and she's never done any work on it herself and doesn't know. She expected me to be able to stand there and give an instantaneous and detailed account of how I had used the prep time, as though I should be able to say *well, it was 5 minutes on this, 10 minutes on that, and whatever...* It's just ridiculous. Moreover, it is Stella who should have prepared and led PS2, but she bottled it and dropped it on me – *at very short notice*. Clearly *she* didn't fancy it. She had also timetabled it badly and I've struggled to make it all fit into the time she has allowed. She also told me I did too much preparation because I do too many seminars. I don't know what she means by 'too many seminars'. What I do is in line with what I've seen in other places, as both a student and lecturer.

On Tuesday afternoon I was supposed to be joint marking student presentations with Patricia. She told me she did not want me there. The reason she gave was that attendance is so poor it doesn't justify two lecturers – she'd prefer to do it alone. She said this in front of Stella, who was delighted, as she wanted to dump some more of her admin work on me. Presumably in a day or two's time, this will be more evidence of my being in the office doing admin work when I should be teaching.

On Wednesday morning I was supposed to be team teaching with Stella – group tutorials with Year 3. The class started at 9.30. Stella wandered into the seminar room, flustered, at 10 o'clock. She had forgotten she was supposed to be teaching. She then said she could see I was doing OK without her and vanished again.

Also this week I went in to see Frank. I told him that my Staff Development Review last year had not been treated in confidence, in fact Stella had used its content as a weapon against me, and I wanted this year's with him instead. He had a think about it, came back to me and said I must have it with Stella. I don't agree with this but have no alternative.

Phil Flanagan tells me that on Friday, Stella was pacing up and down and ranting in the office to him, Linda and the others because she was angry at me for not putting up a poster advertising the intro to Professional Studies 2. There were cries of despair and disbelief at my laziness and incompetence, apparently. I'm half time: I finished on Wednesday lunchtime and wasn't around for the rest of the week. She and I are joint leaders of it: why couldn't she do it? And why tell other members of staff instead of me if she has a problem with my work?

*****

Monday lunchtime. Dan hung his overcoat behind the door, plonked his old leather briefcase on the floor and flumped into his blue office chair. His 2.5 days this week were about to start. He looked at the timetable, carefully, anxiously. It was on the computer now. Progress. When it was on paper it stayed largely unchanged throughout the year. There were odd bits that needed to be altered now and then – when someone went sick or swapped a session to fit in a dentist appointment or whatever – but those concerned would be involved in the alteration and evidence of it would be permanently visible in crossings-out and pennings-in. Now it could be changed over and over again, electronically, without any trace of what had been there before. And it was. Unlike all of the other Course Directors, Stella had not managed to produce a timetable by the beginning of the academic year. It had taken until three weeks into term for her to produce

Barsteadworth College

something, but even that was far from complete. Then, and at any given time since, the few days immediately ahead might just make sense, or something reasonably close to it, but beyond that there would be just a scarcely coherent scattering of names and events, which Stella would address as things started to come uncomfortably close. And then she would address and address and address some more... This was February, halfway through the academic year, and she still spent much of her working day fiddling around with the timetable, shuffling people and events from place to place without telling anyone what she had done. She was of the view that it was up to the lecturers to monitor the timetable to see what changes she had made. There were over 4,000 teaching slots in a year, each represented by a small rectangular cell on the computer timetable. Stella's way of working meant that a lecturer's initials could appear or vanish at any time, without notice. In order not to be caught out, you needed to check all of them every day. And, of course, unlike the old wall-mounted chart, you could not scan the whole thing at once; the screen would only allow sight of a small part, and panning around looking for comparative changes could be a confusing, vertiginous experience.

However, in spite of all this uncertainty, a clear pattern had become visible since Christmas in what was being timetabled for Dan: as the sketchy, embryonic future timetable was firmed up, his admin time was being erased and replaced with more teaching, to the extent that he was by now timetabled to be in class 100% of the time. Four weeks into the Spring Term, he had worked for three consecutive weeks with no admin time, with only half a day's admin the week before. In other words, half a day's prep for a month's teaching. As a half-timer Dan should have had at least half a day per week for admin, and occasionally a full day. However Stella had readjusted the timetable so that he had to teach for every moment that he was in college and was forced to do his lesson preparation and admin in his own time. He had confronted her with this, and she'd said that they had such an enormous workload that it was necessary. Yet Dan was the only person this was happening to. In the same period, Linda Froggatt – another half-timer – was in class for no more than

1½ days a week, and some times as little as 1 day a week. This had to be clear, visible bullying: punishment for going sick in November, probably, and all the other things she held against him.

Dan again scanned his inbox, looking for a reply from Stella to his request to claim back the hours he'd had to work in his own time for prep and other admin tasks. 'Overtime' was unheard of at Barts. 'Time Off in Lieu' (TOIL) was the customary way of getting back extra hours worked. TOIL, however, was not permitted for routine over-working: as a professional you did the hours necessary to do the job. The only exception was if your manager formally organised additional work, and since Stella had deliberately timetabled Dan's admin time out of existence, she *was* forcing him to work in his own time and he should have been entitled to TOIL. But Stella walked away when he tried to speak about it and would not answer his emails. Predictably enough, there was nothing from her in his inbox today, and she was increasingly hard to catch in person; there had been lots of meetings and conferences that she'd had to attend, lately.

Amongst many other admin tasks demanding Dan's attention, there had been the Staff Development Review document to prepare. Stella gave Dan a deadline for this, but allowed no time for him to do it. Then there was the Lesson Observation he was supposed to do with Bill Waxmold, the Course Director of the 3-D Design BA. It was planned and cancelled several times over, as Stella serially eradicated the time in which it would have taken place. Dan was part of the MA Development Group, but had not been able to attend its meetings since November. Stella had also scheduled a date for the spring Course Board meeting and then timetabled Dan out of availability for it. He'd emailed her on this in late January, when she first mooted it, and twice since. He'd received no replies.

As Dan started work on this Monday lunchtime, his teaching programme was set to be as follows: Monday afternoon – Third Years; Tuesday all day – Second Years; Thursday all day – Third Years. As had become usual, there was no admin time. His work would be 2.5 days of teaching from 2.5 days in college. At least, that was how things were when he'd last seen the timetable, last week. However, the paranoia induced by Stella's constant alterations made him give the timetable one last look before setting off to greet his Monday-afternoon students.

He did a double-take. The session had vanished from the timetable.

The squat figure turned from its computer screen to face Dan, who stood in the doorway of the office. The timetable's familiar digital coloured rectangles were on Stella's screen.

"Stella, I was timetabled to be with the Third Years this afternoon. The session has vanished from the timetable. Do you want me to do it or not?"

"Yes."

"Well, would you make sure it goes back on the timetable, so that it shows a true picture of the teaching I'm doing."

At the end of the day Dan went back to his desk and looked again at the timetable. The session had not been reinstated. Although Dan would teach for 2.5 days this week, the record would show that he had taught for only 2 days – and had had half a day for admin. He emailed Stella to ask again that the session be put back on the timetable, so that an accurate record of his teaching hours would exist. He knew there would be no reply and the timetable would not be corrected. He was beginning to feel that the end of his tether was not very far away.

*****

Tuesday morning. Dan spun the clutch and whizzed the Escort into a rapidly moving gap between a yellow Renault Megane and a huge Scammell truck, which completely filled the rear-view mirror. Borchester Road roundabout was huge and had six roads connecting to it; two of them derestricted dual carriageways. Traffic going from one dual carriageway to the other would try to get across whilst losing as little speed as possible. To get on the roundabout from one of the side roads, as Dan had to, you needed the wits of a fighter pilot. It wasn't a good way to start the day for a man who was losing as much sleep as he was lately. The closer he got to work, the more he felt the tension build in his body: tight tendons in his forearms, a dull ache in the back of his neck, pressure in his sinuses, and discomfort in his gut. Second Year tutorials all day today. But the Course Board would start at 10.00, and he would normally have expected to attend. This time, however, Stella had timetabled him for tutorials *and* given him the categorical instruction that, when in these circumstances, he should not leave the studios for any reason whatsoever – even if there was no-one around to teach. Possibly he could leave if there was a fire; maybe not even then. There had been the strong hint that if he defied her she would see it as insubordination, a direct challenge to her authority, and there would be consequences. The emails in which he'd asked for permission to break the 'never leave the studios' rule and attend the Course Board had been ignored.

It was of very little surprise when at about 12 noon the door to Studio 2 burst open and Stella appeared. She'd obviously been setting this up. Dan was the only person in the studio. It was cold. He was seated on one of the desks in his overcoat, reading *Art of the New Millennium*, from a pile of books one of the students had borrowed from the library.

"Why weren't you at the Course Board?" said Stella.

"You know why I wasn't at the Course Board. You've given me absolutely rigid instructions to be in the studios on tutorial days, come what may, even is it's a complete, stupid waste of time."

"That's ridiculous. You should have been at the meeting."

"Ridiculous? Damn right it is. But it's what you insisted I had to do. I've emailed you three times and asked you for permission to come to the meeting and shelve this moronic practice. You ignored me."

"Emailed me? When?"

"In January, when you first scheduled the Course Board; and twice since."

"You should have told me you'd emailed me. How should I know you've emailed me?"

"By looking at your email."

"I don't have time to do that. It's up to you to tell me you've sent me an email, if you want me to look at it."

"So I'm responsible if you don't look at your email?"

Stella said nothing and stomped off back to her office. Dan paused for a moment, then followed her.

The door had been left open. Dan strode in and closed it firmly behind him. Stella turned and glared at him. Hateful, slitty eyes. An almighty row erupted. Dan's body flooded with outrage. His face and eyes were hot. Normally, self-control would have taken over by now, held back those external signs of his rage and distress. But not this time. Everything was wide open. If he had ever felt so angry before he could not remember it. But he mustn't swear. Within the perverse protocols of our society a person can subject another to months of coded violence, to the extent that the victim is made ill, and nothing much will happen. But if anyone swears there will be anger and indignation, and the swearer – the user of a disapproved arrangement of vowels and consonants – will, whatever the provocation, be deemed to have gone too far and will be punished. It wouldn't matter that they all effed and jeffed in the office as a routine response to routine frustrations. That was different: different context. No. Said in anger, a swear word is one of the few remaining heresies. Dan could feel his hands shake. No doubt she would have made a big deal about the preposterousness of his absence in front of the others at the meeting. He accused her of conniving, bullying and deliberately backing him into a corner. At moments he could scarcely speak, such was the build up of rage within him. He had to pause, take a few breaths, compose himself. Months of outrage at the injustices and humiliations he had suffered at the hands of this manipulative, spiteful woman now poured out. The heat and pressure continued to build up. There was a noise in his head – was it in his head or in his *mind*? – a rushing, swishing sound. His temples throbbed. He could hear his own blood stepping up the pace to cope with the stress. It almost drowned out his thoughts and his ability to speak. And for once the normally inscrutable face of Stella Jobby looked worried. She was like a giant turtle, her head periodically withdrawing into the collar of her brown funnel-neck cardigan as Dan repeated back to her the things she had done to him, then bursting forward again as she came up with some new slant that would justify her actions or condemn Dan for something he had or hadn't done. They would never get anywhere. Stella had engineered this confrontation, but did not have the ability to follow it through. She could not convict Dan of the things she would have liked to. And nothing Dan said meant anything to her.

*****

Dan left the room shaking with rage. Moments later he was in Frank Fuller's office, still shaking and periodically breathless. He laid the whole wretched last ten months out before Frank and went home, sick. That evening, composure slightly restored, he sent the following email and copied it into his bullying diary.

To: Frank Fuller
From: Dan Ripley
Subject: Today's Meeting
10 February

Dear Frank

I am writing to confirm the conversation we had this morning.

Barsteadworth College

The exchange with Stella arose after I had been timetabled to do tutorials at the same time as the Course Board was taking place. I am not unused to acting on initiative and would normally have cancelled my teaching and gone to the Course Board. However, back in January, the first week of term, Stella told me in no uncertain terms that she was unhappy with the amount of tutorials I had done and the amount of time I was spending in the studios. This of itself was an unfair observation on several levels: for one thing I had a period of sickness in the autumn term, plus, uniquely within the department, I think, I am able to work highly effectively across all three areas of the course – on studio, theory and careers-related modules – and am therefore timetabled to do less tutorials than some because I do more seminars etc. I was compared unfavourably with Linda Froggatt, who works mostly with the first year and does a large number of very brief tutorials. I tend to work with the upper years and do much longer tutorials. Stella went on to insist that when I was timetabled to do tutorials I must make sure that the time devoted to them is used to the maximum potential, including, if students failed to show up, staying in the studio and seeing if any other students would like some 'help'. In effect, giving tutorials to the same students who have had one the previous day because it is always just the same handful who attend on a regular basis. It is a stupid and wasteful practice, but with Stella's position having been so vehemently stated, I felt it would have been unwise to cancel any tutorial time in favour of any other activity without her express permission. So when I found out that the Course Board would coincide with today's tutorials, I emailed (on three occasions) to ask for permission to reschedule. I never received a reply, so I never had that permission, and so carried on with the timetabling as it had been given to me. The exchange occurred this morning when Stella accused me of inflexibility. I find this extraordinary when it is Stella who has set up such a rigid position and ignored my request to exercise flexibility. Stella, incidentally, told me she had not read my emails and held me responsible for not telling her to read them.

I am also concerned that when faced with the above this morning, Stella had started to shift her position, saying that she had not said the above and instead had simply asked that I followed the tutorial tracking sheet to monitor and catch up with students who were seldom seen. This had not been what she said at the time. I am further concerned that the tutorial tracking sheet has shifted from a device to monitor student tutorials to one for monitoring staff performance, which, since it takes no account of other factors, is a task to which it is not suited.

I am also concerned that for the last 3 weeks I have been timetabled with 100% contact time – 2.5 days contact out of each 2.5 days in college - no admin time whatsoever. Even when I have taught at Further Education level, there was a day a week for 'departmental duties'. One would have thought that Higher Ed would need at least the equivalent. Indeed, I only had half a day for departmental duties in the week before these 3 weeks, which means that I have had only *half a day's preparation time to support a month of teaching*: an almost impossible position. I emailed to ask for permission to cover other duties through time off in lieu – my SDR preparation in particular, which has a nearby deadline – again, I did not receive a reply.

I fear I am on the verge of being forced into incompetence and I am most definitely, through no fault of my own, being forced into letting other people down:

- I have had to work on my days off and cancel other, private activities to get teaching prepared,
- I am losing contact with the MA Development Group (indeed Stella has expressed the view that I do not have the time to work on that),
- I have put off Bill Waxmold, whose lesson observation I am supposed to be doing, so many times it is beyond embarrassing,
- and it is the same problem in effect (the demand to be in two places at once) that has also excluded me from this term's Course Board.

I am also becoming increasingly worried about timetabling in other ways. There is no hard copy of the timetable and the one on the server seems to change endlessly. Things appear and vanish without notice. And since it is digital information there is no physical trace of the change. Yesterday was a case in point. I had had a session for yesterday afternoon diarised for some time, but when I arrived at the start of the afternoon it had been erased – retrospectively in effect. I still had to do it, but the record says I didn't. I diarise and plan for things for quite some distance in advance, like all lecturers, and this is especially important for a part-timer. Sooner or later I will miss something because it has changed, and again be made to look incompetent as a consequence of someone else's unfair and unreasonable actions.

Regards
Dan

*****

Dan looked at his barsteadworth.ac.uk inbox. There was Frank's reply to yesterday's email: mostly a bollocking for Dan's audacity in confirming their conversation in writing, but also setting up a 3-way meeting.

*****

Dan took a seat at the end of the big light wood table in Frank's office. Moments later Stella knocked and sat at the side. They did not acknowledge each other. Dan just caught the familiar dumpy brown shape from the corner of his eye. Frank sat at the other end of the table and made some sort of introductory speech.

Dan again found the anger erupting inside him as he described what had happened to him. He gripped the small white coffee cup and pressed it hard into the saucer to prevent his hands from shaking. The row that had started in Stella's office continued. Dan expanded on what he had said in his email to Frank and set out in detail all of the stuff that had been going on over the last few months: the ambushes in meetings, the ever-changing timetable, the sequestration of his teaching material, the erasing of his prep time, the lot. Well, not quite 'the lot': he still couldn't bring himself to talk about the penis/botox incident. For Stella's part, she said that she couldn't understand what he needed prep time for. In her experience fine art teaching was not of a sort that needed much preparation. Dan repeated that the Professional Studies modules, on which he was currently working, required a large amount of admin time for their apparent size – loads of additional organisational work, especially for a half-timer, who not surprisingly, had half the prep time of a full-timer, like Stella. Moreover, it was Stella who should have prepared and led these modules, but she had dropped them on Dan – at very short notice – because of her own apparently onerous administrative workload. And she'd messed up the timetabling for it, which had made the task even harder. Stella went on to tell Frank that Dan did too much preparation because he did too many seminars. Dan said this made no sense to him because weekly seminars were a routine part of BA fine art teaching in all the places he'd had experience of, and the prep he did for them was normal for the level. He repeated that all of his existing teaching had been eradicated because Stella had allowed Patricia to take it over and put it into Year 1, and he'd had to start again from scratch and research and write a whole year's worth of teaching. Where was the time for that supposed to come from? Dan asked how, since he had a set number of teaching hours, which Stella programmed and which he had to cover, he could possibly be spending too much time on other things. None of this seemed to register with Stella: Dan spent too much time on prep; that was that.

After two intense hours the three made their way to the door. Frank watched Stella vanish down the gloomy corridor before turning to ask Dan if he wanted to make a formal complaint. Hadn't he just done that? He'd placed a huge body of evidence of workplace bullying in front of the Director of the School of Art, who had seen the truth of it through Dan's detailed accounts and Stella's admissions and failures to explain herself. If this wasn't enough to prompt action, what would be achieved by filling in a form and saying all the same things again? Dan paused for a moment. What would the atmosphere be like, how could they work together with some sort of official complaint procedure going on? The bottom line was that he just wanted to get on with his job without being abused. He decided that getting things off his chest and allowing Frank to see Stella for what she really was would do. Now exposed, she would no longer be able to bully anyone.

Barsteadworth College

*****

"Ah, Patricia. Glad I've caught you," said Dan, as he opened the office door. It was one of his lunchtime starts, and there was Patricia at her desk, hunched over a pile of marking. "I was thinking, maybe one way we could resolve the issue of second year theory teaching could be to do *electives*. Each of us could do seminar sessions based on our own specialist skills and allow the students to pick and mix according to their interests."

"No. It would never work," came the reply. "We tried that before; before we were devolved to the various departments. It didn't work. Much too complicated to control and administer."

"Oh. Just a thought..." He wasn't going to give up on this, but thought it best to leave it for now and think his arguments through more carefully, later. He had a lesson to start shortly. "Anyway, I have come up with something I can teach straight away from my existing material: you remember last year I did that lecture – The Two Modernisms – where I set out the orthodox tale of how modern art developed, and then started again from the same point, this time with the deconstructive, postmodernist version?"

Silence

"You remember", continued Dan, "I told you about it at the time: I started both accounts with a slide of Manet's *Bar at the Folies Bergere* and then worked forward with the two different interpretations. The students loved it. It went down really well."

"Er. Yes. Well. I've got that covered now."

The bustling burgundy trouser suit was across the room and out of the door before Dan could find words.

*****

A few days later it was time for Dan to have his Staff Development Review with Stella. With the 'clearing the air' meeting, as Frank called it, still so close, they were polite and distant with each other. Cool professionals. This would be OK. They were seated in Stella's claustrophobic office once again. The red door with its narrow, vertical strip of glass was closed. SDRs were private things.

Dan kicked things off, talked in outline terms about some research he had in mind, then went on to bring up his elective seminars idea.

"Yes, Patricia told me you'd brought that up. She's against it and I don't think it'd work. They tried that before, you know; before Theory was devolved to the various departments. It didn't work. Much too complicated to control and administer."

"It seems to me, Stella, that it would be the ideal way of resolving this. Patricia can't take on all of the non-studio teaching, even if she does see it as her empire. She doesn't have the time. And it's hardly healthy that the students get only one voice on these things. Everybody has some theory knowledge, and in every place I've ever worked studio lecturers also do seminars. We've all got specialist interests that we could teach and the students would be able to choose what they wanted to study and leave what they didn't. They'd be happier and it should improve attendance too. I'd be doing less theory, which saddens me, but at least I'd be doing *some.* "

"Well, I'll have a think about it," said Stella. And then it was her turn to bring up her issues regarding Dan's performance.

"You know my view", she started, "I think you are working inflexibly and spending too much time on prep and admin."

Jesus. This again. "And your evidence is?"

Stella ignored the question. "Well, you are. It's obvious."

Barsteadworth College

This isn't about further discussion; it's about saying it at the SDR so she can record it on an official document. He'd better do his part of this stupid dance. "Do I have to repeat myself Stella? I'm having to do additional preparation because my existing teaching has been taken away *and* because I'm doing the Professional Studies modules. You already know all this. And what's this 'working inflexibly' thing? I work with every year group and on nearly every subject we cover. I'm the most flexible lecturer you've got."

"I still think you're spending too much time on admin and prep."

"Well, what is the correct amount of time?"

"Now you're just being ridiculous."

"I take the appropriate amount of time it needs to do my job properly. I set high standards for myself. As far as I'm concerned, when I go into class what I teach should be very good."

"Well, that's just it isn't it? Just 'good' will do."

*****

Dan took his buzzing head for a walk around the block.

Just 'good' will do. We don't want to provide 'very good' teaching; just 'good' will do. Professionals!? Ever since he'd started at Barts he'd tried to convince himself that he could shake at least his immediate bit of it out of its fluffy, off-the-beaten-track cosiness. He and Phil Flanagan had committed themselves to trying out new teaching material and techniques, and trying, against the odds, to drag the degree up to proper university standard. Now it was clear: they were an embarrassment to old-school plodders like Stella. She hadn't come all the way from London to the rural south at her age to be presented with new challenges and new ways of teaching. She didn't want to have to read difficult new books on art theory. She'd done all of that stuff when she was a student; had to wade through Sartre, Kafka and that lot. And she owned a book on feminist art criticism. She'd wanted everyone to know about that. One day in the office she'd shoved it under Dan's nose, with this sort of triumphant grin on her face. The front cover carried a picture of a flower with a prominent, penis-like stigma; the back was the back of the flower, with a sphincter-like indentation where the stem connected. Provocative stuff. She was clearly proud of being associated with that cover, though she had never said anything about the book's content. As far as she was concerned, this gesture showed that she knew what she needed to know, and besides, as she'd made clear in her various diatribes on how fine art should be taught, it wasn't about *that* kind of learning. Making art should be like trees giving leaf. She wanted the studios to be as they'd been when she was a student in the 70s: everyone sitting around chatting, drinking coffee and smoking roll-ups – when they could get it together to come in to college, that was – and making a bit of work occasionally, slowly, when the urge took. All very laid-back, with a bit of 'free love' every now and then, perhaps. That was how an art school should be. Nothing too strenuous. All these lectures and seminars – what were they for? She'd said several times that if she had her way they would go back to the old system, when the only examination was the degree show – right at the very end of the course – and students could arse about for 3 years and thus *find* themselves. That was the real way art should be taught. It was system that had done her no harm.

Dan deftly avoided a dog turd and trudged on down Tebbit Drive. The cold was starting to work its way through his dark blue overcoat. He tucked his bald head as far as he could into the deep, tipped-up collar. From the start, Stella had been trying to find ways of forcing academic teaching out of the department. She could not rationally oppose it because, rationally, it belonged in the syllabus. Across the UK and beyond, BA-level Fine Art students could no longer be artisans. They now studied in academic institutions and were expected to be able to contextualise and theorise their work in terms appropriate to BA graduates. So Stella was left with only irrationality and bullying.

Barsteadworth College

He reflected further on the exchanges in the SDR meeting. Stella had come up with the idea that he should write down everything he did in his preparation time on something like a timesheet – perhaps he could devise something suitable, she suggested – then hand it to her so she could inspect it (and presumably pick it apart). He refused on the basis that this created a new and special level of disciplinary control, exclusively for him, and operated on the basis that he was guilty until proven innocent. And there had never been anything to show he'd been doing anything wrong in the first place.

He turned back into College Road. The low red-brick buildings of Barts were a few hundred yards away, shadowed by the taller, beige concrete towers of the university. He'd need a coffee to warm up when he got back. She'd told him that she wanted him to become Year 3 coordinator: the 'manager' of the course's final year. He had carried out this task when he was Course Director but handed it over to Stella along with the rest of the job. The Course Director was always Year 3 coordinator – on every other degree in the college, that was. It was the final year of the degree and the one in which the students needed guidance from the most senior available member of staff. He pointed this out and also expressed the view that if he was going to coordinate something, his natural place – because of his integrating role between theory and practice – was Year 2, though Phil currently did that coordinating role and would be unlikely to want to relinquish it. Perhaps they could share it or something…. Stella wasn't interested in his protestations or in the idea of reshuffling. She insisted he took the role on, and he reluctantly agreed. Stella would become the only Course Director in Barts with no coordinating role whatsoever.

Stella also revealed that there had been time set aside in the autumn for him to work on the development of the new Masters Degree. She had never mentioned this before and it had therefore never happened. The time would have taken the form of remission: money had been made available to bring in visiting lecturers to cover some of his work and release him for the MA development workshops. So what work did those visiting lecturers cover? Oh yes, Stella had been away on quite a few conferences lately, hadn't she.

*****

It was a Wednesday afternoon and a month since the 'clearing the air' meeting. Dan had finished work at lunchtime and was at home. With hands clasped behind his head, he leant back in the swivel chair and gazed at the Hewlett Packard monitor with its clip-on loudspeaker ears, framed by the canary yellow wall of the study. Not his choice of colour. It had been there from its previous life as a kids' bedroom when they moved in, but it was cheerful enough and it gave him a lift when he came into the room. The bullying diary was untouched since just after the SDR meeting, three weeks ago. Things seemed to have started to normalise in the office. He felt that for the first time in ages he was actually being treated fairly and with respect by Stella and Linda. He seldom seemed to see Sky and Tim, and they were just natural, measured and businesslike on the odd occasion when he did have dealings them. He had stood up to the bullies and now that they had seen that he would do this they would leave off, and a proper, professional regime would now reign in the department. And he would do his bit too: with the air now cleared, he would look to the future in a positive frame of mind and say no more about what had gone on in the past. He would leave the bullying diary to gather whatever the cyberspace version of dust was. There was nothing to report and he felt confident there never would be again.

*****

The Year 3 students had settled quietly into their seats in the crowded seminar room. By this stage of the course things had got serious. No one was playing anymore. They had to think earnestly about how they were going to get their degrees and what grade they might get. Two modules were about to be introduced in this morning's session. Dan would kick things off, introducing Professional Studies 2 and, after coffee, it was Stella's turn: she would introduce Final Major Project. This was the big one, the most important module of the course, the one where the students made work for their final degree show-cum-examination.

Dan welcomed the students, explained to them how the morning would unfold and handed out copies of the Professional Studies 2 module handbook. Taking them stage-by-stage through the slim A5 booklet, he described in detail what would happen and what was expected of them. He turned down the lights and showed visuals to illustrate points and clarify things. With the lights back on he then took questions and chaired a discussion. It took about an hour and a quarter in total. Everyone then traipsed off for coffee. When they returned, it was Stella's turn. The students quickly settled back into their seats. Stella clicked a black VHS video into the machine, pressed 'play' and then 'pause' and smiled benevolently at the class. "I'm going to show you a movie: *Babbette's Feast*. I don't think I need to say much; I think this says it all." She pressed 'play' once more, Dan hit the lights, and *Babbette's Feast* got underway. By about halfway through, when it was apparent that Stella was going to show the whole, unexpurgated thing, a few silhouetted heads turned towards each other, and muttered.

A group of three mature students then got up and left, silently but for the shuffling of coats and the scraping of the odd chair leg on the vinyl floor. Light flooded the room momentarily and vanished again as the door opened and clunked closed. Later, after everyone else had sat through the whole 103 minutes, Stella switched on the lights, marched to the front and smiled once more at her blinking, stretching audience. Wringing her hands, she announced with great enthusiasm: "*that's* what it's all about – you have to put everything into it". And that was, apparently, *it*: the end of the lecture. The class remained seated, expecting a critique, an explanation, a discussion or something. Stella rubbed her palms together and said "Right. Have a nice lunch. I'll be seeing some of you for tutorials later in the week." At this the students slowly and quietly extricated themselves from their seats, picking up bags and lifting coats from chair backs. There were a few bewildered glances between individuals and back at the lecturers as the group trailed off towards the door. "I think that went pretty well, don't you?" said Stella.

*****

With another mentoring meeting concluded in Stella's office, Dan drew his various files and papers to his chest and stood up from the visitors' chair. "Well, if that's everything Stella, I'll get back to class."

"I never finished telling you about Tim, did I?"

"Hmm?" Dan was caught in the short space between the chair and the red plywood door. He turned and looked at Stella, still seated in her swivel chair.

"He's a sexual submissive, you know."

What? This isn't happening. It's a dream. Thoughts flooded thick and fast into Dan's mind. None of them useful. How was he supposed to deal with this? Why was she telling him this? He felt embarrassed. He tried to control it. What was the correct response? We're all supposed to be open-minded nowadays. And he was. He didn't give a stuff about what those two got up to in bed. He just didn't want to hear about it. This was a treat, he supposed. The clique held itself together with its little secrets. She was giving him one of hers. He was being invited in, again. He couldn't think of any equivalent he could offer in return. Tim's a submissive. *Well, he'd have to be, really. But why tell me about it?* Instinctively, he wanted to make a run for it. The door was *so* close. With an outstretched arm he could reach that worn old aluminium handle and be gone. But he had to stay. He had to be cool. That expected open-mindedness had to shine through. He had to be seen to be a man of the world: cool and not judgemental. All the same, he couldn't think of anything to say, and Stella continued.

"He likes my big peachy bum. Most submissive men are bum fetishists, you know."

Barsteadworth College

Was it possible for skin to sweat on the inside? His felt like it was. Why didn't someone come to the door? *Does she think this is going to turn me on? Am I supposed to reveal something about my sexuality?* 'Big peachy bum', though. Since she'd started, a mixture of chivalry and political correctness had prevented him from acknowledging that thing. It had been the big pink elephant in the room that no-one would allow themselves to see, though he'd heard a couple of the mature students – Harmony and Gloria – calling her 'bum woman' once. He'd pretended not to hear or that he'd not got it. But since she'd brought it up: yep, it was big alright. Or maybe it wasn't big. On a six foot, eighteen stone woman – or bloke, for that matter – it would probably be about right. But Stella was small, and that seemed to make that backside the focal point of her whole body, like it was a secret energy source or something. Those big, patch-pocket fawn cords she always wore did her no favours, either. Or was that deliberate? Did she think it should be highlighted? And *'peachy'?! What's that all about? You can't have an arse the size of Shropshire and call it 'peachy'.* Past Stella's fruity head, across the candyfloss courtyard, two grape-like students pushed open the liquorice doors of the marshmallow woodwork shop and disappeared inside.

"He says it makes him feel more alive when I'm dominating him", she continued.

More alive? Dan was losing the will to live. But there was something familiar about this. Something from a Conrad novel staggered vaguely into his mind and took a few moments to dust itself off. In a terrifying storm, the captain of the ship said to the lead character (*was it Lord Jim?),* who believed he was about to drown, 'aye, but you know yer alive don't yer'. So that was it. An encounter with Stella's colossal arse was like a near-death experience. That figured. Dan finally mustered some words:

"Hmm. Yeah. I've heard that. Y'know, not about you and Tim specifically, y'know, obviously, but...er..."

At last, the door opened. Dan barged past two students before they had chance to speak and made straight for the car park where he breathed in the fresh air deeply.

*****

The two men sat in the subdued light of Poxy's Bar in the town centre – Barsteadworth's trendiest nite spot. Not that it was nite yet, just Friday teatime. Later it would fill up with the town's bright young things, and even the bouncers would make Dan feel old, but he would have beaten a retreat long before then. Also, he was drinking Stella Artois and, as much as he enjoyed the stuff, it wasn't something you could drink for very long without needing a long lie-down in a darkened room. Phil nursed his pint of 'proper English ale': 'Old Dog-Breath' or something.

"That really happened? She really said *that*, all that 'bum' stuff?" said Phil.

"Yeah. Absolutely. Just a couple of days ago. Well you couldn't make it up, could you," replied Dan.

"So it's true then: you *do* have to kiss her arse to get on in that place."

Dan guffawed and spluttered into his beer. "It would certainly seem that way."

Phil shook his head. "Where are the loos in here?"

Dan pointed. Phil stood and turned.

Dan gazed absentmindedly at the computerised mood lighting behind the bar: pink, then indigo, then peach... It had been Phil's idea to go for a pint. It was funny; he'd worked with Phil for a few years now, but had never been for a pint with him before. It wasn't that he didn't get on with the guy, they worked very well together, shared the same passion for what they did, it was just that 'not mixing work with social life' thing. He'd had the odd drink and chat with him at Stella's place, and met his missus – she seemed all right too – and Sophie seemed to have got on well with both of them. But Stella's parties turned out to be what he should have known they'd be: forums for intrigue and backstabbing; classic examples of why it wasn't smart to socialise with work colleagues. Phil appeared back at the table. Dan hadn't noticed, before, just how tired he looked.

"So, how are you doing, y'know, in general?" asked Phil.

"Me? Yeah, I'm fine. Fine. You know I had that run-in with Stella? Well, ever since they've been off my case. Yeah. I'm enjoying my work again. And you?"

"I'm just fucking sick of it. I'm going out of my mind with all the stuff that's happening."

"What? What do you mean? What *is* happening?"

"It's just this whole 'fear and favour' thing that Stella uses to run the department", said Phil. "She's had me in for God knows how many times criticising my teaching, and yet the sun shines out of every corner of her bloody pets."

"Criticising *what* about your teaching?" This was all starting to sound very familiar to Dan.

"It's hard to say really. It's all very vague. But she's threatening to have me in for evaluation and send me on retraining courses. She reckons I'm incompetent. No doubt it will be Stella herself who evaluates me and will discover – surprise, surprise – that she was in fact *right*. She's just trying to humiliate me. And when I stand up for myself she accuses me of insubordination and threatens me with disciplinary action."

"Have you been to see Frank?"

"Yeah, but she's primed him. She's learned from her experiences with you and she's made sure she's got to Frank first and given him a full, detailed story. And you now how convincing a liar she is."

"Indeed."

"So when I go in there now, anything I say to Frank myself is clear evidence of how unmanageable I am. She's told him I'm a trouble-maker; always complaining. But the thing is, I saw what happened to you and I thought *right*, that's not going to happen to me; I'm going to operate within the system, and every time they dump more crap on me I'll complain, and sooner or later they'll have to take me seriously. And since they're dumping crap on me all the time, I'm complaining all the time. If they won't let up, I won't let up. You're half-time; you don't see it. And they're being nice to you at the moment. But the bottom line is that she's persuaded Frank that my complaining is evidence of my unmanageability, so when I complain it makes matters even worse. I've got nowhere to go."

"Shit. You can see why she likes Kafka."

"You don't know the half of it. One of the second years, Tracey Loaf, came to see me the other day. She was upset and embarrassed, but she thought there was something I needed to know. They were being given a team-taught session by Linda and Sky, and the two of them were pulling me to bits to the class; telling the students what a twat I was."

"Jesus. How far will they go? I mean, I knew they were bad, but I didn't think they'd go as far as trying to recruit students to their hate campaign. And why are a husband and wife teaching together anyway? Sky isn't even a lecturer – he's a technician."

"Oh there's more. I went to see Stella to complain. I thought there's no way she could ignore this one. But she just laid into me. She told me she was just about at the end of her tether with my trouble-making. She talked about 'serious consequences'. I think she's going to try and sack me. Tracey had already been to complain to Stella herself, saying she thought that was an unprofessional way for lecturers to carry on in front of a class, and Stella threatened her too."

"Did you go to Frank?"

"No. I daren't. That *would* be it. I went to Personnel, but they referred me back to Frank. I told them what had happened with Frank, and they said that all they could do was make a note of it on my record."

"Shit. I don't know what to say. You need to join the union."

"I'll think about it."

"No. Don't just think about it, do it. This could get really serious. You're going to need help and protection. I think we both are. I'm a member."

"Yeah. Well, OK. But there's something else you need to know: they're using you in this as well."

"What? How?" asked Dan, though the answer was dawning on him before Phil spoke.

"They're saying that you're on board with them now and that makes it clear that I'm the only one who is out of step."

"I knew that was coming. But, you know, I'm not doing anything different from what I was doing before. They're just treating me differently and picking on you instead. I can assure you though; I'm not going to kowtow. If they do anything, if I see anything, I will stand up to them. But I'm just not seeing it."

"You will."

*****

With Easter and the end-of-term recess fast approaching, it was time for the team meeting. Today it would be in the seminar room. This was an improvement. Same dazzling blue tables, but much less cramped than the lecturers' office.

Dan was tense. Nothing had happened to him for a time, but he was so used to being attacked and undermined at these events that the effect was by now Pavlovian. But that wasn't the only reason he was feeling uncomfortable. This new peaceable relationship with Stella had come at a price: his acquiescence to her other dubious practices. She'd stopped bullying him, but was bullying Phil instead, and the process of making life as cosy as possible for herself and favoured members of staff seemed to be continuing apace. She had already brought in guest lecturers to cover many of what should have been *her* teaching sessions, and part-time lecturers now conducted all year-group coordination. Offload a few more things and she would be free to sit around and chat all day, which was evidently the way she thought things should be.

With everyone else distributed liberally around the cluster of tables, Stella and Linda came into the room together and sat down together. This wasn't a good sign.

Stella declared herself pleased to announce that Dan would be taking over the third year coordinator's role. Everyone already knew this, but the meeting was the opportunity to make it official. Dan thought he picked up on the odd murmur of approval from here and there around the table. He said nothing. Stella continued:

"And module leadership will now go with year coordinatorship."

What?! What the fuck?! He had never agreed to this. It hadn't even been mentioned before. As things stood, three part-time lecturers would run the three year groups of the course. Even that wasn't right – Stella should be doing the third year. But the individual modules – of which there were many – had always been shared out on the basis of a fair distribution of workload. As the full-timer amongst part-timers, Stella's contract gave her a quarter of the course's teaching hours and, correspondingly, a quarter of the modules. Now she was offloading the lot. It was perfect:

No year-group coordinatorship = no module leadership

and

no module leadership = no module design, no handbooks to write, no lessons to plan, no research, no handouts to make, no admin, no collating of statistics, no pursuing poorly-attending students, *no lecturing*....

If this went through, Stella's entire teaching workload would amount to conducting a few tutorials on modules other people ran, whilst monitoring things from a distance.

"Of course, I'll lead *some* modules", she added: "I'll do the Professional Studies modules".

And that's the sweetener? This is a fucking outrage. The only full-timer on the course, and she's going to teach two half-modules... from material she's just made me rewrite! Nearly all of the teaching would now be headed and administered by the part-time lecturers. *She'll be running 4% of the course –* with 25% of its teaching hours. *And the modules she's chosen to lead are the ones where you get guest lecturers in. They're mostly taught by other people.*

Why was everybody so silent? Even Phil wasn't saying anything. Mind you, he daren't. But Dan could no longer stay silent.

"You're not on Stella. You can't do that. It's just wrong." The zombies round the table turned their heads towards him in silent curiosity. "You're going to do two half-modules? *Two half-modules out of a whole year's work.* That's a disgrace."

Again, he looked around the table. Surely someone else would speak up on this. She was effectively relieving herself from the routine management of the course and all of the complex teaching; just giving herself, essentially, a presidential role with, perhaps, a few tutorials here and there as the mood took. This affected everybody, not just the departmental scapegoats. They'd all be lumbered with the extra workload.

"Look at it: you'll lead no year groups and almost no modules. Who's the manager here? We'll be managing you. You're making yourself a guest tutor on modules run by everyone else. You can't get away with this one Stella." But it looked like she would. No one else seemed to mind, and complaining to Frank Fuller had become a dangerous sport. Rapid-fire argument continued between Dan and Stella, with the rest of the course team seemingly in stasis. The pressure told, a little: Stella agreed to take on one more module.

"Great", said Dan, "the course's only full-time lecturer will be running the equivalent of 2 modules."

*****

It was Easter. In the study the two-tone grey monitor narrated the computer's start-up ritual. Dan clicked on 'My Documents', then 'Barts', then 'Bullying Diary'.

Bullying Diary - Easter
Having left this bullying diary alone for some time, I realise I have to reinstate it. The situation has two sides: 'fear and favour', as Phil Flanagan puts it. It isn't just about bullying. Whilst he and I have been abused in all sorts of ways, Stella is according herself special privileges and bestowing them on her chosen few when it suits her. Play the game – and it's a rotten game – and you will be rewarded; oppose it, try to be professional, and you will be bullied and undermined. There may come a need for whistle-blowing. What happened last week has tipped the balance and I am therefore continuing with this.

Dan recorded the events of the pre-Easter team meeting.

*****

A couple of weeks later, he made the following entry:

Bullying Diary - Week Ending 24 April

This was the third week of the Easter recess. The official public holiday is over, the students aren't back until next week, but it's a whole, normal working week as far as staff are concerned, unless you've got holidays booked. Phil, Linda and Patricia are officially away on holidays and research, but Stella and Sky should have been in this week. On Monday Stella wasn't in, though her office light and computer were miraculously switched on. Sky was in, briefly, visibly hovering around for a while in the morning. He has a key for Stella's office. From about 10 o'clock onwards I was the only person around. On Tuesday morning Stella was in. She made a point of popping her head round the door and saying 'hello' to me. She's never done that before. Sky was nowhere to be seen, but there was a fleece slung over the back of his chair. I took it off and put it on a coat hook. There it stayed. I wondered if I'd got it wrong, so I checked with the School Secretary's office. Neither Sky nor Stella had any holiday booked and they weren't on training courses or anything. The day panned out the same: for all of the rest of the day I was the sole presence in the fine art department. On Wednesday morning the same pattern was followed again: there was no Stella, but Sky was to be seen pottering about the studio for a short while, and Stella's office light and computer were on again. It is pretty clear that these two had given themselves an extra week's holiday by setting up an arrangement where they could take turns at putting in brief, token appearances and leaving signs of their presence in the office. And I was the only person honest or stupid enough to be at work.

*****

It was the May team meeting. It felt like a duplicate of the previous one: same room, same time, everyone seated in the same place. And once again Dan was tense. Anticipating more rows and confrontations, he'd scarcely slept. Not that he could think of what she could pull this time.

Stella opened the meeting with, as usual, an agenda of which the only copy was the one in her hand.

"As you will recall from the last meeting, we agreed that Linda, Phil and Dan would now all be year coordinators. I've done some thinking onwards from that, and the most sensible step now would be for you all to take over the timetabling, so that you have proper control of things."

So there it was: this week's coup. It was breathtaking, and there was a laugh of disbelief in Dan's throat as he started to speak. "You really are going too far this time, Stella. The timetabling is a fundamental part of the Course Director's work. It's the means by which you deploy your staff. Its how you ensure there's a fair spread of responsibilities. It's how you ensure that people are allocated work that suits their skills and knowledge. It's central to how you manage people. You *can't* offload it."

"I don't see anybody else objecting", said Stella.

What arrogance. She's bribed and cowed them, and now she's behaving as though that amounts to willing endorsement.

"Well you wouldn't would you... Apart from anything else, Stella, it won't even work. The timetabling has to be done by someone who's in a position to oversee the whole thing. We all contribute teaching to all of the year groups. How can I plan to use any of the other lecturers for something when I don't know what anyone else is planning for them or what they're planning for themselves? I can't even plan *me* because someone else may have planned to use me at that same moment. Can you imagine a train network where each of the drivers timetables themselves?!"

"You could compare notes."

"For the whole year? Oh my godfathers! We would just keep comparing notes and shifting things around forever. It's absurd. It's endlessly attritional. It would waste a monstrous amount of time."

Stella addressed the room: "Those in favour?"

Barsteadworth College

All hands went up except Dan's and Phil's

"Those against?" asked Stella, triumphantly.

Only Dan's hand went up. Phil – evidently feeling his job was on the line – abstained.

Dan cast his eyes around the whole table. "Well done. You've just agreed to do something that isn't actually possible…" *Silence.* "I'm not doing it, Stella, and you can minute that."

*****

"Stella? Stella?" Dan poked his head round her office door. The computer was switched on with the timetable on the screen, as usual, but no-one was home. He went to put his wadge of duplicate tutorial sheets on her desk. On top of the large pile of papers, forms and files already present was something that caught his eye. He shouldn't, but he had to look. A pay claim. Tim Small's name was there in spidery writing at the top; and Stella Jobby's signature, clear and assertive, at the bottom. Though not officially an established member of the course team, Tim was by now largely a permanent fixture in the department, albeit on a part-time basis. His wife awarded him lots of visiting work. However, all Dan had ever seen him do was conduct casting workshops with the first years and help Sky put up exhibitions in the foyer: technician work. But the pay claim form showed 'visiting lecturer' pay rate. For showing students how to mix plaster and for handing screwdrivers to Sky Gelding he was being paid what Tracey Emin would have been paid to give a lecture on her work (in the singularly unlikely event that anyone could persuade her down from London). Tim was on nearly double the rate of pay he should be on for the work he was doing, and this was being sanctioned by his wife. What a great situation to be in. If household funds were looking a bit short towards the end of the month, or if perhaps they needed a new hoover, Stella could find her husband something to do and sign it off. Come to think of it, he wouldn't really need to do anything. The whole thing could be fiction. Who was to know? Frank had to counter-sign these things, but he had no way of knowing who had done what, and with a ton of other stuff on his desk to deal with he'd trust the Course Director and sign it off without question. Another question dawned on Dan, whilst he was gazing at this outrage: *who had actually interviewed this guy in the first place? Who checked his credentials? His wife?*

*****

Bullying Diary - Week Ending 12 June
There had been a notice on the board outside Stella's office for a couple of weeks to say that the Summer Course Board would take place on Tuesday 15th June. I booked go to a conference of Friday the 18th June. Phil Flanagan would also be away on the 18th on a recruiting trip to Iceland. This week a new sign appeared to say that the Course Board had been rescheduled to Friday 18th June.

*****

Bullying Diary - Week Ending 31 July
A few weeks ago a message came through from Finance to say that there was an amount of money left over that the department needed to spend quickly. It was one of those institutional things, when spending has been too frugal and money has been left hanging around that needs to be spent before the end of the financial year, otherwise future funding will be jeopardised. Stella came into the office asking for ideas quickly on what we could use the money for. There was 8 or 9 grand, apparently. Someone suggested that we could do with more computers, but it couldn't be spent on hardware or materials, only on staff time. I said it might be a good idea to pay me for my outstanding TOIL, since there doesn't seem much chance that I'll ever be able to take back the time I'm owed. Stella ignored me. In the event, the money has been spent on employing Tim Small's sister, Emma (our Course Director's sister-in-law). Her 'task' is to sort out Stella's paperwork in advance of the Quality Assurance inspection. This involves collating things, putting them in box files and writing what they are on the spines with nice swirly calligraphy. After a couple of weeks of this she seems to have done most of what it is possible for her to do, but she's still around and it seems she will be a fixture in the department for the rest of the

summer. She comes in about 9.30; she and the clique go off for a coffee for half an hour or so; she comes back and does some 'work'; and then they all take a long lunch. There's then another long break for coffee and chat in the afternoon, and she knocks off at 4pm. I don't know what hours she's meant to do, or indeed, what Stella's still able to find for her to do, but everyone else's hours are 8.30 – 5.00. There was no advert, there were no interviews and no one else has had the chance to apply for this cushy little number. Emma has been brought in because of who she is and because there was money there to give her.

The departmental family tree now looks like this:

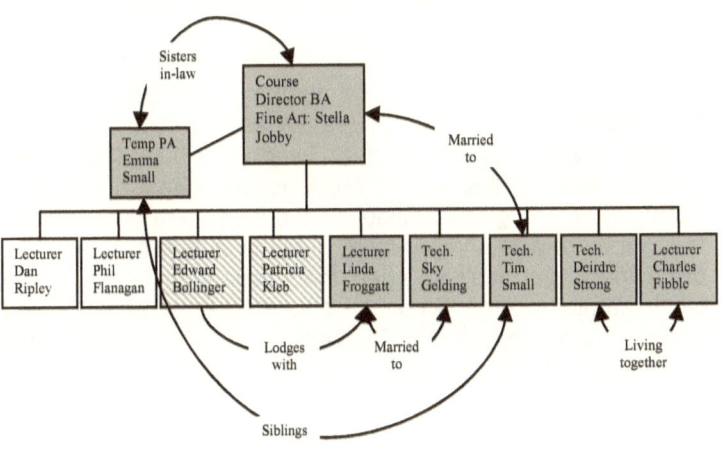

Key:

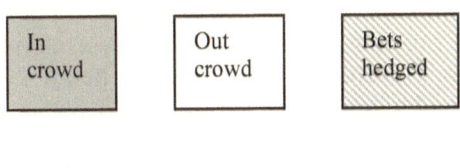

*****

"Nepotism? Don't get me started," said Phil. The Uni refectory was quieter than their own. Two thirds of it were in a tall atrium, but the hard acoustics of the umpteen square metres of Pilkington's finest were toned down by soft furnishings: a few drapes strategically placed to deflect the midday sun, two leather sofas that faced each other across a newspaper-strewn coffee table, a scattering of tall parlour palms and rubber plants in white plastic tubs, and three curly wooden screens that were waved-shaped at the top, made a scroll-like footprint on the floor and served to break up the space into different zones. The two men sat at a small circular table. It had a wooden top, which distinguished it from the stainless steel ones over in the coffee bar zone. Before each was a polystyrene plate with a plastic knife and fork and the last scrapings of lunch on it. "We have *institutionalised* nepotism. Have you never weighed up the number of relationships in that place?" continued Phil.

"I can't say I've weighed up the number," said Dan, "but I do know there are a lot, and that Beasley and Ledlock encourage it. They talk about 'added value', by which I think they mean that husbands and wives will continue to do Barts things and think Barts thoughts outside of work, though I've always thought there was another more dubious side to it: it's a great disciplinary tool, isn't it, when the husband and wife – the whole family income – rely on one establishment? Did you know, union membership in Barts is virtually zero? Silas doesn't approve of unions."

"Yes, I know," said Phil. "What concerns me more though is the impact on other people: the people that policy turns into outsiders. Elliot Boodle, Course Director – Graphic Design is married to Jemima Song, one of his lecturers. And that situation cost Daisy Denim her job. She was a Senior Lecturer. She walked out in a fit of pique and never came back; couldn't take any more of being bossed about by Jemima, who always had Elliot to back her up. That's just not right. No one should be forced out of their job because of filial connections in a public institution. Then there's Mindy Buxton, Course Director of the Illustration degree. You know her, don't you?"

"Yes, of course I know Mindy. I like her. She was really helpful when I was feeling my way as Acting Course Director. I feel sorry for her, though. Whenever you go to her office, on the shelf behind her there are always fags, cans of Red Bull and those Kalms herbal tranquilisers. I don't think she knows if she's coming or going."

"Yes, well, there's a reason for that. Her second-in-command, Tracey Roper, is knocking off James Ledlock, and of course everything Mindy says – and we all say lots of things we shouldn't in the heat of the moment – goes straight back to Ledlock. Pillow-talk. So Mindy feels like she's walking on egg shells all the time."

"Ledlock and Tracey, eh?" mused Dan. "I know that Russell Hobbs, who runs the Photography degree, is married to Amber Filigree, Course Director – Textile Design, and Christopher Trowel from Foundation is married to Patsy Boddington the Photography technician, and one of the other photo technicians, Dave Ponkridge, is engaged to Rebecca Fulcrum from Finance. Oh, and Rob Ramsbottom, who runs BA Model Making is engaged to Gail Cartilage, one of his Senior Lecturers."

"Engaged? They're married now." continued Phil "There's also that new bloke, Clive something, who's been appointed to teach Photographic Theory; his wife is Perdita Box, Personnel Manager. How much influence could she have on his career in this place? How much did she have on his appointment?"

"Well, I don't think much. It's usually the line manager who has the biggest say."

"I dare say you're right, but it still feels a bit uncomfortable, doesn't it? And she may or may not have influenced his appointment, but she'd normally be the one who'd draw up the contract and she may well have chosen which pay scale point he started on. Who knows?"

"Hmm. Yes: who knows? That's the point. Who polices situations like that?" Dan stared thoughtfully into the middle-distance. "And there's Pam Spooler, Director of, er... Circumstantial Affairs? Something like that...?"

"Something like that"

"...She's married to Bill Spooler, Senior Lecturer – Photography."

"Yes, a Director. But it goes up still further," continued Phil. "Guess who's been made Commercial Manager of the new Genesis Centre?"

"Dunno."

"Clarissa Macadam."

"Who's that?"

"You'd know her better as 'Mrs Silas Beasley'."

Dan leant back in his seat; a look of disbelief shot across his face. "You're fucking joking. How've they got away with that? His pet project and he installs his wife as Commercial Manager?"

"Who's going to stop them? Anyway, she might have got it on merit", suggested Phil.

"Yes, well, who knows? And who would the interview panel be? And if Silas wasn't on it, which seems unlikely, who'd want to be the one to tell him they'd rejected his wife?!"

"Apart from the pressure Silas's presence would have, I suspect they get away with it because she uses her own name. The paperwork would show no visible connection. Did you know, when I complained to Personnel about Tim Small being appointed and managed by Stella, they didn't know she was his wife? He used his name; she used hers; they didn't declare the truth of the situation and no-one asked."

Barsteadworth College

Dan leant forward again and gripped the edge of the table. "There were no circumstances in which anyone *could* ask: there was no application form and there were no interviews. Anyway… that brings us to our own illustrious department: the Grand Duchy of Small-Jobby-Gelding-Froggatt-Land. And to that cosy situation we can now add that Edward Bollinger, who Stella taught at Twickendean, lodges with the Gelding-Froggatts when he's teaching here. And the new technician, Deidre Strong, lives with Charles Fibble, that one-time Visiting Lecturer who now seems to be on an open-ended, running contract, like Tim's."

"Yep, Stella likes taking on more couples – it adds validity to what she's doing for herself and Tim – and doing it that way means there are none of those nasty, inconvenient interviews and such."

"Well, yes", said Dan, "the rest of the interview panel might want someone else… Who knows what might happen if you go down that road?"

"Quite. And so we've ended up with a department in which out of ten staff, six are married or living together. Seven, if you count Edward living part time with Linda and Sky. And like Graphics, we've lost someone for the wrong reasons: Mervin jacked because he couldn't take the way the place was now being run. I don't know if that was because of the nepotism or the bullying. The two things seem inseparable, anyway."

"Yes, it's all massaged into the shape Stella wants… except that you and I are still here."

"Speaking of which, we'd better get back to work", said Phil, pushing back his plywood chair.

The two wove between tables of noisy diners and reached the door. "Oh", said Dan, "one more for your delectation: the library has a new painting. Have you seen it?"

"Can't say as I have", said Phil.

"Between the Derek Jarman AIDS thing and the Eduardo Paolozzi machine print: a new abstract by Royston Dimley."

"Who's Royston Dimley?"

"Just graduated from Bristol. Son of Aileen Dimley – Director of Infrastructure Services."

"I see. Money left over at the end of the academic year again, perhaps?"

"Who knows…?"

*****

Bullying Diary – Week Ending 24 July

There was a team meeting on Tuesday. I again brought up the idea of running elective seminars. Stella said that Patricia had already suggested this and she thought it was a good idea. Amazing: they both rejected the idea out of hand when I first mooted it 6 months ago. Now Patricia has had this highly original idea – electives – and selective amnesia has kicked in again, so my suggesting it never happened. Seems it must be contagious – they've both got it now. I really am getting fucking sick of this. I am sick of being treated like this. I am sick of the fucking job. I am sick of it all. I feel physically sick as I write, thinking about it. I don't know why I didn't kick up about it at the time, but I didn't. I just pressed on and set out my plan as though nothing had happened. I've been trying to keep the peace lately – since the 'clearing the air' meeting. Apart from when I've just had to say something – like when Stella was offloading most of her job onto us – I've kept quiet, let things go. I don't know what's happening now: if I feel I can't change my new workplace persona – can't fight my way back from that position – or if I'm just defeated by it all.

*****

It was a Monday morning in early September and although it wasn't yet 8.30 the sun was up, untroubled by clouds and bringing an agreeable warmth to the Borough of Barsteadworth. Dan had just got back from two weeks in

Barsteadworth College

Menorca, though the laid-back feeling the holiday had induced retreated noticeably as he approached Barts' car park. He locked-up the red Escort, slung the long leather strap of his briefcase over his shoulder and scrunched over the stone chippings towards his new office, checking out the changes to the department's other facilities en route.

The summer had brought yet another reorganisation of the Fine Art Department. The second of two factory-style, grey, north-light studios had just been completed. These would house the second and third year students. The first years would be in the original fine art building; the one that used to accommodate all three year groups, though there would now be excess space that would be given up to other departments. The old GNVQ Art and Design studio building would be occupied by the newly inaugurated part-time version of the degree, and the long-disused ceramics block had been cleared out and would house the computers, the seminar room and some of the lecturers. From the previous situation, where the Course Director occupied one office and the lecturers shared another down the corridor, things would now be more disparate. This was on Stella's instructions. She had worked with Infrastructure Services to get things the way she wanted them. Patricia, Edward and Dan would now occupy the draughty, narrow room that had been the clay pugging area in the old ceramics block; a space designed to be kept damp and cold so that the clay would stay workable for as long as possible. The room still reflected its original purpose: there were large vents in the door and there was a row of grilles along the ceiling line that led directly to the outside, so that air could pass through unhindered. Naturally, there was no heating. The technicians, Sky and Deirdre, had their base in the new store room in the third years' studio. Stella and Linda would occupy a large, purpose-built office at one end of the second year studio. It was the only one that was carpeted, and it was equipped with new, modular, beech-veneered desks that fitted together and made an 'L' shape along two walls of the room. Atop these were two spanking new computers and above were rows of neat white shelves that Sky and Tim had installed over the summer. Phil Flanagan – if anything hated more by the departmental clique even than

Dan – was to be housed alone in a small glass kiosk in the corner of the part-timers' studio.

Phil poked his head round the door. "How's it going then?"

"Fine, I guess", said Dan "Just weighing-up my new home. There's not much room in here. When Patricia and Edward get in we'll be falling over each other. It can't be more than, what? About 12 feet by 6? They've staggered the desks so the chairs fit into the recesses between. Edward's will get clobbered every time the door's opened."

"It's probably not legal", said Phil.

"I'm sure it's not, but I can't see anything much being done about it. Can You? I'll need to order a heater."

"I think one's been ordered for you."

"That's good. I'll need a new chair as well. Mine's been snaffled and someone's dumped this bloody thing on me." He pulled out a filthy old beige office chair from under his desk. It was the one that had originally been Ronnie's, been Dan's for a while and had then been retired to the studios, where it had become subjected to every imaginable abuse. Blobs of what looked like paint, glue and chewing gum were stuck to it, and it was impregnated with several years' worth of diverse studio dust: soil, stone, sand, cement, plaster, charcoal... It had picked up some from what had been airborne but accumulated far more from its routine use as an improvised ladder and sack truck. "Anyway, how's you lunar module then?"

"So, you've seen it. It'll be OK. Mind you, Sky was supposed to have fitted it out and installed storage racks for the students' artworks on top if it, but I kept asking him, all summer, and he just ignored me. In the end I gave up and did it myself – in time I should have spent preparing my teaching."

*****

Bullying Diary – week ending 17 September
I got my Staff Development Review report back (the one from
February), now with Stella's comments on it. She's supposed to
complete the review form straight after the meeting and give the
reviewee and personnel a copy. Yet this is the first time I've seen
my SDR at this stage of completion (I didn't get last year's one
either). She's evidently just been sending them off to Personnel
without my seeing them. This time she *had* to give me a copy (albeit
8 months late and left on my desk with just post-it note saying
'oops, sorry, I forgot to give you this'), because it's needed for staff
reviews that Beasley's running and I have to be able to speak from
it. When I read it I was horrified. It was a skewed, antagonistic and
a dishonest review of the discussion: the victor's history, intended
for others to read with my having no opportunity to object. It
contained a lengthy and patronising diatribe about the need for
'flexibility in the workplace', this to disguise Stella's abusive
manipulation of the timetable earlier in the year, when she'd shifted
things around to deliberately overload me. This could be handy stuff
for her. In the event of action being taken against me, she'll be able
to refer to the SDR, which now shows in an official document just
how she has struggled to bring me into line.

*****

Another Monday morning. The new chair still hadn't arrived.
Disappointed but not surprised, Dan lowered himself into the
filthy old one. He felt dirty and degraded every time he had to
use it, though it was looking a bit cleaner nowadays: he had
taken much of the crap that had been on it home on his
clothes. The old computer clicked and whirred and stumbled
into lethargic wakefulness. As always, he clicked on the little
yellow rectangle labelled 'Timetable'. At last there was
something there. He looked for his initials. They were densely
packed early in the year and they thinned out progressively
into the future. Everyone's were like this. He scrutinised
things carefully: the latter part of the year wasn't yet done,
and even the sessions for the near future only made sporadic
sense. There were clashes of rooms and staff, incongruous
pairings of modules, study trips that coincided with lectures...
He'd given up trying to argue about this. That was wasted
energy and start of term was too close for comfort. He took

down the bookings that Stella had made for him, worked it all out on a year planner, rescheduled them to make them make sense and emailed her with a long list of things he wanted to change. If Stella had conceded, as she seemed to have (albeit silently), that it was not feasible for everyone to design their own timetable and somehow make it work with everyone else's version, then this was her way of dealing with it: set out a crude framework that they would have to modify and conclude if they didn't want the frustration of dealing with the cock-ups and the embarrassment of explaining the mess to the students.

*****

Bullying Diary - Week Ending 24 September
An interesting turn of events. They wanted to appoint a Course Director, on a secondment basis, for the new MA. The course is nowhere near ready yet and it won't be launched until next year. The main task for now is to write it. There was an internal advert. Stella applied. I didn't, but I sent a mail to Ledlock to say I wasn't interested in the job but thought I was well-equipped to do the writing and I could hand it over to a Course Director proper when it was more developed. Stella got the job and I got a letter thanking me for my application and hoping I wasn't too disappointed – and that I'd continue to help Stella to write it. I never applied. I guess that's a way of making it look like there was competition.

Anyway, it's a 0.4 (2 days a week) appointment. So Stella now spends 0.6 or her time on her usual job and 0.4 on her new one. And, of course, another secondment necessarily came up for grabs, filling in for Stella: 0.4 Course Director of the BA. The job has been given to Linda Froggatt. Stella's best friend. There was no discussion in the department. It was simply announced. No one else was offered the opportunity even to declare an interest, let alone be considered. I feel sick again.

Also, something even weirder than usual happened this week. It was just before five, Stella was stood in the office doorway, talking to Patricia and me, when Sky popped his head round the door, said he was leaving for the day and placed a long, lingering kiss on her lips! What the hell was that all about?! I've seen them give each other the odd peck on parting – which is weird enough behaviour amongst colleagues – but this was loaded: lingering eye-contact, the lot!

*****

It was early October and time for the first Course Board of the new academic year. Staff and student representatives filed into the new seminar space. It wasn't quite a room; more a tall corral: three and a half walls of white-emulsioned MDF boards isolating a space in the middle of the old ceramics block. One side touched the end wall; two made an 'L'-shaped computer area; and the third – the part-open one – led to the office that Dan used and out to the entrance. It was a bit like the wriggly-board space they'd had when Dan first started, but at least this time it was properly made and wasn't in the midst of a busy studio. The only noise from the other side of the boards should be the tapping of computer keys.

As usual, minutes had not been distributed in advance. Dan scanned quickly the papers now in front of him. For the first time he had chance to read the minutes of the June Course Board; the one that had been rescheduled to when he and Phil Flanagan weren't available. He could see that that earlier team meeting – the one when Stella had redistributed the workload – had been erroneously reported to the Course Board: the bit Stella wanted had been recorded – that the lecturers would be year coordinators and year coordinators would run the modules – but there was no mention of the modules she had grudgingly agreed to do.

Stella started things off by asking those present to agree that the minutes were a fair record of what took place at the June Course Board. Dan said that they might well be an accurate record of what was said at that meeting – he hadn't been there – but they included a misreporting of what had been said at the earlier *team* meeting. He described the discrepancy and asked that the minutes recorded this error and that things were corrected. A thin, nervous-looking young woman – *Jenny something, wasn't it?* – scratted down minutes on a wire-bound jotter.

Stella announced that they would now be doing elective seminars in place of the old second year theory programme. She handed round photocopies of a chart showing how it would work – *the one Dan had produced for the July team meeting* – and went on to say what a great thing she thought this was, what a boon. She then began to congratulate Patricia on coming up with such a fine scheme, but looked at Dan and stopped herself. Dan felt a kind of sinking feeling mixed with burgeoning anger. Could he react to that? Was there enough there? Had the others noticed what had happened? A thing part-said, but not entirely. If he kicked off at that, Stella might say he'd missed the point: that wasn't what she was going to say at all. And then he'd look an idiot. He was trapped in confusion with rage burning up inside.

The meeting moved on and eventually reached 'Health and Safety'. Dan said that he wasn't quite sure if this was the right place in the agenda for what he wanted to say, but it would do, and then brought up a whole series of issues that he was worried about, particularly concerning the state of the reorganised office accommodation: how cold and overcrowded some of the offices were; the fact that he had been lumbered with an ancient and unreliable computer whilst everyone else's had been replaced (and whilst the convention was the oldest was replaced first); the fact that he was having to put up with a filthy chair that had been salvaged from the studios; the office demographics, which had separated the team into four different buildings and damaged communications…

Stella muttered something about bedding-in, getting used to things, seeing how it went…

*****

The meeting ended and Dan trotted off upstairs in the main building to see Jamie in IT. On the way back, at a junction in the corridors, he bumped into Stella. She looked flustered and embarrassed. What was she doing up there? *The only things along that corridor are the staff rest room and the admin office – where Jenny, the minute-taker, works.*

Barsteadworth College

*****

Bullying Diary – week ending 16 October

We all put our orders together in September for materials, stationery and such, as we always do. I also ordered a new office chair because the one that had been dumped on me was so beaten-up and filthy. Everything else arrived some weeks ago – Stella was running around the place with one of the new pairs of scissors saying 'look, this is me castrating men' (joke?) – but the chair did not arrive and still hadn't by the middle of this week, so I went to see Sky to see if he knew anything about it. He said yes, he'd crossed it off the order because he thought it was an unnecessary expense. I was livid. I went to see Stella to ask if she thought it was OK for a Technician to cancel an order made by a Senior Lecturer without consultation, notification or anything. Stella said she thought it was – she knew about it and agreed with Sky. She's perfectly happy for me to have to use a filthy chair, long since discarded from the offices and used as fucking cart in the studios. Would she want to contradict a man who gives her long, lingering kisses anyway? This the process of disempowerment promised by Linda Froggatt at that summer party made tangible. They are treating me like shit and I don't know what I can do about it. I want to leave. I am so pissed off and sick. I am reaching the end of my tether.

*****

Tuesday morning. Dan arrived early, excited about launching the first of his new elective seminars: 'Postmodernism and the Sci-Fi Movie'. He'd enjoyed putting it together. This would be a good one. The students would enjoy the references to such familiar movies, but he'd be able to get some really important points over to them about the nature of postmodernity. This was going to work really well. The session would start at 9.30 in Portakabin 2. He had various bits of projection equipment booked out – video player, slide projector and TV monitor – but had no idea whether or not they would arrive. He had been briefly back in fashion in the spring and Sky had been grudgingly helpful, but things had become hit-and-miss again lately. At 8.45 Dan gathered up all his teaching materials from his desk – notes, handouts, video tape, packed slide carousel – and strode purposefully across the car park to the portakabin. As he unlocked the door his heart sank. The room was a mess with chairs and tables scattered about all over the place, plus a liberal sprinkling of empty cardboard coffee cups and sandwich containers. There was no projection equipment of any sort in there. The heat and tension shot through his body once more. He went to the store. It was locked-up. Sky wasn't around. No one was around. Deirdre was half-time and this wasn't one of her days. Dan rushed to Stella's office. She was the only other key holder for the store, but she wasn't around either. And her office was locked, so that meant that Linda wasn't in, so he couldn't even find out what had happened to Sky and if and when he might arrive at work.

Dan was beginning to panic. He ran to the college gallery to see if, maybe, Sky was setting up an exhibition. But he wasn't there either. Dan asked around: students, staff, reception, and technicians from other departments... No one had seen him; no one had any news of him. The sense of panic was increasing. It was 9.20. Most of the students had taken their seats in the portakabin and were waiting for something to happen, but he had nothing to give them. He found himself, by turns, going into the classroom to reassure the students, then frantically running around the site trying to find Sky. This was how it always was – *they fuck up and you end up stood in front of the class looking ridiculous. You can say what you want to the students, but their experience is of incompetence and you are the one stood in front of them. You're made to look a twat. Try and blame someone else and you just look even worse.* Dan stood in the middle of the car park, looking this way and that. Physical and emotional sensations threatened to overwhelm him. He was hot, sweaty, tense, panicky. He could feel pressure in his tear ducts. But he could no longer trust himself. This was surely an overreaction. He was embarrassed that he felt this way. He should just be cool. But he couldn't be. Anything his mind might have wanted to happen was overwhelmed by the way his body was making him feel. Back to the class. More excuses. The physical traces of the state he was in had to be noticeable. His throat was tight; his voice strangled and high-pitched. He went outside again, partly for another look for Sky, partly to hide. He paced up and down the car park.

At 9.40 Sky strolled through the gates, chatting and laughing with Edward.

*****

Half-two in the morning. Dan hadn't wanted to wake Sophie. The sound from the TV was scarcely above the threshold of hearing. Nevertheless, something had woken her. He heard the floorboards of the spare bedroom creak and then the door open. She appeared on the open-plan staircase, eyes blinking at the light. "Are you all right?"

"Go back to bed, love."

"No, I won't. Are you all right?" She sat next to him in her pale blue towelling dressing gown.

"No, I'm not. I'm not." Dan's face was in his hands. "I can't stand it. I just can't take it anymore. I'm cracking up Sophie. I don't know what to do." He rubbed his hands over his eyes, onto his cheeks, onto his forehead and then down onto his thighs, which he squeezed repeatedly and involuntarily. "I was in a meeting today with some fairly senior people. We were working on the MA. And I just lost it. I set off to speak and then had no idea what I was talking about. I just stopped. I had no idea what I was going to say. I felt ridiculous."

"Oh, it probably wasn't as bad as you thought. Everybody loses their train of thought now and then. It happens. Everybody will have completely forgotten about it by now."

"It isn't just that. At other meetings lately I've had these kind of Tourette's-like moments. I haven't sworn, at least I don't think I have, but I've just burst out with things that were a mile off the tone and meaning of what was going on. It was like it had nothing to do with me. My mouth just went off and I was sat there watching... or listening. I'm losing control of myself. Everything's just pressure and stress. Stella's dumped most of her workload on the rest of us and the timetable's a fuck-up again. I sorted a load of it out at the beginning of term, but as usual she keeps fucking changing things. That's creating more work, there's more to do because of the stuff she's offloaded and there's the new seminar programmes to write. She just sits in her office, holding court. She likes everyone to come in and gossip with her: first the lecturers, and when they go off to teach, the students, and it's *oh, I'm so busy, everybody seems to want me. I can't get anything done.* And then something else gets offloaded or she hires a visiting lecturer to come in and do some of her work. I'm supposed to do 2 ½ days a week. I'm doing more like 3. Meanwhile, she's managed to whittle things down to the extent that she can take Fridays off as a 'research day'. She doesn't do any bloody research. An extra day at home with Jonte, more like. She does four days a week for thirty-odd grand a year, and I do three days a week for thirteen grand a year. It's just. Fucking. Sick."

"I've had enough of this. It's time someone blew the top off what's happening in that place."

"But what would I say? It's subtle. It's lots of little things that might seem trivial. But it's cumulative. And who would I say it to? Frank doesn't want to know. I have tried to talk to him again about it. You know what he said? 'I have to back the Course Director'. I said 'where does that leave me?', and he just repeated himself. I've heard, sort of trickled back via his secretary that he's 'fed up with all the tittle-tattle'. That's all it is, for him, 'tittle-tattle'. That's fucking Frank all over though: anything for a quiet life. Phil Flanagan's had several goes at complaining, but from the reaction he's had it seems complaining about Stella Jobby is now virtually a sackable offence. He's in a bad way as well, by the way."

"But what about the famous 'Fuller Fudge'? Doesn't he try to please both sides?"

"That's how it starts, but if things go on long enough he chooses sides and then he gets entrenched. Whoever gets to him first, or most often, wins the day. If you can persuade him of something, get him onside, he'll back you. And of course, I have no access to him now. Stella does and she's the arch-manipulator, so he 'has to back the Course Director'."

"Then I'll go in and say it."

"How can you? How can you really? And what does that make me look like?"

*****

Stella had asked Dan into her office for a quick word. When he arrived Linda was there too. They'd be right with him; just had a few things to finish off. Dan took a seat whilst the two Course Directors, with their backs to him, shuffled papers around and muttered between themselves. What did they want? There'd been a couple of peculiar incidents recently, when they'd sidled up to him and said some pretty weird things: on one occasion they'd kind of shaped and schmoozed around him and said something like 'ooh, hasn't he got nice lips'; then, on another, they'd asked him what part of a woman's body he found most attractive. At one time, back in prehistory, he might have felt included in the joke. Now he just felt awkward and embarrassed. He'd tried to say something pithy in response, as though he was cool and on top of the game, but if he'd convinced either of those two, he'd certainly not convinced himself. He'd just got hot and uncomfortable. He wasn't sure if they'd been having a bit of genuine, grown-up fun – flirting even, though that seemed unlikely, given all they'd been through – or if it was simply that they'd registered his collapsing confidence and were putting further kicks in. Was there going to be some more of that? From where he was seated, on one of the visitor chairs, the women's backs filled his vision. They stepped left and right, reached arms across each other, exchanged words that were scarcely audible and placed papers on this, that or the other pile. Since her promotion, Linda had started coming to work dressed as a dominatrix. Previously, she'd turned herself out pretty much like everyone else: black jeans, sweater and comfortable flat shoes. Now, her hair was yanked back tight in a Croydon face-lift, exposing the dark roots, removing any fluffiness and making her features hard and pronounced. She painted her lips a startling red. She'd always done that, mind; it just seemed more visible now. She still wore the black sweater, but below were a bum-hugging black leather skirt, black nylons and jackboots. And there was something else: her bum had definitely got bigger; quite a bit bigger. In fact, he couldn't ever remember noticing it before, but you'd definitely notice it now. Was it a sympathetic response to Stella's? Maybe he'd been right about Stella's being a secret source of power – like Samson's hair, perhaps – and now Linda had become a Course Director, maybe hers too was expanding to cope with the new level of responsibility.

"Can I help?" Dan heard himself say, boredom having got the better of him.

Stella turned. "You could get some coffees."

He stood bolt upright and marched assertively towards the canteen. Rapid communication to the bit of his mind that dealt with body language said *I don't want to reveal that I feel any affront at being sent for the coffees, at least until I work out whether or not it is an affront.* Get the coffees… was this a put-down? In the canteen, when they were all together, anyone could go for the coffees – not that that happened anymore. Same in the meetings. So why did this feel wrong? Was he being paranoid? Was it OK to send him for the coffees – nearly fifty years old, a doctor, a former Course Director – or was it wrong? Was it more deliberate humiliation? In his body it certainly felt that way, though in Politically-Correct-Land maybe it wasn't… How could you tell? This was all part of the deal: his judgmental skills had been worn way by the cumulative effects of months – was it years now? – of psychological violence, and they didn't work anymore. He didn't feel good, but wasn't sure if that was the correct feeling for the circumstances.

With the paper shuffling and muttering evidently completed, the two women sat and faced Dan and smiled indulgently. Dan tried to smile back, but wasn't sure if it came off. Stella began:

Barsteadworth College

"Dan, we've asked you in because we want you to introduce more flexibility into your teaching hours."

"How do you mean?"

"Currently, you do Monday, Tuesday and half of Wednesday."

"Mostly, yes, but not entirely. That's the basic framework, but there are several weeks per term where it's not like that, where it's adapted to suit the timetable, and of course it changes now and then for unforeseen events."

"Yes, well, we'd like you to work more flexibly. It would be really helpful to us if you could be available any day of the week."

"But I'm half time."

"Yes. That's fine. We don't want you to work any more hours..." Linda and Stella looked and smiled at each other. *An obvious misunderstanding. As if they would be so demanding.* "... just to be more flexible."

"I am flexible. I *do* do other days besides my routine ones. I *do* fit in changes at short notice. What else do you want?"

"Ah. I think the word 'routine' captures it. It's this Monday, Tuesday, Wednesday thing. It would be far better if you could be available any day of the week."

"So how do I plan the rest of my week then? For all you know I have a second part-time job," reasoned Dan.

Linda joined in: "But you don't, do you. All you do is spend time in your studio."

"That's none of your business. What I do in my own time is my affair, nothing to do with this place, and I don't have to discuss it with you. And what about the other part-timers? Will you be asking them for the same 'flexibility'?"

"Linda's hours need to be fixed because she'd got children", said Stella "and Edward commutes from Surrey; he needs a set routine too."

"Yeah, well, so do I."

"You only live 20 minutes away and you've got no kids," pressed Linda.

Dan could feel that now-familiar heat and pressure building up inside. "My spare time is as important to me as everyone else's is to them. I don't see why I should be especially singled-out for worse terms and conditions than everybody else."

"Oh, it's not worse terms and conditions, Dan. Your contract won't change," said Stella with another of those indulgent smiles.

Fucking patronising cow. I don't mean my contract, I mean the special private working arrangements you create down here. "You want me to be available all of the time, anytime, during a 40 hour week for half-time pay. How am I supposed to make plans for the rest of my week when you can change things at any moment?"

"Well it wouldn't be like that a lot of the time, Dan. We would be able to work things out. Keep things as simple as possible. We just need flexibility."

"No. I am not going to be pushed about from pillar to post in order to accommodate everyone else's cosy lifestyle."

"Well, if that's your attitude…"

"It is."

As Dan left the office, he wondered about the extent to which these plans had been driven by necessity and to what by other motivations. Sure, someone as disorganised as Stella could make use of someone who could be dropped into a class at any time in any place, and it would be him because she wouldn't dump this kind of crap on any of the preferred members of staff. But was it more than this? He was the only person this was happening to. So, was it another way of rubbing his nose in it? Was she trying to see just how far she could push him?

*****

Bullying Diary – 19 November
There was a study trip to Barcelona. If there was any discussion about who was to go on it I was not party to it. It was organised by Linda. The staff she chose to go on the trip were and her husband (he has a thing for Spain) and Patricia. I was not invited. I was not on the previous one either. At least it wasn't Stella's extended family this time.

*****

The cold November wind picked up the dust and blew it down Burlington Street. He squinted to keep it out of his eyes. A gallery-hopping day in London was a good way to remind himself of what it was all about, keep things in proportion. He'd spent the morning at Tate Britain and was now on his way to Cork Street to check out a few of the commercial galleries. The first were the gilded-frame sort, the ones that have more to do with heirlooms than art. He glanced without stopping. Behind glass and security bars were cheesy images of faithful spaniels with pheasants in their mouths, spates in the Highlands and sheep coming home through the snow. There was always some good stuff further down the street, though, if you looked; in Waddington, Flowers, Cristea and the rest.

It took a few moments to recognise the large shape coming towards him; something once very familiar but not seen for some time.

"Kinell! Bill Bulwark!"

"Gor! Dan Ripley! You old bastard!"

The two men shook hands and embraced. 'Don't be a stranger', Bill had said when Dan moved north. And he'd never meant to be. They'd had a great time working together at Woodheath Tech in the mid-90s, but somehow time had passed and he'd not been back in touch.

Bill didn't look much different: still hefty, still with that wedge of brown hair and possibly even still with the same leather jacket. No. It had to be a different one by now… but it looked the same.

"So how are you?" said Dan.

"I'm fine. Yep. Still at Woodheath. Married now. Got a son: young Jack."

"Good for you! Did you marry anyone I know?"

"Nah. Don't think so. Bella. Met her in the camera shop."

"Right."

"And how are you?" asked Bill.

"Well, fine, yeah, you know, sort of." Dan's mind ran quickly around his problems and the question of how much he wanted to reveal to Bill. The whole thing was humiliating. He didn't want Bill to see him like that. "Yeah, I'm doing OK. I'm at Barsteadworth."

"Oh, got an art college down there now have they?"

"Yeah, yeah, it's pretty good. I ran the Fine Art BA for a couple of years, a couple of years ago. It was a secondment. I let it go when it became permanent and went part time, which is great. I'm getting to spend some time in the studio now. The person who took over is someone called 'Stella Jobby'. Don't know if you'd know her?"

Barsteadworth College

Bill Bulwark recoiled: the top half of his body pulled away from Dan and his eyes widened. "Stella Jobby! STELLA FUCKING JOBBY!! My God! God 'elp yer!"

"So, you know her then. I wasn't going to say anything but..." Dan paused. He didn't know where to go next with this.

"I used to work with her at Twickendean. Years ago. How are you finding her to work with?"

"To be honest, Bill, she's fucking poison. She's devious, spiteful and manipulative... and I think she has gender issues."

"GENDER ISSUES?! Ha! Well that's one way of putting it, I suppose. Personally, I prefer to cut the crap: she *hates men*. She's a misandrist. Can't stand men unless she can control them, and the more discomfort she can create whilst she's doing so, the better."

"That rings true. It's only the men she's had it in for. One guy's left already – Mervin Botwinch; he couldn't take any more of her – and she's been going out of her way to make my life and Phil Flanagan's as wretched as possible."

"She was just the same at Twickendean. She picked on people – just the men, of course – though eventually the women saw through her too. She picked on me. I had a really terrible time with her."

"What did she do?"

"I don't want to talk about it. It's in the past now and it was just such an awful, negative part of my life. But you know what she does: plots, undermines, bullies... No doubt you know all about it."

"Yes, and she's just so skilful at it. You get the sense that no-one will believe you if you complain."

"Of course she is. She's been doing it all her life."

"Do you think it's a feminist thing?"

"No. She's not a feminist. When she first started at Twickendean she was all over the male lecturers like a communicable disease. They were older, more empowered than her and she wanted a bit of what they'd got. Eventually, she'd shagged her way round the college and everyone was fed up of her. Then all the digging and conniving started."

"She came with a really good reference."

"Well she would, wouldn't she? If you thought she was leaving your place, wouldn't you give her the most glowing reference imaginable?! But she's a poor lecturer: disorganised and lazy. The only thing she's any good at is what you've seen: dodging things and manipulating people."

"But is she a good artist or anything? She must have had something that pushed her career along", reasoned Dan.

"No. Not that either. Everything's derivative and contrived. When she started at Twickendean it was that 70s-80s period of macho metal art. All the male lecturers she was sucking up to were making great big welded-steel sculpture, so she made some of that. Then feminist art was the thing, so she started hanging tampons on washing lines. And then when feminist art softened a bit she started copying those Anna-Marie Pacheco head-on-a-pole things. That was the early 90s. I don't think she's made anything since."

"Neither do I. I haven't seen anything and there's nothing on the internet."

"Anyway, Dan, great to see you. I really don't envy you, the circumstances you're in. I'm serious: your best bet would be to look for another job. Stella Jobby is a vindictive, manipulative bitch. It won't get any better. But, hey, you know, do call in and see us."

"Count on it. Great to see you as well, Bill."

Barsteadworth College

Dan strolled on down Cork Street, stopping every few yards to look through the windows, though he was no longer really taking in what he saw. What Bill had said was hardly news, though it helped Dan to know that it wasn't just him; that he wasn't going out of his mind. Or maybe he was, but at least that part of it was right: Stella was a vindictive, manipulative bitch who had a problem with men. That was corroborated now. *And it wasn't going to get any better.*

Memories of events drifted into Dan's mind. A few months earlier he and Phil had taken a group of students on a study trip to London. It had been a really exceptional trip, just one of those days when everything falls perfectly into place. They had got lucky with the weather – it was still early autumn then – they had seen some fabulous new art work and stumbled by chance onto a couple of exciting performances at the ICA. It had been a very rewarding day and the students had loved it. The next morning Stella asked Dan how it had gone. He started to enthuse about what a great day it had been; probably the best London trip since he had been at Barsteadworth, he told her. He started to expand on things, but Stella threw her head back, visibly irritated and, without speaking, turned on her heels and walked away in a huff without letting him finish. The news that a trip organised by Phil and Dan had gone supremely well was evidently unendurable. There was no doubt that she'd had it in for Mervin, Phil and Dan from the start. The only tolerable males around the place were Tim, Sky and Charles – Stella's, Linda's and Deirdre's subservient husbands – and Edward, a quiet and amenable chap who'd been to the right sort of schools and was one of Stella's former students. It was clear why Mervin, Phil and Dan had been the targets of her hate campaigns: Mervin was the most commercially successful artist in the department, by a long chalk. In fact, he didn't even need to teach for a living – nearly everything he painted sold – he did it just to get himself out of the studio now and then. Phil Flanagan, of course, was a high-flying Saatchi Collection artist. And Dan was the only one in the department with a PhD. Plus, he had read an awful lot and had a level of knowledge that Stella, by her own admission, found intimidating. Worst of all, though, they were all good lecturers and the students liked them. Competent, popular and male. Bastards.

*****

The rain hammered down onto the tarmac. Headlights were on and trucks were producing deep waves of spray. It was a horrible morning and Borchester Road roundabout was even more frightening than usual in the poor visibility. Dan's Escort swooshed into a gap and came off at the Long Lane exit without incident. A truck had gone straight over the roundabout the other week when its Portuguese driver had fallen asleep at the wheel. His tyre marks were still etched into the grass. He'd missed the second Borchester Road exit and taken the front off the Methodist chapel on Woodleigh Lane. Amazingly, no one was hurt, though the driver was rather shaken… and in quite a bit of trouble.

Dan tried to clear his head. He'd taken a sleeper at 3am and was still struggling with the wooziness. He hadn't wanted to – not at that time – but it had been the third consecutive night with no sleep, and he had to do something. He was going crazy. It was a good thing he was half time. If he were full time he'd probably never sleep at all. Once, a glass or two of red wine could be trusted to knock him out. But not any more. All that did now was give him the choice between lying in bed stone-cold sober or lying in bed half-drunk – rigidly awake in either case. That tape loop in his mind was an unstoppable force now, endlessly playing back to him all the awkward, embarrassing positions he'd been placed into, all the humiliations, all the things he'd wished he's said but never had the presence of mind… God, he hated his life.

The queue at Petley Cross traffic lights took an age. A bit of rain and everything grinds to a halt. *Ha! The irony!* Here he was being impatient about getting to *that place*. And then a deep feeling sadness came over him. He used to love going to work. Even when it was tough; even when he was overloaded as Acting Course Director he still loved it. There was never a day when he didn't want to go in. Now he'd rather be anywhere else. He'd been fantasising as he lay awake about driving off to Cornwall, changing his name, reinventing his history and getting some work on the fishing boats. Just working with his hands out in the elements. Just some physical reality, not a job that's all stupidity and mind-fuck. But it *was* a fantasy. He knew he'd never do it. For one thing he wasn't even sure if there was still a fishing fleet any more. Hadn't that all been written off by EC quotas or something? There was probably only one fucking fishing boat in the whole of Cornwall. Tourists probably gathered round with their cameras every time it was launched. In any case, the state his bowels were in nowadays he wouldn't last two minutes on a trawler. And Sophie wouldn't exactly be pleased if he did a Reggie Perrin.

Brake lights started to come on in front of him as traffic backed up from Dean Bridge roundabout. He slowed and then stopped. The windscreen wipers flicked off the rain left and right. Beyond the queue of traffic he could see the tall buildings of the uni, right next to Barts. He felt that awful, icy grip in his guts.

Chapter Eight
Two years ago

First week back after Christmas. Dan's 10.30 tutee hadn't shown. Handy, he needed a quick word with Stella to sort out a few timetabling anomalies. Amongst other things, he'd been timetabled to do two lots of things in one space of time and something had to give. He ducked into his coat and cut across the car park to Studio 2. All that was visible from the door of Stella's office to where she was presumably seated were backs of student heads. It would have to do later. He shoved his way through the heavy double doors and back out into the cold air.

Back in the office Dan clicked on the white plastic Pifco kettle, spooned Sainsbury's Light Roast Coffee Granules into his Manchester United mug and waited for the water to boil. Dan carting around his coffee mug from tutee to tutee in the studios was a familiar sight and a source of mild amusement for the students. He didn't mind and shared the joke. He jotted down a brief message on a green post-it note to remind himself to make sure he spoke to Stella before the end of the day, and stuck it on his computer screen.

This had become the norm. Stella boasted of her 'open door policy' at meetings, explaining proudly that students were permitted to call into her office for a chat *at any time*. She saw this enlightened practice as one that put her some way ahead of colleagues, in and outside of the department. What she didn't say anything about, however, were the consequences: her other duties were neglected and in some cases abandoned altogether, and as for time management – which had never been her strongest point anyway – that had gone completely out of the window. There just wasn't time for teaching amidst all this caring. Her day now revolved around gossip, which she justified as 'pastoral care'. Students queued, eager to tell her their tales of woe: boyfriend or girlfriend trouble, money issues, things not working out with room mates, not feeling able to cope... All very worthy stuff and, of course, popular: everyone loves an agony aunt. And if someone were to question her spending so much of her time doing this, they would be guilty of not taking *their* pastoral care duties seriously. Still better, Stella recorded her informal student tête-à-têtes as 'tutorials', and there were lots of them, thus the tutorials chart demonstrated incontrovertibly just how hard she work compared to everyone else. On top of this demanding schedule, there were of course the various meetings a Course Director necessarily attends, as well as other extra-departmental duties that she had to perform. And then there were Fridays: these she spent at home, researching and catching up on things. As a consequence of all these many important tasks, Stella had achieved a state of serene semi-retirement, and it was necessary for others to take on much of what she might otherwise have done in the studios or lecture theatre.

Bullying Diary – week ending 15 January
This week was the January Course Board. I suspected that Stella had had the minutes of the October Course Board altered. I was right. I saw the minutes for the first time: I'd complained in October that the June minutes were an inaccurate record of the previous team meeting and that there were numerous problems with the revised staff accommodation. Yet, if you were to believe the minutes, these subjects were never raised. In fact, there is no record of my having spoken at all during the whole meeting. I complained about this. Phil Flanagan similarly complained that things he had said were not recorded. Again, according to the records he appeared not to have spoken. Also, severe criticisms that had been made by Year One Student Representative, Noreen Stretch, about timetabling cock-ups were ameliorated to something innocuous. Stella reckoned it was incompetence on the part of the minute-taker – the one she had evidently followed back to her office and no doubt pressurised into editing the minutes to her liking. A different minute-taker was there this time so the previous one was not around to defend herself.

*****

Bullying Diary – week ending 22 January
On Monday evening as I was about to leave, Stella called me in to her office to help her with a presentation she was preparing. In her

role as MA Course Director she was to lead the rest of the MA Development Group – which included me – and give a talk on Tuesday morning to Barts' Validation Committee (Fuller, Ledlock and the rest of the top brass) on how far we had got with the project. She was lost. She was trying to download images by fine artists whose work involved elements of theatre, performance art and costume design. She had got three and run out of ideas. She simply did not have the breadth of knowledge. I worked with her well into the evening and helped her put together an impressive presentation involving about 30 such artists. The following morning the meeting took place. Stella put on the presentation to an impressed and delighted audience, and took the plaudits all for herself. There wasn't the slightest intimation that I had been involved, and she studiously avoided my gaze for the rest of the meeting.

*****

The red Escort swept smoothly along the neat suburban roads that led to Barts. Black plastic dash. Red brick semis. Grey winter trees. Roads familiar to the point of invisibility. Sweaty hands on the steering wheel. He was anxious. His body was now ahead of his mind. He didn't even have to think about what kind of shit he might be dealt today; his body already anticipated it and assumed it would be something pretty bad. It usually felt that way about things now. His mind picked up the pace, joined in and got anxious about the totally unpredictable timetable, the relentless criticism of his work, seeing Stella's fear-and-favour strategies going on around him, being denied the basic requirements of his job, having his teaching taken away, being made to look incompetent by the subversive actions of his protected colleagues... He found himself trying to anticipate the next undermining plot, and got anxious about that... He was pressurised by his own fear, and then felt humiliated that he was allowing these fools to create these sensations of fear within him. Going to work was now one with humiliation. His self-esteem had collapsed. He might have left the place, but could no longer imagine being able face an interview panel. Psychological pressure was fixed tightly to unpleasant physical sensations. His body did things he couldn't control and his mind followed. An invisible force would press on his chest or his head and trigger a kind of deadening in his hearing. This created a kind of closed-out quality that became especially apparent in meetings, when the conversation would suddenly involve him and he would have no idea what was going on and then panic. Then there were those occasions, of which there had been several now, when he had started to talk and then lost it entirely, forgotten what he was talking about. He became, by turns, withdrawn and then loud. He would feel incredibly shy, like a child and blush for no reason, then blurt out loudly things that seemed to come from nowhere and have nothing to do with him. Insomnia was relentless, as was sinusitis. Irritable bowel syndrome and fatigue had returned, as had that easy susceptibility to colds and infections. These reduced his ability to cope still further and burdened him with additional pressures, above and beyond what Stella and her cronies were creating for him. As things multiplied and compounded he had started to get anxiety attacks; at home, at work and especially as he approached the car park. And there it was now. His felt sick to his guts.

Bullying Diary – Monday 31 January

It's approaching the half-way point of the academic year, the timetable is still incomplete, causing chaos and spreading stress liberally around the staff and students. I have once again found myself with a dense period of contact time and other things not accounted for:

I have Year 3 Major Project Proposals to read and give feedback on. But I am timetabled to be in class with other groups *all of the time*: no time has been allocated to deal with the Project Proposals. There are about 30 proposals, each the size of an essay. The procedure is to read them, write a page or so of feedback on each student's planned project and, where necessary, ask for the proposal to be revised and resubmitted; at which point the process is repeated, with me now, hopefully, being able give my approval. If I read them and then have to ask for about half to be amended and returned for re-consideration, and if each takes roughly half an hour to deal with (and that's pretty conservative), then that is twenty-odd hours of work. That's over a week's work for a half-timer, like me, *and there's no time allowed for it.*

I could, of course, deal with them in my own time. But that would mean doing a forty-odd hour week for eighteen hours' pay. That's just not right. To do it would be to give in to bullying, or to shoulder the consequences of Stella's incompetence, or both. But the situation is 'live' there in my face: the students are anxiously waiting for their feedback so that they can start their projects, whilst I have no time to read the things on which I am supposed to be feeding back. They're stressed. I'm stressed. I've scarcely seen my manager(s) for weeks – they don't seem to have been around when I have. I don't imagine I'd get much sense even if I did. I don't know what I'm supposed to do. Go mad with the fucking anxiety, presumably.

The Year 3 students have also been anxiously awaiting 2 days of tutorials that Stella had listed in the timetable, but put down as 'lecturer tba' (*to be advised*). However, she never got around to putting names to these sessions, so when the time came there was no one available to do them. Everyone was doing something else and it was too late to book a visiting lecturer. By this stage of the course students start to panic about the degree show and, at last, they value and badly want their tutorials. But these ones are not going to happen. It is a disastrous cock-up, lousy for morale and stemming entirely from Stella's failure to write a proper timetable, but as far as the students are concerned the buck stops with their Year Coordinator – me – and although it is outside of my control it looks to them as though it is my fault. I really can't take much more of this shit.

*****

Wednesday afternoon. Dan had knocked off for the week after the lunchtime MA Development Group meeting, but had emailed himself things to work on at home. He wasn't going to do much right now, just recheck he'd got the material he needed and email Stella to confirm his plans. He'd scarcely seen her at work, but this was a straightforward thing. His next block of seminars was coming up soon, but because of the work he'd had to do on the MA and the over-cramming of the timetable he'd had no time to prepare for them. Every minute and more had been spoken for. But, at last, recess week was coming up – next week – and there were two clear days on the timetable when he could get the thing done.

Bullying Diary – week ending 5 February
The following exchange of emails took place. They are self-explanatory.

To: Stella Jobby
From: Dan Ripley
2 February
Hi Stella,
I wasn't able to catch you at work or by phone. Next week – Monday and Tuesday – I've got nothing timetabled, so I'll use the time to get on with the prep for my upcoming seminars – I just wanted to confirm with you that it's OK…?
Best,
Dan

*****

To: Dan Ripley
From: Stella Jobby
3 February
Hi Dan,
Sorry. No. We need you for interviews.
Regards,
Stella

*****

To: Stella Jobby
From: Dan Ripley
3 February
Hi Stella
There's nothing timetabled for me and I've been relying on that time to do the prep for my seminars.
Best
Dan

*****

To: Dan Ripley
From: Stella Jobby
3 February
Hi Dan,
Sorry. Out of the question. We need you for interviews. You'll have to do your seminar prep some other time.
Regards,
Stella

*****

To: Stella Jobby
From: Dan Ripley
3 February
Stella
There is no other time. There are those two days then that's it: after that I'm in class all the time. I have no other available time to do the prep before the seminars start. And those days are blank – you haven't timetabled me for interviewing.
Best
Dan

*****

To: Dan Ripley
From: Stella Jobby
3 February
Hi Dan,
We need you for interviews. You'll just have to find time for your prep. I am in any case getting concerned about the amount of time you devote to prep and the level you're teaching at, which I think is creeping towards MA level. I did my prep in a few hours over a couple of evenings. I'm also concerned that you're not using student-led seminars when you might.
Regards,
Stella

*****

To: Stella Jobby
From: Dan Ripley

4 February
Stella
I say again - there is no other time. I'm in class all the time, right up to when the seminars start. I don't know how you can say my teaching is creeping towards MA level and doesn't include student-led seminars when I haven't started preparing it yet. And I'm completely at a loss to understand why, when there are so many staff now who could do the interviews, that it's me you need so badly.
Dan

*****

To: Dan Ripley
From: Stella Jobby
4 February
Dan,
You are placing me under intolerable pressure. Do your prep. We'll cover the interviews.
Stella

*****

To: Stella Jobby
From: Dan Ripley
4 February
Stella
I do not wish to place anyone under pressure. But you placed me in an impossible position. I will now get on and prep my teaching.
Dan

*****

I am just exasperated with all this shit. If I was supposed to be interviewing it should have been shown on the timetable, but there was nothing there. This has been going on for months: each time some prep time looms, Stella slots something else into it. Moreover, on any given Monday there should be Stella, Linda, Phil, Patricia, Sky and available, and possibly Deirdre – as well as me. That's at least 5 people without me, and since only 2 (max) are needed for interviews there's more than enough cover. And on the Tuesday

Edward is in as well. That could be as many as 7. Why is it vital that I do them? I think what's going on is pretty clear. It'll be the same as last Easter: the Small-Jobbys and the Gelding-Froggatts will have alternative plans for the week, and I bet Edward's been told he needn't bother travelling as well. And in support of that, all this crap has been thrown my way. She's accusing me of pressurising her unfairly, alleging that I'm over-preparing, that my material is of an inappropriate level and that I'm not involving the students sufficiently. All of this before I've even fucking done any of it. And I bet that goes back to Frank Fuller, as well. No doubt there's a 'Dan problem' now, just like there was a 'Mervin problem' and still is a 'Phil problem'.

My seminars are on a subject I've never taught before – I'm starting from scratch with new research and preparation. And as regards student-led seminars: it was me who introduced that teaching method to the fucking course. I always use student-led elements in my seminar programs.

It's bad enough to face the absurdity of my teaching material being criticised before it has even been written, but knowing that this whole thing is almost certainly to do with the clique scamming extra holidays again is beyond bearable. And this from the laziest fucking lecturer I have ever seen: Stella Jobby. Her downer on prep stems from the fact that she, herself, scarcely prepares anything at all. She lives with the double-bind of not wanting the strain of doing any prep or complex teaching herself, whilst resenting others who do, because they exaggerate the contrast. She described how she did her prep in her own time in a few hours. Well that's hardly surprising: for the 3 sessions that made up her last seminar set, she got a guest lecturer in for the first day and the other two days were student-led projects. All she did was arrange it and walk away. I have never seen her give a lecture, as such, and her office contains no books, periodicals, abstracted texts or lecture notes – nothing but the box files of course documents and student records that her sister-in-law dreamily labelled, sorted and filled last summer. Stella is that very rare thing: a senior academic who possesses no reading material. Of course, many fine art lecturers do have fewer books than their more academically oriented colleagues, because their explorations are in the form of visual art and their output is represented in exhibitions, not books. But no one has ever seen any artwork by her either.

Barsteadworth College

*****

The drive into work a was a blur Dan was more involved with the ructions in his mind and body than the world around him as he approached Barts things started to go off the scale sweating but cold in his guts a feeling of fear and panic rising through his tightening chest. Car park. Office. Eyes hot head throbbed a wall some sort of wall between him and the world invisible but there. *Please don't speak to me leave me I'll be OK. OK.* Kettle on. White plastic click. Computer on. *Settle settle. OK OK let's sort out next week for the third years. Professional Studies 2 module starts Monday. Fine.* Computer. *Come on.* Timetable. Monday. *It's blank. BLANK.* It was one of the modules Stella was supposed to run, but there was nothing there. Nothing. *She hasn't planned it, hasn't set it up, hasn't done anything.* Dan chilled and sweated. His head filled with noise; a wowing, throbbing sound; huge quantities of liquid roaring down a massive pipe. He couldn't query it with her because she was away all week at a conference. He wouldn't see her before next Monday morning, and possibly not even then. His year group; her fuck-up. The students would arrive in the seminar room expecting to start the module, and he'd have to stand in front of them and try to explain this away. He'd be made to look a fool. He'd feel like he felt now, but have to try and speak through it. Another humiliation. More mental and physical convulsions to anticipate. Meanwhile she was completely fucking separated from the consequences of her actions.

*****

Wednesday afternoon. Dan's half-day. He threw the old leather briefcase onto the passenger seat. The tyres of the grubby red Escort scrunched slowly, gently over the sandstone chips, up the ramp to the exit. He had started at 8.30, done tutorials until 12.30, attended a lunchtime meeting of the MA Group, then gone back to the office to finish off the paperwork generated by the morning's teaching. He was probably hungry, though he couldn't tell. The dashboard clock showed 2.30. Half a day: six hours. That's about right.

Home. Everything was grey. The house was grey. Outside was grey. No wind. The street was silent and still. No other people at all. Dreamlike. But the noise in his head wouldn't go away. Wowing and throbbing. And that awful, mind-numbing, rushing sound, like billions of gallons of filthy water smashing its way ferociously down some colossal storm drain.

He needed a walk. Fresh air. Try and clear his head. He was in the wood. Silent, but for his own private noise. Above, a towering green-grey canopy; below, a soft russet cushion built up from decades of fallen twigs, leaves and pine needles. It normally smelt nice – tree smells and the comforting primal scent of damp, decaying bark and undergrowth – but he couldn't smell anything lately. A 'wood'. That seemed a bit over the top – it was just half a square mile of mostly conifer forest that separated his estate from the next one – but it reminded him of holidays by Lake Constance and it was quiet and a good place for a short, undemanding walk and a bit of peace and contemplation. But there was no peace to be had today. The noise would not go away and nothing would come clear. There was just the relentless drone of confusion in his mind.

In a place somewhere much too close to the throbbing and rushing for clarity to survive, thoughts were engaged in their own life-and-death struggle. In a grey, claustrophobic space they flew hopelessly around, hit the sides, hit other each other, became dazed and stupefied and then crashed to the floor, at which point they were descended on by countless other thoughts which nourished themselves before taking off and repeating the same stupid, hopeless process.

His ankle started to hurt, a bit at first, then a lot, then a *real* lot. He hadn't twisted it or anything; he just became aware of pain, which rapidly became more and more piercing. He felt anxious. His ankle hurt so badly now that he was worried that he might not even be able to make it home. *That's irrational. Home's only half a mile away. It isn't even a real forest. People walk their dogs in here.* And then it wasn't just his ankle. The pain shot up through his legs and throughout his whole body. Every joint, bone and muscle. It was as though he had fallen unconscious for a few moments – gone to sleep on that soft inviting forest floor – and in that time someone had bashed him about with a big, heavy stick. It was like a dream. Maybe it was. The sensations were like those in a dream, like when you need to move or run, but are fixed to the spot. When your body is like lead – too heavy to shift. By the time he got home he could scarcely walk. He dragged his dead leg onto the sofa in the grey room.

His consciousness was filled with small buzzing shapes. Dots. Fast-moving dots. Insects. Filthy black malevolent things. A swarm of them that grew and grew. Within no time a huge black cloud fizzed and rattled around the room. The hateful little beasts were so fast and numerous and angry and aggressive that they constantly collided with each other, which made them even more angry and aggressive. And so densely packed were they that they blocked out the light. The grey went ever darker. The sickening black cloud swept over and through him, through his body, heading for his very soul, where it devoured anything good it could still find. There wasn't much left there anyway. Confidence, self-belief and happiness had gone some time ago. Of the few things still surviving, resilience was the second last to be consumed, shortly followed by hope. Dan could see his dying self from across the room: a small, cold, desiccated thing, shrinking and shrinking, curled up like a dead, grey foetus on the cold black leather.

*****

'Banff' it said. 'Banff'. He could see it vaguely in the dim light of the early-morning bedroom through partly open eyes. White letters on a black ground. *What the fuck was that? Banff? A town in Canada, wasn't it? No. That can't be there. It must be something to do with a dream...* though it seemed pretty real. He had no connection to Banff whatsoever. Scarcely knew it existed. Couldn't think why he should be dreaming about it. *Fuck off Banff.* He stuffed his head back into the pillow and went back to sleep. Some hours later he awoke, and there it was again: Banff, in rather better light this time, on top of the pile of yesterday's clothes dumped where he'd climbed out of them at the side of the bed last night. It wasn't Banff the Canadian city, but BAN and FF: the join in the waistband at the back of his Jeff Banks underpants.

Some indeterminate but not very large number of weeks into Dan's madness, this was how things were. The dread, anxiety and hopelessness of his initial mental collapse back in February had retreated somewhat, and for the most part he spent his days in a state of largely passive confusion, which was interrupted by irregular but fairly frequent periods of unwarranted panic and desolation. In the immediate aftermath of the breakdown he'd been unable to go outside, answer the door or the phone, or even open letters or email. The thought of doing any of these things brought on an overwhelming sense of terror.

After a time he was able to go to certain, selected, 'safe' places, but Sophie had to deal with his mail and other incoming communications. Going anywhere near Barts, however, was out of the question. Even being on the road that led to it would bring on a feeling of appalling dread. There would be agitation and anxiety followed by a cold sweat, breathlessness and a profound desire to be anywhere but there. Dan's counsellor told him that, without wishing to be over-dramatic, this was equivalent to Post Traumatic Stress Disorder. She didn't mean, she explained, that Dan's experience equated to that of a terrified solider trapped behind enemy lines, wondering if he would be butchered before the helicopter arrived, but the effects on his body and mind were similar. It had been cumulative. Because of the circumstances he was in, his body produced naturally the 'fight or flight' chemicals over and over again, but he couldn't react to them. His defences were restricted to rational arguments and complaints to senior managers, both of which were futile, and running away meant finding a new job, which he neither wanted nor felt able to do. Lots of small moments and sustained periods of stress that had never been resolved had built up into one massive, overwhelming force, and he had gone under. And as happened with ex-soldiers suddenly confronted with sounds, places or events that brought back earlier high-stress experiences, Dan's mind and body were fiercely telling him that this was a place he should not revisit.

In the early day of his crisis, some time before appointments with the counsellor could be arranged, the prescribed (and still ongoing) treatment was anti-depressants. There were many sorts and Dan's GP tried him on several before the most appropriate ones were identified. The first were the notorious ones that make you want to commit suicide. He didn't take those for very long. Then there was Ecitalopram. It was relatively new to the market and apparently an improvement on Citalopram, which had been around for some time. So effective was it as a mood-enhancer that it reduced him to the state of chuckling buffoon. Had there been a nuclear strike on Greater Barsteadworth it would have done no more than bring on a fit of giggles, right up until the moment he was vaporised. The pills they had settled on were Citalopram. Though far from perfect, they seemed to bring about the best balance of preventing panic attacks and dips into despondency, whilst still giving him *some* access to his intellect. Nevertheless, they did have the effect of making him so nonchalant that things tended to be met with disproportionate levity. When driving, for example, it did not seem to matter all that much whereabouts on the road the car was. The size and shape of the increasingly tired-looking Escort seemed to be similarly negotiable, especially when parking, and he drove into many bollards, walls and bumpers, always finding the whole thing pretty amusing. But then, at other times, the feelings of irrational fear and not-so-irrational dejection would return without warning. Between the two extremes there could be a whole mixture of confused emotions, which would seldom have anything to do with what was going on around him.

Then there was the visual stuff. Things would appear fleetingly in the corner of his eye, but when he looked they'd be gone. Sometimes it was as though a person had just left the room, as though he'd just caught sight of a heel as it vanished through the door. Was this why, traditionally, the demented would sometimes see ghosts? Or maybe it was the cat just sneaking behind the armchair. But when he looked he'd find her still fast asleep on the windowsill. Sometimes it would be cockroaches… or something like that: dark, black, shiny things that moved around shiftily in his peripheral vision. Normally, such filthy little beasts living in the whites of his eyes would be the object of revulsion and a reason for panic, but the Citalopram had the situation covered and he was persuaded that this was just a hallucination and he shouldn't worry about it.

The weirdest things were the dreams. They were so intensely real that, when remembered, they were inseparable from events that actually *were* real. And since most of his dreams were fairly negative, each day would bring something new to worry about. A battle of wills would then take place between his conscious mind and the sub- or semi-conscious one, which stubbornly refused to give up on the belief that the event had really happened. That bank robbery in Barsteadworth: he had nothing to do with it. In fact, it had never happened. *But would that wash with the police?* That incident with that gang of fraudsters at that hotel had never happened either, but all the same he wouldn't be able to settle until his credit card statement arrived and he had checked it over. And how could he make it up to Bette Midler, after he had been so rude to her? How could he explain that he had not really meant what he had said and had not intended to upset her? No. He had *not* had a row with Bette Midler at a New York party and she had *not* stormed off crying. He had never met her and never would. This was clear and irrefutable. Problem solved. But then again, she *had* seemed very upset, and he did feel pretty bad about it…

*****

Dan's fingernails pressed hard into the arms of leather chair as Sophie stood in front of him and opened the letter. It was May and for the first time in quite a while a letter had arrived that wasn't instantly recognisable from its outside, wasn't in the familiar livery of the bank, council or utilities, or in the recognisable handwriting of a relative or friend. She it read out loud. It was from an Occupational Health Officer appointed by Barts. In view of the fact that he had been off sick with 'stress and depression' – as it said on the GP sick notes – for three months, he would now need to be assessed from an Occupational Health perspective. Like everything else that was other than Dan's daily routine (he would mostly just potter about the house, go from room to room without quite knowing why, take the odd daring trip to Tesco Express and at the end of the day not remember very much about it, anyway) this was a source of great anxiety. Trying to clear his head, he told himself there was no cause for concern. Indeed, this was a good thing in terms of his recovery, because he could now tell someone other than the counsellor what had happened. It would be good therapy, especially as the Occupational Health Officer would be connected to Barts whilst not a Barts employee as such, and would be able to feed back what had happened with objectivity. However, he felt he had to set the scene, tell the officer what had happened to him before they met, partly because he did not feel he would be able to hold himself together explaining it 'live', but also because he wanted her to be ready for what she would find when she arrived. He would write her a letter based on the bullying diary.

Dan had largely avoided the study. It contained the computer, and that contained his email, and that meant connections to the outside world, and that was just too alarming to face. He took a breath and pressed the button at the top of the stubby grey tower. Above, the impassive grey face filled slowly with warm electronic colours. His bullying dairy looked as though it had been written by someone else. The events it described seemed to have happened in another time and place, and to have been recorded by someone who was articulate. He wasn't. Nevertheless, this was a barrier that had to be overcome. He clicked on the tiny, white rectangle at the top left corner. A large, white rectangle filled the screen. He started to write.

*****

Dan's union representative, Tony Rice, leant into the open back door of the metallic green Astra and gathered up a black briefcase and a couple of coloured cardboard files from the seat. Dan watched him furtively from behind the curtains. He'd heard the car pull up and needed to be sure it was Tony before going to the door. His palms sweated. Dan's delicate condition had meant that, until now, the few conversations he'd had with Tony had been pretty brief and only by telephone. But buoyed by the support he felt he had received from the Occupational Health Officer, Dan asked to meet with Tony to discuss a way forward, though it would have to be at Dan's house.

Tony set out his files on the glass dining room table, produced a lined reporter's pad from his briefcase and flipped over yesterday's written-on page to reveal a clean sheet for today's business. Dan set down two mugs of tea and handed a couple of pages of stapled A4 to Tony.

"That's my letter to the Occupational Health Officer. Basically, it's a thinned-down and simplified version of my bullying diary," said Dan.

Tony scanned the document. "How was the meeting?"

"It was good. She was really constructive and sympathetic. Writing the letter and having to discuss things has been good therapy. It's helped me get my mind back under control, to some extent, and to feel a bit less guilty for being off work."

"You shouldn't feel guilty about being off work. You didn't create this situation."

"I know. I don't always feel that way. My mood swings from one thing to another. Sometimes I just feel intense rage about what's happened to me. But I think it's just that it's something so intangible. If I had a broken leg or something it would be there plain for everyone one to see, but this isn't visible."

"Look," said Tony, leaning across the table and looking Dan squarely in the eyes, "keep this clear in your mind: this is not your fault. What has happened to you is despicable. Your breakdown and consequent absence from work are not things you should feel guilty about. *They* should feel guilty about it:

the ones who did it and the ineffectual managers who stood by and let it happen."

"Thanks. You should have a copy of this too." Dan spun a letter with a blue logo through 180 degrees and slid it over to Tony. "It's a copy of the Occupational Health Officer's report, as sent to Barts' Personnel Department. She says she agrees with my GP, that I *am* suffering from stress and depression and should not go back to work until that improves *and* until the circumstances that caused my problems have been rectified."

Tony placed the letter on top of his other papers and read it quickly. "They always say that. It's a Health and Safety thing. You must not be allowed back into the circumstances that caused your injury: they have to be rectified."

"Right. So where do we go next with this?"

"Do you want to submit a Grievance?"

Yes. Absolutely."

"Well, I think that's the right thing to do. Not only does this stuff need exposing, you've got a mental health problem that has no proper explanation without it. You need to submit a Grievance and that will then set their Grievance Procedure in motion."

*****

Crisp white A4 envelope in hand, Dan walked past the neatly trimmed gardens of Tennyson Road towards the post box. It was one of those 1960s ones, built mostly out of crusty brown brick with concrete capping on the top and a red, cast iron panel on the front, carrying the motif 'EIIR'. If he actually did this, posted the thing, everything would change. One way or another he would not be able to go back and work with those people, not in circumstances like those he had been in, probably not at all. He had modified slightly the letter he had sent to the Occupational Health Officer and addressed it to

Frank Fuller. It was twenty pages long and gave a detailed account of the bullying he had experienced and the other abuses he had borne witness to over the previous three years. He described how he had been subjected to deliberate and systematic undermining through public humiliations and other forms of workplace bullying; had his competence attacked on the basis of irrational and non-existent evidence; had teaching that he had developed over a period of years taken off him and given to a more favoured member of staff; had his stress levels raised though incompetent timetabling and administration; had to work on the outside of an aggressive clique; seen favoured members of staff given preferential treatment; seen rules bent and broken on behalf of favoured members of staff; been excluded from work, meetings and information that he should have been involved with; had his comments expunged from minutes; been the object of unfair reports about his performance and been denied the opportunity to comment on such reports; had his workload increased on highly questionable bases; and had his health damaged by all of this.

Everything did need to change. He posted it.

*****

June: Dan and Tony had eased themselves into Tony's cramped Portsmouth office. Surrounded by shelves, ring binders and endless mounds of paper, they drank Lidl coffee from pastel coloured mugs and discussed how things were and how they might develop. Driving the fifty-odd miles from Barsteadworth had been a nerve-racking challenge for Dan. Parking had been tricky too, and leaving the car had been marked by much neurotic fussing over whether it was properly secured and things were hidden away from thieving eyes.

"Presumably Barts has a proper, formal Grievance Procedure?" asked Tony.

"Oh yes, I've seen it in the Staff Handbook, but I haven't got a copy. It's at work. You know something," reflected Dan, "as far as I know, no-one has ever used it. You've never been there, have you? As Higher Education establishments go, Barts is very small. It's essentially the private domain of Silas Beasley, with James Ledlock as his sidekick and fixer. And no-one rocks the boat."

"It's a publicly funded institution", said Tony. "It can't work like that."

"I dare say that's an oversimplification, but it's not far off the mark. I can remember being at a validation meeting with these officials from Waterhead University who expressed concern that Barts was run by 'two men in suits' and wasn't properly accountable. No action was ever taken, though, as far as I know. Another thing is that it's very difficult to leave: the next nearest art and design college is forty-odd miles away and with a much higher profile, so they're a lot pickier about who they'll employ. Basically, if you get fed up at Barts you have to sell up and leave the area, and lots of people just don't want to do that."

"Yeah, kids settled at school and everything," offered Tony.

"Well, yeah, and family and friends living around you. And, you know, whatever the pros and cons of working at Barts, Barsteadworth was a very pleasant part of the world and people who live there tend not to want to leave. One way or another, it's just about unknown for anyone to stand up to authority at Barts. If there's anything wrong, they just grin and bear it."

"I'll get Barts to email me a copy of the Grievance Procedure," said Tony "The next move after that will be a meeting between us and one or two people from Barts'. It will be an informal one in the first instance. It'll then get more serious if we can't resolve things there."

"Well, fine, but I can't go anywhere near Barts. I just can't at the moment."

"That's OK. That's not unusual. They'll probably book a room in a hotel or something."

*****

Dan eyed his pinstriped Austin Reed suit hanging in the wardrobe, unused since Sinead and Dave's wedding, nearly two years ago. It was probably best to look formal for the occasion. He could only speculate on why it had taken until now, September, for Barts' administrators to set up the meeting. Holidays, probably. But still, three months? With the suit he wore a black round-neck sweater – a shirt and tie would be going too far – and his favourite black Loakes lace-ups. He shook the contents of his briefcase onto the study floor and placed in it copies of his bullying diary, the letter he'd sent to Frank, the Occupational Health Officer's report and the Grievance Procedure, plus a lined, blank A4 pad and a biro. The meeting would take place at Treetops Hotel, between Director of School Frank Fuller, Senior Personnel Officer Nerys Crimp, Tony Rice and Dan. Treetops was a medium-sized hotel, built in the 1920s in the neo-country house style that was popular in Barsteadworth at that time, and then extended fairly unsympathetically in the decades since. It was three miles away from Barts on the other side of town. Nevertheless, this first re-encounter with former colleagues caused a great deal of anxiety for Dan.

He felt a cold sweat and tightening of the chest as he approached the room, and had to take deep breaths to try and bring himself under control. The function room was small: a forty-foot parquet square with a tiny, hole-in-the-wall bar on one side and French windows leading to a courtyard on the other. Most of the furniture was stacked at the sides of the room, awaiting its next wedding, wake or bar mitzvah. In the middle of the small dance floor, one rectangular table had been extracted and set out neatly with four chairs – two on each side.

After brief introductions, the four sat down; Frank paired with Nerys on one side of the table; Dan paired with Tony on the other. Tony, in tweed jacket and grey slacks and just a touch less than average height, was a tenacious terrier of a man who liked an argument and had a substantial knowledge of employment legislation to support that. Nerys, a sharp-featured Presbyterian who had been at Barts longer than anyone, was deeply loyal to the place and knew her stuff as well as Tony knew his. She was someone who was not given to smiling unnecessarily. Nevertheless, as form dictated, everyone smiled to some extent as they settled into their chairs.

Frank, as was his way, did his best to make it as friendly an encounter as possible. He started the meeting with that tone well known to Dan which, even before the words are unpicked, says *look we're all friends here, all reasonable people, I'm sure we can come to an agreement that there has just been a bit of a misunderstanding, and I'm sure we can all sort things out quickly and amicably and get back to work*. Frank passed round a document. Dan was expecting the Grievance Procedure, but that wasn't what it was. The two-sided sheet of Barts-headed paper contained a hastily compiled list of points and provisos, evidently thought up and typed especially for this meeting. So quickly had it been cobbled together that it was full of embarrassing typos, and point 3 of the 14 simply did not exist. As a recipe for a Fuller Fudge it would no doubt have served admirably; as one for solving the problems before them it was hopeless. Frank had decided how things would go and written a procedure that would guide them through to the predetermined conclusion. Within seconds of reading the document Tony was visibly agitated.

"Do you want me to leave?" said Tony, angrily.

"What?" said a startled Frank, in that way that people do when they realise that they've affronted someone but don't really know how.

"*Do* you want me to leave?"

"Well, erm..."

"I am not just here as a 'friend and advisor' to Dan, as this document suggests. I have legal right to be here and I have an important task to perform, and if all you are recognising me as is some kind of 'friend and advisor', then this meeting is over before it has started."

"Well, you see, I thought we could just deal with this informally," said Frank.

"Yes, but you've produced this document and you want us to commit to it. Look at some of the things it says: look at this one," – the pitch of Tony's voice raised in disbelief – "*that you – YOU – will listen to what everyone has to say, take a decision on what will happen, and that will be binding on all parties...* This case can NOT be limited in its scope by you or anyone else. It could, conceivably, go all the way to the European Court of Human Rights, and no one has the right to prevent it from doing so. Not you, not me, not anyone. If this is all that's on offer then we don't have anything to talk about."

At this, there was little else to say or do. There were quiet, damp handshakes and the meeting was terminated.

*****

A week later Dan got a letter from Nerys to say that he should submit a Grievance in the terms of the Grievance Procedure. He wrote back to say that was what he had done; the way it was *handled* was outside of the Grievance Procedure.

*****

A few days later, another Nerys letter arrived, saying he should resubmit what he had written but add onto it what he thought should happen as a consequence of his Grievance. That would make the document meet the terms of the Grievance Procedure. Dan resubmitted his letter adding that all evidence that would support his case should be protected – taken away from those who might destroy or alter it – and that disciplinary action should be taken against those who did the things that he described in his complaint.

*****

Barsteadworth College

The credits on yet another History Channel programme on Hitler rolled up the screen. Dan would be quite an expert on the bloke by now, if he could remember any of it. It was well into autumn. He was feeling a lot better, but by no means recovered. As he regained more control of his mind he become ever more dismayed at the extent to which it was still beyond his control and at how long his recovery seemed to be taking, even though the doctor had told him that this was not unusual and that it could still be quite some time yet before he got back to normal. Years, even. He felt the need to do something, but he was keenly aware of his fragility: he was OK, but only as long as nothing out of the ordinary happened. That made him passive. He was the passive recipient of drugs and other people's attempts to make him better. This was a situation that needed to be challenged if progress was to be made. It was as though there was a barrier that he needed to break through, and if he did everything would be all right again. He needed to be more assertive. It was important to go out and try to spend time with people, even though company was something he found very difficult to cope with.

On the shiny veneer of the coffee table lay a small, colourful card that had arrived in the post a few days earlier. It was from Harmony Morris and friends: an invitation to attend an exhibition of their latest work at The Art House. Harmony, along with Petra Finlay, Marshall Thomas and others of Dan's former (mostly mature) students had established The Art House in the town's old industrial quarter. It was a disused packing plant of some sort, that they had converted into studios and an ad hoc gallery space. He couldn't face the opening night. All those people. There would almost certainly be a Barts contingent too. He decided to go the evening before: show his support for the group's endeavour, but avoid the crowds.

When he arrived they were busy putting the final touches to the exhibition: sticking up labels, sweeping the floor, setting out pricelists. A battered old radio provided entertainment, playing pop music he didn't recognise. They were very kind and welcoming. It might just have been that they were pleased that someone had been interested enough to visit, though Dan got the feeling that they had some idea of what had happened to him. The group had all been longer out of Barts than he had, but the art community rumour mill in Barsteadworth was a very effective instrument. Marshall made him a mug of coffee, and Harmony showed him around the exhibits. It was a charming space: Victorian... possibly older. The ceilings were low with exposed beams supported by cast iron pillars that marked the space out into a kind of grid. The floors were worn, unadorned timber and the unplastered walls were painted brilliant white, as was the done thing in art spaces. Paintings, prints and drawings of all kinds and sizes were hung on the wall and the floor was dotted with sculptures, made mostly from found objects, printed cotton and manikin parts.

After his informal lap of the place, resisting Harmony's mischievous attempts to get him to say which pieces he liked and disliked – he wouldn't fall for that; any negative comment would be bound to get back to and offend its maker – they all pulled up chairs to drink their coffees and chat.

To Dan's utter astonishment, the group, one-by-one, started to tell him their own horror stories of the way they had been treated by Stella Jobby. Their tales were remarkably similar to his own. As they relived their experiences, they became ever more upset and angry. They too had felt the effects of not being part of Stella's group of preferred people and they felt that their tuition and possibly even their grades had been damaged by not being part of the right crowd.

Harmony, Marshall, Petra and the others all had tales of threats and bullying, and of seeing other students given preferential treatment. John Driscoll, who came from Derry and was of an age where the province's turbulent history had played some significant and unpleasant role in his life, had been pressured by Stella to make the Troubles the focus of his work. He refused: he felt that he'd left that part of his life behind and didn't want to keep raking it over. Also, the fact that he'd had to live with the Troubles didn't mean that that was what defined him. There were other things in his life. The affront meant that he was placed with the others of his cohort's out crowd; the group of people who now surrounded him. Refusing to suck up to Stella, they explained, would bring about subtle punishments, like a verbal demolition of your work in front of fellow students in a group critique. How similar this was, thought Dan, to his own experience of being ambushed in front of colleagues in team meetings. Complaining, Petra explained, would result in the silent treatment, cancelled tutorials and would cost you marks. The consensus seemed to be that being favoured was worth a grade. The three individuals who had got Firsts in their cohort had all been mature students with a sad story to tell, and had all been Stella's favourites. For everyone else it was a Two-One or less. The beatified trio comprised two females – Marta Burns and Jenny Poppleton – and a male – Charles Shipton-Bellinger. Marta and Jenny had both been battered wives, and Charles had been adopted; something he had never quite come to terms with.

Dan's mind flitted to another student – Ellie Sudge – and a particular incident he had experienced when marking her work with Stella. Ellie had gone through all kinds of traumas, tried almost every known mind-altering substance and was borderline certifiable. She had joined the course in Ronnie's time and dropped out, done the same when Dan was Course Director, and come back again with Stella in charge. On a very particular level Ellie was the ideal student for Stella. She seldom came to college, never did any work, and when she did put in an appearance it would be to sit for hours moaning semi-incoherently to whichever Course Director was now in place about what a fuck-up her life was. For Dan, the thought of his lengthy and pointless pastoral tutorials with Ellie threatened to bring on a headache. But for Stella, such events were manna from heaven. The hopeless, destructive rollercoaster ride that was Ellie's life was a thrilling, vicarious experience for Stella, and each instalment was avidly consumed and then relayed enthusiastically to the rest of the staff as part of the office gossip. For the whole of her second year Ellie's studio space was occupied by a part-broken mould of a hoola hoop that she had made at the end of the first year. Somehow she managed to re-present it over and again for each assessment and get a mark. Possibly it had been fresh tutors each time who didn't know the history of the thing. For the final mark of the year Dan was marking jointly with Stella. As they walked into Ellie's deserted studio space, clipboards in hand, he pointed out that there was in fact nothing in the studio to mark; only the hoola hoop mould and that had been hanging around collecting dust for at least a year to his knowledge. Stella leapt to Ellie's defence and insisted that the lack of any change to the hoola hoop mould, the absence of any new work or, indeed, of any evidence that Ellie had spent any time whatsoever in her studio during the last 12 months was in fact a *statement* in itself, and she was going to give it a mark. Dan refused to mark it, whatever 'it' was: it couldn't be the thing in front of them because that was old work.

Stella tried to argue that what they might be in the presence of was a piece of conceptual work hidden cunningly from view by its lack of any material existence; some sort of fine art treatise on the concept of *absence*. When that didn't wash, she said that they should give 'it' a mark because of all of Ellie's personal problems. Dan said that although he sympathised with Ellie as a person, they really should not be awarding marks for work that did not exist or, by extension, telling the outside world and potential employers that this person had achieved a level of skill and understanding which she patently had not. Moreover, what mark would you give to something that wasn't there? Was it a 2-2 nothing or a 2-1 nothing? Perhaps it was a first class nothing? At this suggestion Stella told Dan he was being silly. The conclusion of this increasingly absurd debate was Stella's insistence that she was Course Director, it was her decision and she was not going to fail poor Ellie simply because she hadn't done anything. Dan abstained and Stella thought up and applied what she felt was an appropriate mark for Ellie's 'statement'. Dan didn't bother to find out what it was.

Students like Ellie and the three Firsts, as different as they were, had all, wittingly or otherwise, said and done the right things to endear themselves to Stella, whilst Harmony and the others had spotted the game and refused to play it. It was not that they did not have the necessary ammunition. They too had seen a lot of life and had tales of woe with which they could have wooed Stella, especially Harmony, who had probably experienced as much pain and misery as the rest of the cohort put together, but for their various reasons – pride, a need for privacy, or the conviction that it should not be necessary to deal in this currency in order to receive respect, fair treatment and a good quality of education – did not do so. Needless to say, the Art House lot vehemently disputed the rights of the three chosen ones to first class degrees and to the favours that had come exclusively their way: Stella had given both Jenny and Marta teaching jobs in the department immediately after graduating, even though several years' experience as an artist and tutor and a postgraduate qualification are normally called for. Ironically, most of the work they were covering was that created by Dan's absence. The vacancies generated *had* been advertised... *sort of*: two part-time, temporary lecturing jobs were listed internally on the staff newsletter and thus seen only by people who were already teaching fine art or were working in other disciplines and therefore not qualified to do so. So it was that when Jenny and Marta applied – as they were told to do by Stella – there were no other applicants. Stella had also canvassed energetically and successfully to get Charles into a London college to do his MA. Even Ellie left with a degree of some sort, though Dan had no further dealing with her and did not know whether the award was in any way contingent upon her having produced any work.

Along with the astonishment Dan felt at hearing the group's tales of woe came a twinge of guilt. He had been the person who had given these people their places on the course and then, when they were part way through their studies, given up the Course Directorship and placed them in the hands of that awful woman. To keep things in perspective, he pointed out to the group that his Course Directorship had not been some form of Golden Age. There had always been resentments, arguments and complaints, and there always would be. He had had his share of rows with staff and students and had been complained about periodically, as Course Directors often are. It went with the territory. There were lots of tensions: marks, careers and egos were constantly in the balance. The group's response was that at least with Dan you knew where you stood. He could be blunt and annoyingly unmoveable by the routine bullshit and sob stories that were supposed to excuse late or inadequate work, but there were no favourites and no enemies, and everyone was treated equally.

Dan was itching to tell them about what had happened to him, but he could not. Although he had not seen the inside of Barts for eight months he was still a Senior Lecturer there and still had to behave professionally and not take sides against a fellow member of staff. In spite of everything, he was still shocked at what he heard. It was typical Stella, of course, but he was still amazed that she would risk treating students like this. Students were money tokens for colleges. That gave them power with senior management. Piss them off at your peril.

From the way the group had brought this to Dan's attention it looked as though they too regarded him as partly responsible for their predicament and were hoping that he would take it up on their behalves. But, apart from the fact that he was on sick leave and was far too mentally battered to pick up arms for any new battle – dealing with his own was scarcely manageable – he had no official capacity in this. Stella was not answerable to him. He was answerable to her. He tried to come up with a suitable course of action for them. This was, however, difficult, as they were no longer Barts' students, and even if they were still hurting and resentful, their relationship with the place was over. The time to complain was when they were still on their course, though, as they told him, they were too frightened to do so. All he could suggest was that they went back to Frank Fuller or spoke to the Student Union rep.

*****

It was November. Dan heard the letterbox clap shut. On the mat lay a white D5 envelope with Barts' familiar franking mark on the front. He had been opening his own mail for quite some time now, but it was still by no means easy. There would be anxiety and sweaty palms every time. He would take deep breaths, whilst urgently scanning the outside of the envelope, looking for clues that might take the edge off the dread of tearing it open. That first couple of letters from Nerys Crimp, seeking modifications to his Grievance submission, had been followed by several more, though each time the required modification was ever more slight. Other Nerys letters had offered him additional bits of news or procedural information. The most important, in Dan's view, had been the one that said that since the Grievance Procedure was still in progress, it had been agreed that his sick pay would continue at its normal level for the time being. It normally drops to 50% at 6 months, then stops completely at 12 months.

He ripped open the envelope and skimmed today's Nerys letter. It announced that Barts' management was finally happy with the form of his Grievance Submission and offered him a choice of Investigating Officer for his case. He could choose from Mary Ledger, Director of Finance, Pamela Fringe, Director of the School of Design, and Aileen Dimley, Director of Infrastructure Services. It had to be Aileen. Dan knew nothing of the other two, whereas, from the few dealings he'd had with Aileen, he felt that she was a straight, down to Earth person and someone who was going to be absolutely fair and honest. OK, on the light bulb shelf of life she was more the 9-watt energy-saver than the 1,000-watt halogen, but that needn't matter. What he was going to lay before her was an injustice so clear and indisputable that she couldn't fail to understand and find in his favour.

*****

Another week passed and another Barts envelope arrived with another Nerys letter inside. It acknowledged Dan's choice and announced that Aileen Dimley was now undertaking an investigation. She would interview all of those named in Dan's Grievance submission, including, of course, Dan himself. It set out how the Grievance Procedure would work:

Stage 1 - the Investigating Officer interviews all concerned.

Stage 2 - the Investigating Officer listens to a presentation of the Grievance by the complainant.

Stage 3 - the Investigating Officer produces an outcome: a summary of the evidence, evaluation and recommendations. Action, such as is appropriate, is then taken by senior management.

If the outcome is not to the complainant's liking, s/he can appeal to the Principal, and if that fails s/he can appeal to a panel of the Board of Governors.

It didn't say anything about the stage after this, which would be to take things outside of the academy to a tribunal.

*****

A few weeks later yet another Nerys letter brought the news that all of the interviews had now taken place, except for Dan's, but since it was nearly Christmas his would take place in the New Year. The function room at Treetops Hotel had been booked for the 2nd February – a few days short of a year since Dan's breakdown.

Chapter Nine
One Year Ago

On the morning of 1 February another Barts-franked letter lay on the welcome mat. It was from Aileen Dimley: a few platitudes followed by a long list of questions that formed the core of what she wanted to discuss at tomorrow's meeting. As Dan read it his heart sank. He was not going to get a fair hearing; that was plain from the questions now set out before him. Instead of seeking to find out from Dan what had exactly had happened to him, as one might expect, they were all geared to undermining his position or seeking material to use against him. Dan rang Tony Rice, copied the list to him by email and asked if it was still worth attending the meeting. Tony had seen this a hundred times before. He told Dan that it was clear that Barts' management had closed ranks. He would not get a fair hearing, but they should go to the meeting regardless, otherwise they would appear to be acting in bad faith and wouldn't be able to make any progress.

*****

Dan was not in good shape for the start of the meeting. He was still shaking off the pills that had enabled him to get a few hours sleep and was rigid and sweaty with anxiety, though he was so angry that that would probably carry him through. A table and four chairs were again grouped neatly together on the dark parquet flooring of the function room, in the same place they had been for the previous meeting. It was Nerys, Tony and Dan again, but this time with Aileen seated where Frank had previously been.

Aileen's list of questions was the agenda. There were 20 of them, many with sub-clauses. Many read like a test of Dan's knowledge of Barts' policies and management systems: cheap, smart-arse provocations that deconstructed to: *perhaps, since you're saying that Barts' procedures have failed to protect you, you would like to recite those procedures and say what is wrong with them.* His complaints had become the departure point for a trawling exercise designed to seek flaws in his arguments and find holes in his knowledge that might discredit his allegations. What made Dan even more angry was that Aileen, the inquisitor, did not even have the honesty to say that what he had said had shown a gap in his knowledge or that he had misunderstood anything; she just presented him with open ends in the hope that he would say something that would demonstrate his ignorance and undermine him in a way that she could not. This was hardly the strategy of a neutral investigator seeking the truth.

The first question read 'What is you understanding of the latest Quality Assurance Agency Review.' Dan asked for clarification: it was a very large report. When Aileen got to the specifics the question seemed to fizzle away to almost nothing. She just wanted to know if he'd picked up on the bit where they'd recommended a reduction in teaching hours. He had. Everyone at Barts knew about it. But if he'd tried to answer the question as posed he would have probably have tied himself in knots.

Things moved on in a similar vein: Aileen asked Dan to define particular words used in his submission. To Aileen's surprise and irritation, this was not a problem. Dan remembered Aileen's performances at Barts' training days: she was often taken aback by people not being as stupid as she thought they were.

Aileen put it to Dan that he resented the fact that Stella had got the Course Director's job, instead of him. Dan told her what he thought to be a matter of common knowledge: that he had not applied for the job and had been happy for someone else to take over. The issue was not *who* was Course Director; it was the *behaviour* of the Course Director.

Next, Aileen suggested to him that what had triggered his depression was having been in Phuket at the time of the 2004 tsunami. "That must have been a traumatic experience" said Aileen, with remarkably transparent phoney sympathy. She was no Stella. Dan explained that he and Sophie *had* been in Phuket at that time – in hotel on a hill top, far away from the beach. They had been completely unaware of what had happened until television and other reports came through. They saw no more of it than they would have at home.

With each question, Aileen's face took on a kind of superior, condescending, smiling quality that seemed to say *I've got you now*. It was especially so for the next one. She put it to Dan that he did not understand his contract and teaching hours. She had picked up on a figure that Dan had used in his Grievance submission; one that he had learned during his time at Leeds University and seemed to recall having discussed with Frank Fuller, though Frank had by now denied that any such conversation had ever taken place. It was a widely accepted guideline: that when preparing new teaching material at higher education level, it takes roughly 3 hours of research and writing to produce 1 hour of teaching. Aileen had, however, misconstrued this: she had read it as meaning that, in Dan's view, for every hour of teaching there should be 3 hours of administration time. He explained that this was not what he thought, was not what he'd said and, indeed, would be an absurdity if he had. What she was in fact suggesting to him was that he believed that each time he did an hour's teaching – a 1-hour tutorial, say – he should sit in the office for 3 hours afterwards staring at the ceiling (since there was in fact no appreciable admin or preparation associated with tutorials). She looked at him vaguely, so he repeated himself: "Are you clear on what I mean, Aileen? I mean it takes 3 hours of preparation to produce 1 hour of brand new teaching material at this level, not that there should be 3 hours of admin associated with every hour of teaching." She said she was.

Aileen went on to suggest to Dan that Sophie's job as a cosmetics practitioner, who routinely used botox in her work, might be the reason why Linda Froggatt thought it was fair enough to tell him he should have his penis injected with the stuff. Dan put it to Aileen that if she accepted that as justification, then she would also have to accept that it would be OK for a male member of staff to tell a female one she ought to have her vagina injected with botox, just as long as her husband was a cosmetics practitioner.

Aileen asked Dan what made him think that the Small-Jobby's and the Froggatt-Geldings were friends outside of work. She seemed to believe that this was not the case and that there would be no evidence for it. Dan told her that the fact that they went out together, went on holiday together, looked after each other's kids and routinely kissed each other might have something to do with it.

With the question and answer session finished, Aileen declared herself satisfied and announced that she would now go off and produce her report. Tony and Dan looked at each other. Were they imagining this? Dan spoke first:

"What about Stage Two?"

Aileen looked confused and took on an indignant tone, that of someone who is trying their best to hold on to their patience in the face of unreasonable provocation. "I have listened carefully to what you have had to say, I have taken notes and I have heard enough to be able to form my conclusions."

"But what about my opportunity to present my case?" pressed Dan.

Aileen became even more angry and indignant. "Well, what was *that*?"

"That was me answering your questions."

"Well, I've heard all I need to hear."

"No you haven't: you don't know what I'm going to say."

Aileen breathed out, heavily, and glared at Dan. "What about Stella and her team? Have you any idea what you're putting them through? I promised them I would have this sorted out before Christmas, but we ran out of time. I told them not to worry, but they've had to go through Christmas with this hanging over them." There was more than a hint of emotion in her voice.

Good grief. She's told them they've got nothing to worry about; said she'd have it all sorted for them by Christmas. "Er... It's me who had the mental breakdown, Aileen, not them. What about my stress?"

Aileen's mind seemed to come back into the room, having been somewhere else entirely. Her tone became conciliatory. "Er, yes, of course," she said. "I'm obviously aware of that. Obviously."

"So, what about Stage Two, then?" Tony asked it this time. Aileen's face was a study in confusion.

"Excuse us for a moment," said Nerys, taking Aileen by the arm and walking her gently over to a corner of the room.

After a few moments, Aileen looked back towards the table, smiling. "Oh! Stage *Two! Stage Two* – of course. Yes, yes, obviously: there has to be a *Stage Two*. I think we must have all been at cross purposes there for a moment."

"Yes, we'll be setting up another date for Stage Two. We'll get back to you on that", added Nerys.

Aileen and Nerys left first. Dan and Tony shoved papers into briefcases and strolled slowly through the hotel lobby and into the bright cold air of the car park, talking as they went. "You could hear the ranks closing like doors, couldn't you," said Tony.

"That was not an Investigating Officer," said Dan, "it was Stella Jobby's attorney."

"I know. It's what always happens. Unless they want rid of the person you're complaining against, they close ranks to protect them."

Dan climbed into the silver Rover 400. The clapped-out Escort had had to go. The Rover was a hand-me-down from Sophie. She did so many miles nowadays that it had rapidly closed in on the point where the mileage would have made it unsellable. Dan hardly went anywhere, so it made sense for him to use it in its dotage. It might have done 95,000 miles and have a chuggy old diesel engine, but the bodywork was spotless, and after the Escort it felt like a limousine. He was pleased with it; it made him feel good. It seemed to signify a positive change in the way things were going. He even washed it now and then.

He made a right turn out of the car park onto Bentley Road and after a short distance under the canopy of bare winter trees made a left into the heavier traffic of Cavendish Avenue.

He tried to work it all out: was it that Aileen was so thoroughly the company's woman that she would always protect a fellow Barts manager, whatever the evidence? Or was it that she so sympathised with Stella and co. that the notion that Dan's case could have any validity was one that simply could not be countenanced? He would never know. What was plain to see, however, was that Aileen was no match for the arch-manipulator, Stella. He could picture the scene: Stella as convincing as ever, pouring her heart out to Aileen; and Aileen being both taken in by the act and flattered by the camaraderie and confidence of this eloquent middle-class woman. *All the things she wanted to be.* He passed cemetery junction. Fresh flowers had been tied to the railings where a Chinese student had been knocked off her bike and killed by a taxi. There was something else, too, though Dan had tried to block it from his mind. Aileen had a reputation for having a hair-trigger for any slight – real or perceived – against women. She had famously held up a committee meeting for twenty minutes after she had objected the use of the term 'master plan', because of its lack of gender neutrality. His mind travelled to the committee room. He imagined them all there, Beasley, Ledlock, all the Directors of School and all of the departmental staff representatives, all po-faced and politically correct, all trying to take it seriously. Maybe 'mistress plan' had been proffered. But no, that wouldn't do, for the same reasons, as well as the fact that it sounded pretty ridiculous. How about 'boss-person plan'? Or, maybe 'authoritative-person-of-no-particular-gender plan'? The meeting had, apparently, descended into something close to farce, before

Silas lost patience and they all agreed on just 'Plan'. On another occasion it was 'mandate' that came in for scrutiny, though this was settled rather more quickly, when someone pointed out that the 'man' bit did not come from 'man' as in 'person in possession of a penis', but instead from the same etymological root as 'manual': to do with the 'hands', which, of course, are unisex. Dan turned right into Stanford Road. He would go the long way round, to avoid going anywhere near Barts. With all of this in mind, there was now the additional question of whether Aileen's bias in favour of Stella was to do with the possibility that, when faced with a male-versus-female dispute, she could simply not find it in herself to back the male, whatever the evidence, especially if the male is, within his case, also making allegations of sexism.

*****

Dan slotted the cordless Panasonic phone back into its base on the Ikea Billy bookshelf in the dining room and gazed out into the garden. *Shit.* He felt awful. That had been Kate Flanagan. Phil had had a breakdown. He was upstairs in the bedroom with the curtains drawn and hadn't come down for days. The doctor had referred him for psychiatric help. Over the last few months, Dan had received ever more frequent and desperate calls from Phil, pleading with him to come back to work. In Dan's absence, the clique had just had the one person to give their attentions to. They had closed in like jackals and made Phil's life intolerable. And, like Dan, he had finally snapped. Dan felt partly responsible. Each time he'd spoken to Phil he'd been appalled at what he'd heard and he felt terribly sorry for him, but there was nothing he could do. When it came down to it, Phil's plight was not a reason for Dan to put himself back into circumstances he still could not cope with and, in any case, things had gone so far now that it would be unlikely that Dan could ever go back to Barts.

*****

Treetops Hotel had been booked again for the 21st February for Stage Two of the Grievance Procedure: the presentation of the plaintiff's case. Aileen, Nerys, Tony and Dan took their seats in the middle of the function room, as before. This time the table had been laid with a cloth and there was a large jug of water and four glasses. There were polite smiles. Papers were scanned and shuffled in preparation. Somebody said something about the weather and was met with a few murmurs of assent. The realisation at the previous meeting that he would not be treated fairly had not been without some effect on Dan. The improvements he had experienced over the last few months had gone into reverse and he had started to descend back into depression, and the stress of what he now had to do was causing all sorts of ructions in his body. The outward manifestation of all this was just a slight shake as he spoke.

Using his Grievance submission as a framework, Dan set out his case. He outlined each of the points made in the submission and then read verbatim from his Bullying Dairy to fill in the gaps with specifics, all of which had been recorded at the time, so they were fresh and clear in his mind when written. He went right back to that summer when things started to go awry, when Linda Froggatt announced the new 'us and them' regime and power redistribution project in the department. He then brought things all the way through to his crisis point, just over a year ago. He was able to go through everything. He described each of the events in detail, who was there, what was said, how he felt and so on. It took 3 hours, but at the end Dan felt a sense both of triumph and relief. He could not fail. It was all there, everything he had set out for the Occupational Health Officer and Frank Fuller, but now backed with loads of evidence: dates, times, specifics, *the lot*. Aileen looked shocked, taken aback. Whatever her level of bias, there was simply too much here to ignore. He *must* have won her over.

*****

Stage 3, the publication of Aileen Dimley's Final Report, took place on the 21st April: two months after the final Treetops Hotel meeting. A few days later Dan's copy arrived. He hurriedly opened it and within a few seconds of starting to read felt sick to the pit of his stomach. It was apparent why it had taken Aileen so long to produce the report. She had announced at the end of the February meeting that she would be taking a holiday in March, and that would delay things somewhat. But that didn't account for two months, and it was clear from what Dan now saw before him that she'd needed the additional time to go back to Stella and her team in order to compile answers to Dan's more detailed evidence and come up with a riposte. Between Stages 2 and 3, Aileen had come up with a new one: Stage 2.5. If written into the official Grievance Procedure, it might have read:

Stage 2.5 - the Investigating Officer goes back to the people who have been complained about with detailed the contents of the complainant's Stage 2 submission, and then works with them in order to rubbish it and produce new damaging material to use against the complainant in the final Report.

Stella, her friends and Aileen had visibly worked together to produce a series of counter-allegations. These had now gone into the finished Report, without Dan having the right to read it or respond before it was published. In short, the 21st April Report was an exoneration of Stella and her friends – in some places a eulogy, indeed – and a character assassination of Dan.

After her introduction, outlining what the case was about, Aileen had produced a list of names of all of the people involved. Phil Flanagan, Dan's only witness, was missing from it. This was at least consistent, as reading through the document it was apparent that Phil's evidence would not feature in the Report, though he would be mentioned sporadically, but only where his inclusion could be used to damage Dan. As Aileen went on to set the scene, in which she would discuss only the evidence of Stella and those who would agree with her points of view, she announced that she had 'no reason to doubt' their word. That they would be fighting against disciplinary action and possibly even sacking if Dan's allegations were found to be true, and the simple, pure Mandy Rice Davies logic that *they would say that wouldn't they* might be reasons for doubt for others, but not for Aileen. Her position was that the targets of Dan's allegations were just blameless victims with no reason to lie.

Aileen Dimley's Final Report comprised over 11,000-words. What follows is a summary. The 'team' refers to the *residual* course team – Stella, Linda, Sky, Tim, Patricia, with occasional references to the peripheral figures like Edward, Deidre and Charles – with Dan extracted because he was the complainant and Phil extracted because his evidence was contradictory. Aileen mostly dealt with Dan's allegations in two ways:

1.   Dan's allegation would be summarised. It would be challenged by the team's or a particular team member's evidence. Aileen would uphold the team's or the team member's evidence and dismiss Dan's allegation. The team or team member would make a counter-allegation against Dan. Aileen would uphold the counter-allegation.

2.   Dan's allegation would be summarised. The team or the particular team member concerned would have no recollection of the event taking place, but would go on to explain why it would have taken place, if it had, which it hadn't, and the explanation would be another counter-allegation against Dan. Aileen would uphold the team's or team member's assertion that the event had not taken place, as well as the explanation of why it had taken place, even though it had not. She would dismiss Dan's allegation on the grounds that it never happened, but uphold the counter-allegation: effectively, that Dan was a complete shit who deserved this thing that had happened, even though it had not happened.

As regards the incident where Linda told Dan that he should have his penis injected with botox, Aileen conceded that this *might* have happened, though, of course, no one could remember it. However, it was not the jibe that was out of order, it was Dan's reaction. Dan had conceded that bawdy jokes were not unusual in the department, and this was no different. It was clear to Aileen that the humiliation and embarrassment Dan felt was a consequence of his having dwelt on it too much and worked the thing up into something it was not. Aileen did not discuss the nature of it as a *sexist* remark, but moved straight on to the point that Dan himself was a deserving recipient for the insult because he himself was sexist. However, the team had evidently not been able to come up with any particular incident or remark that would demonstrate that this was so. The best they could do was to describe the occasion when Dan had said that he had once been to see the punk poet John Cooper Clarke (in Bristol in 1982). In the view of Sky in his role of explaining his colleague-wife's behaviour (had she behaved in that way, which she had not), John Cooper-Clarke was sexist and therefore Dan must be too. Aileen accepted this evidence. The tenuousness of the link between Cooper Clarke's and Dan's attitudes on gender was not an issue for Aileen, even though by the same logic, if Dan had been to see Sid Vicious instead, it had to be a virtual certainty that he would shoot his wife to death in a drug-addled rage in a New York apartment. And there was, in any case, nothing revealed about John Cooper Clarke to demonstrate that he was sexist, other than that Sky Gelding said so.

To Dan's recollection John Cooper Clarke was spiky bugger who didn't defer to anyone. Men and women came in for his vitriolic observations in equal measure. But then, Aileen had predicated her Report on the notion that she had 'no reason to doubt' anything said by team, so if Sky Gelding said that John Cooper Clarke was sexist; he did not need to provide evidence to prove it. Saying it was enough. To tell someone to have their genitals injected with botox is not sexist; to go and see a poet in 1982, whom Sky Gelding deems sexist, is.

Similarly, since Dan had made allegations of bullying, evidence had to be found that *he* was a bully instead. The trouble was, he was not a bully and there was no such evidence, so more perverse creativity was called for. The team recounted an incident in which Phil Flanagan had had words with Patricia Kleb about her appropriation of Dan's teaching, telling Patricia just how frustrated and upset Dan was at what was going on. Even from the team's description it was hard to equate the conversation with bullying, but of course, it was in any case a conversation that had taken place between Phil and Patricia. Dan had not been there and knew nothing about it. Nevertheless, Aileen was happy to record this as evidence of Dan's being a bully. Guilt by association. And she went further.

She reported 'there have been complaints' by 'students' about Dan. What the complaints were, when they had taken place, whether they were upheld and who the complainants were was not disclosed. And Dan would not be allowed to ask what it was he was supposed to have done, would not have right to reply and would not be able to ask what this had to do with his Grievance. This was the Final Report: fait accompli. Dan's head reeled as he tried to take in the multiple layers of abuse that the Report comprised. Complaints about staff were far from rare – such are the tensions between those who submit work for marking and those who mark it – but of the few complaints that had been made about Dan, none had ever been sustained. He had never been reprimanded. His record was spotless. Nevertheless, there it was: 'there have been complaints', left hanging in the air, loaded with secret and unchallengeable guilt and shame for Dan.

Aileen had another such trick up her sleeve too. She announced that 'some members of staff' had 'refused to work with Dan'. Again, there was no further information; no who, where, when or why. The only thing he could think of was a series of critiques and seminars that he was supposed to be teaching jointly with Patricia. Patricia had not wanted him there and said she could handle the sessions on her own. Her explanation at the time had been that there were so few students showing up for these events that the presence of two lecturers would be farcical. There was, however, the routine issue of Patricia's secrecy and insecurity about her teaching and therefore her discomfort at having anyone else around, especially Dan, whose ability she had openly admitted she found intimidating. But there was no openness now. If there had been any occasion where anyone had *refused* to work with Dan, he knew nothing about it. There was only this occasion, where Patricia had *declined* to work with him because it wasn't necessary. But there it was in the Report:

'*some* members of staff' had '*refused* to work with him'. No information; only innuendo. But what was being implied? That he was incompetent? Evil? Foul smelling? Given to bouts of uncontrollable rage and violence? Maybe he was a child molester...? In the absence of any evidence to use against Dan, it had to be that Aileen hoped that suitable answers would form in the minds of the readers of the Report. With a bit of luck they might think that the lack of disclosure was because the truth was unspeakable.

Dan's mind and body were now in some sort of time machine, hurtling back to that day in February last year when he came apart. It took several days to read the report. Each time he picked it up he would only read a paragraph or two before he would be overwhelmed with nausea and mental chaos.

*****

Dan read on and the assassination of his character continued. The team and/or Aileen had unearthed a remark from Terry Mortice, the department's former technician. He had not worked on the course since Stella's arrival and had not, therefore, been a member of the course team in the period in question and in fact knew nothing about the dispute between Stella and Dan. Nevertheless, he was useful because of the disputes he'd had with Dan, and indeed with Phil, who had found him equally exasperating and had probably had even more rows with him than Dan had. So it was that it had been possible, or at least it was reported as being so, to use a quote from Terry to say that he 'hated' Dan and Phil and would 'like to kill them' (Terry's lack of self-control and predisposition towards murder being reported as evidence of some form of deficiency on Dan's part, not Terry's). Also, the circumstances in which the deposition had been acquired were not disclosed. Terry had not been listed as one of the people interviewed. He probably didn't even know that he was being used like this. These remarks might have been things said years ago at a party, or in the King's Head shortly before closing time, or they might also have been part of a conversation that took place shortly after one of the arguments, when Terry was still steaming. Dan would never know and, as with the bullying allegation, Dan and Phil had been conveniently lumped together as one person. It wasn't possible to know who Terry was talking about if, indeed, he had ever said it. But of course, since this had appeared only in Aileen's Final Report and at no earlier stage, Dan was denied any opportunity to query any of this. And quite what it had to do with finding out whether Dan's allegations against Stella and her clique were true was also unexplained. But then it had long been clear that, both in her investigation and in her Report, examining the veracity of Dan's allegations was not part of Aileen's project.

Just when Dan thought Aileen and the team couldn't stoop any further, they did. Sky had reported that Dan had called 'the students' a 'bunch of fucking cunts'. Again, no context was provided: it was just a crude and random accusation dropped in amongst so many. As sickened and horrified as Dan was at seeing this, he also felt somehow vindicated. As far back as his first letter last May to the Occupational Heath Officer and then to Frank, he'd said that he knew the clique would say anything to get themselves off the hook. And here it was. They'd gone past the pale. And if there had been no context given for the alleged outburst – contexts for things that haven't happened are, after all, notoriously hard to find – there was a context for Sky having chosen to say it. At one of the Treetops Hotel meetings, the discussion had gone to the fact that swearing was not unusual in the office. Aileen had asked Dan for an example, presumably hoping he would say something she could use against him. At first he couldn't think of anything. Expletives from frustrated lecturers are hardly noteworthy things. Then he remembered something: the day that Stella had stomped into the office after a row with Benny Pederson, one of the Norwegian students, and called him 'a little fucking troll'. This had presumably gone into Nerys' minutes and had to be dealt with. Thus the team had had to up the ante and claim that Dan had said something even worse, though in reality no one ever went further than the 'f' word. No one had ever, to Dan's knowledge, used the 'c' word in the office. But even with this suitably fierce riposte concocted, Aileen would have not wanted to use anything that showed Stella in a bad light. Thus, the 'little fucking troll' remark was not reported, and all that was left was the riposte, hanging in mid-air without a context, without the thing being riposted.

The nepotistic appointments by Stella of her husband and sister-in-law were dismissed as 'expediency'. Things were tough at the time, and these brave souls stepped selflessly into the breach. Though, quite what was so urgent about Emma's summer job of sorting out Stella's filing and labelling her ring binders was not made clear. Also, Frank had suddenly remembered having interviewed Tim, having previously confirmed to Dan that because of the need for expediency he had not done so.

Tim's overpayment – his being paid a lecturer's rate when he was doing a technician's work of demonstrating plaster casting – was not explained by the fact that it was his wife who decided what he would be paid, but instead by the fact that casting was a technique used by the famous sculptor Rachel Whiteread, and Tim mentioned her in his workshops. This meant that there was a 'theory' element in his delivery, therefore his plaster casting workshops were lectures and he was a lecturer.

Bizarrely, whilst conceding that expediency had been at work and that family members had been appointed in a careless and privileged manner, Aileen concluded that this was not nepotism. Expediency doesn't only excuse nepotism; it changes it into something other than nepotism.

Aileen dismissed Dan's complaint about Linda Froggatt's privileged and unopposed appointment to Acting Course Director on the basis that no such appointment had been made. According to Aileen, all that had happened was that Linda had been asked to step up and take on a few of Stella's administrative burdens for a short period of time. This was quite simply a lie, though Aileen had not realised that she would be caught out. Frank Fuller had carelessly left Linda's letter of appointment on the staff server, and anyone with access to a Barts computer could read it. It congratulated her on the appointment and gave her a long list of duties: 2 pages worth, which amounted virtually to the same duties and responsibilities as the Course Director. And as for the 'short period of time' assertion: at the time of Aileen's Report, Linda had been in post for a year and a half.

Aileen also lied about Sky and Stella's extra holidays scam, again thinking that she would not be found out. She said that she had checked the records and had discovered that Sky and Stella *did* in fact have holidays booked on those occasions. When, during the investigation, Dan and Tony asked for sight of these records, Aileen refused to release them on the grounds that this would have been a breach of data protection legislation. Eventually, she was persuaded to release the whole team's holiday records, but with the names removed. This, she thought, would provide sufficient camouflage to make the truth impenetrable. However, given the small number of staff in the department, the different kinds of holiday allocation that different posts were entitled to and other fragments of information, Dan was easily able to work out which were Sky's and Stella's holiday forms, and sure enough, they had no holiday booked and they should have been at work. It also would not have made an awful lot of sense for Sky and Stella to have kept nipping back into the office to switch on computers and hang up coats, as they had, if they really had been on holiday. Sky and Stella had ripped-off the system and public money, and Aileen Dimley had chosen to lie to protect them.

Aileen's response to 3:1 teaching-to-prep ratio debate was to ignore Dan's explanation, that this was a figure used only for the research, design and planning of *new* teaching, and to conclude in her Report that Dan believed he should do 3 hours of admin for every hour of his teaching, whether it needed any preparation or not. He wasn't clear if she had failed to understand his explanation (which he had by now given to her twice: at both of the February Treetops Hotel meetings), or if she was simply falsifying the Report to show him in the worst possible light. There was ample evidence for either possibility. It would take an idiot to believe what Dan was alleged to believe. Aileen was doing her best to make him look like one.

Barsteadworth College

The issue of Stella dumping an unfair workload on Dan as a means of bullying was brushed aside. It could simply not be countenanced that Stella would use such a strategy, even though it is a classic workplace bullying tactic and Dan had provided abundant evidence of it. Far from evaluating this evidence, Aileen made no reference even to its existence. The fact that there were periods in which Stella had gone out of her way to change things in order to eliminate all of Dan's admin time so that he was forced to work extra days to catch up (and that records in timetables still contained the evidence of this) was ignored. It had to be something else. It was bad behaviour on Dan's part of various sorts. He was a 'jobsworth': he had an old fashioned industrial view of working arrangements, like a 1970s factory worker. He thought he should work his routine hours and then be paid for overtime. Dan's disgust at this brought another hiatus in his reading. He picked up the thread again 24 hours later.

It could hardly be further from a true description of Dan's working ethos. But the fact that this was simply not what had happened and there was no evidence to suggest that it had were irrelevant issues for Aileen. The fact that Dan routinely worked far more hours than he was contracted to without comment or claim was ignored, as was the fact that he had made clear in his submission that the only time he had tried to claim back was that which was wilfully, artificially, and unnecessarily pressed on him by Stella, for no reason he could think of other than spite.

The report moved on: a person like Stella, said Aileen, in her complex management role needed staff who were flexible, and Dan was inflexible.

The reality of the situation was that the kind of flexibility expected from Dan was that he should be available, at little or no notice, to work at any time during the five days of a week, even though he was a half-timer, and that the need for such flexibility usually stemmed from Stella's incompetent timetabling or her wish to dodge elements of her own teaching. Moreover, no-one else in the department was expected to work in this way; only Dan. Dan had explained this at length in the two Treetops Hotel meetings. Aileen, however, had failed to register any of it in the report and went on to attack Dan still further, and indeed to praise Stella.

For Aileen, far from Stella's timetabling being a chaotic mess, it was brilliant. Far from her falling short on one of the Course Director's basic tasks, she outstripped it. Stella had invented the idea of 'fluid' timetabling; a revolutionary new concept in which the relationship between the appearance of an event on a timetable and its actual occurrence was entirely arbitrary. Stella's 'fluid' timetable was the way forward, though it was clearly the case that this kind of advanced thinking was too much for a stuck-in-the-mud jobsworth twat like Dan.

And on it went in same vein. The team's counter-*arguments* were expanded into counter-*allegations*, which were either unsupported or supported by innuendo or invention, and then recorded as 'fact', and with the indulgence of (and, indeed, further input from) Aileen, the Report ceased to be an analysis of Dan's complaint and instead became a scathing appraisal of him as a person and tutor.

In the opening remarks of her conclusion, Aileen launched straight into a negative evaluation of Dan. His Grievance was nowhere to be seen. It was simply not the topic that Aileen was dealing with. She was not the concluding an investigation into his complaints; she was summarising her own and the team's rancorous demolition of Daniel Ripley. In case it was not already abundantly clear from the rest of the Report, reading through the conclusion made the existence of Aileen's separate agenda unmistakable. The additional covert meetings that had taken place between Aileen and the course team, which were not mentioned in her description of her methodology or permitted in the terms of the Grievance Procedure, were evident if only implicit: the Report contained the team's responses to things said at the 21st February meeting. She had given them the opportunity to speak both first and last: to help set the agenda, reset it in the light of Dan's Stage 2 presentation and make further last-minute allegations that Dan knew nothing about. As a consequence Aileen had predicated a substantial proportion of her conclusion on allegations which had been generated by herself and the course team, and which Dan had never had chance to challenge, and these she presented as 'facts'.

Aileen betrayed her prejudices still further. She went on to express dismay that Dan seemed so angry. In his meetings with Aileen, he had described years of subtle and not-so-subtle workplace bullying and the fact that he had been made seriously ill and had probably had his career destroyed by it. He was reliving his shame, anger and humiliation as her spoke. Damn right he got angry. But for Aileen, he had nothing to be angry about. She had long since rejected Dan's allegations and therefore excluded them from her thinking. Dan's anger was inexplicable because nothing had happened.

Aileen went on to blame Dan for what she called Stella's 'inconsistency': her endlessly contradictory instructions to Dan about what she wanted him to teach. According to Aileen, Stella had been 'emotionally exhausted' by Dan. The absurdities of this were multi-layered. For one thing, it had been Dan who had collapsed in a state of emotional exhaustion, not Stella. For another, the contradictory instructions had not come at the end of their exchanges, they had come at the beginning: Stella's condemnation of Dan's teaching and her failure to say what she wanted in its place was the source of their very first argument. She must have started out emotionally exhausted and gradually got better. And it had been Stella who had started the debate on what should be taught by condemning Dan's teaching. She had clearly had enough energy for that. The idea that she had suddenly become exhausted and did not have enough energy for another couple of sentences, to say what she wanted in its place, was ridiculous.

The bottom line in this was something that Aileen completely failed engage with: Stella could not suggest any alternative teaching, because she simply didn't know of any. She hadn't even known what the content was of the teaching that she had denigrated. She had attacked it in order to bully, and that was why she was unable to follow-through with any kind of sensible academic discussion on the topic. Meanwhile, Aileen had nothing to say about the emotionally exhausting impact on Dan of having his teaching publicly rubbished and then seeing lecture slots coming up on his timetable and not knowing what he was allowed to teach in them.

Aileen went on to denounce Dan for not being more sympathetic to Stella's emotionally exhausted condition. For Dan, this was like being punched in the mouth and then condemned for not showing concern for his assailant's bloodied knuckles. Taking this through to what she saw as its logical conclusion, Aileen reported that it demonstrated yet another deficiency in Dan's personality, made it clear that he was in possession of 'low emotional intelligence'. She did not, however, say what qualified her to make such an evaluation. This was one of the many points at which Dan had to put down the Report and walk away. He was simply knocked sick by it.

Each time he went back and tried to start again he was enraged, horrified and sickened once more. There was another feeling, too: betrayal. Having become ill, lost his strength and resilience and found himself in need of help, the people he had turned to, the people who were supposed to have caring procedures and policies in place, had not only failed to help, they had turned on him for daring to speak up. He had complained about Stella's ad hoc bullying, and Barts' managers had responded by formalising it. He felt worse now than he had at the start of the procedure. Yet somewhere, underneath all of this misery, there was something that was funny, ironic: having your intelligence – emotional or any other sort – criticised by Aileen Dimley was rather like having your attention span criticised by a goldfish.

For the further amusement of her readers, Aileen went on to do that thing she did in meetings and at staff development events: unearthed a load of completely irrelevant statistics and policy documents and quoted them in lengthy and pointless detail. Presumably, she imagined that this tour de force of administrative pedantry would impress Silas and the others.

Barsteadworth College

One thing Aileen did concede was that Dan was genuinely ill, though she could find no evidence that his illness was work-related. His GP had said it was; two Occupational Health Advisors appointed by Barts had said it was; the Mental Health Counsellor Dan's GP had referred him to had said it was; and Dan had said it was and had described in great detail the incidents at work that had caused the various stages of his gradual decline. But there was no evidence that Aileen could see.

Aileen had decided that the problem with Dan – well, one of the many problems with Dan – was that he was 'old school', stuck in the past and could not come to terms with Stella's radical modernising project. In addition to what she had already identified, Aileen had spotted another couple of examples to support this theory. Barts' management had decided that it needed to do something about the issue of nearly everyone being a director and had begun the process of change by renaming 'Course Directors' 'Course *Leaders'*. The fact that Dan still used the term 'Course Director' was clear evidence that he was wedded to the past. The fact that he had been off sick for 14 months trying to mend his mangled mind and knew nothing about this change was not considered.

Furthermore, Barts *used* to have a statistical system called 'Student Perception of Course Survey': 'SPOCS' for short (pronounced 'spocks', as in the pointy-eared bloke from Star Trek). This had been renamed too: it was now called 'Student Perception Survey', because someone – quite possibly Aileen – had pointed out at a committee meeting that it wasn't just about the students' perceptions of the *course*, it was about their perception of the whole Barts experience: support services, accommodation, car parking, demeanour of staff, canteen food, the lot. However, Dan, at the 21st February meeting, was still using the term 'spocks'. He was lost in the past – it was obvious. Dan did in fact know that SPOCS had been renamed – this had happened before he had gone off sick – but in common with many other Barts' employees, he still used 'spocks' because it was quicker in rapid exchanges in meetings than 'ess-pee-esses'. But in Aileen's book, common sense was no match for pedantry, and a man who used the wrong acronyms was clearly a fool.

Aileen didn't go into much detail about the ethos or content of Stella's modernising scheme, apart from the 'fluid' timetable. Had she done so, she would have described a rather surprising version of modernisation; one that involved ridding the course of recent developments in teaching and going back to a sixties/seventies hippy love-in kind of studio in which precious little teaching takes place; the eradication of contemporary theory in favour of those mainstays of early/mid-twentieth century thinking, Existentialism and the works of Franz Kafka; and the disregarding of guidelines taken on elsewhere to eliminate nepotism and bullying.

For Aileen, Dan was like a rabbit transfixed by the blinding light of Stella's brilliant new ideas, and it was entirely possible that it was the stress of being unable to cope with such radical change and of not being able to understand this difficult new thinking that were making Dan poorly. Certainly, it could not be the actions of Stella Jobby, who was very nice, and clever, too. Dan wondered where Aileen might have taken her argument, had she been capable of joined-up thinking. It wasn't only Dan who had been damaged by Stella's bullying and incompetence: Phil had complained about the same things as Dan over a long period and had himself gone sick with mental health issues before the Report was written, and Mervin had resigned because he couldn't stand the way Stella was treating him. Would their issues also be blamed on failure to engage with new ideas, when Mervin had never taught on a BA before and Phil was new to teaching, period, so neither had a past model of BA teaching for which to pine?

Dan reflected on Aileen's remark about 'low emotional intelligence'. This was not without significance, though like most of her report, it was 180 degrees out of kilter. It was hardly the case that Dan was unable to read Stella and her mental machinations; he probably read her better than anybody, and that may well have contributed to Stella's need to oppress him. And he was quite sure the rest of the team had worked her out too, though, for some, what they saw was clearly an attraction or, at least, useful. It took time with Stella to work out what she was about. She was devious, manipulative and spiteful, and had spent a lifetime honing those skills. And in the unlikely event that Dan couldn't have worked this out for himself in the long time he'd worked with her, he'd heard it from Bill Bulwark, Phil Flanagan and the Art House lot. Aileen was probably the only person involved in this who'd failed to work Stella out. She'd taken everything on face value. She had 'no reason to doubt' Stella, she had said at the start of the Report, and Stella had played her like a fiddle.

*****

Dan was devastated by the Report. In spite of everything, he'd had faith in Aileen and had believed that she would, on hearing the full misery of his experiences read verbatim from his dossier and corroborated by Phil Flanagan, have found in his favour. Not only had this *not* happened, things had gone into reverse. She had vilified him. Dan had gone from being – at the time of his collapse – a model employee who had never transgressed or been reprimanded in any way, was respected by everyone but his tormentors and would have been the Vice Principal's first choice for Fine Art Course Leader/Director, had he wanted the job, to – a year on – being a depraved, sexist jobsworth who was too dim to cope with new thinking, too awful to work with, so wicked that he deserved to be murdered, and in all probability possessed by the Devil. The Report was not just unfair; it was hateful, nasty, and vitriolic. There was not even the semblance balance about it. Aileen had used her role as Investigating Officer to defend Stella and her team and mount a sickening and cowardly attack on Dan. That was the whole point of the Report. It was far more important to keep things running smoothly, to maintain the facade of respectability, than to address issues such as those that Dan had raised. Problems would be dealt with behind the scenes, and anyone who did something official, like making a formal Grievance, would be punished. Barts' management, as an entity, would not tolerate complaints against itself. To complain was therefore a punishable offence and the Report was part of Dan's punishment.

Dan became ill again. He'd probably only been 50% of the way back to normal anyway, but this threw him right back to where he had been a year ago. He couldn't sleep; he couldn't wake up; not properly. He paced about; got in and out of bed at all times of the day and night. He couldn't concentrate. He'd struggled even to read the Report. At each turn he'd been appalled and devastated again; each lie, each distortion, each insinuation, each wilful omission of the truth; each was like an explosive blow to the guts that sent him reeling. And all the time he struggled to read it, he was reminded by Silas Beasley's accompanying letter that if he wanted to submit an Appeal he had to do so within 7 days.

Dan wrote to Silas to say that he would be submitting an Appeal and had started to write it. He got the letter to Silas within the required 7 days, but Silas wrote back to say that the rule was not that you had to submit *notice* of appeal within 7 days; you had to submit the Appeal *itself.*

The timescale was impossible and unfair: from first receiving Dan's complaint it had taken Barts' managers nearly a year to produce the Report. Yet Dan had to produce a detailed response within 7 days. It had taken him most of that time to read the thing, with the relapses it had brought on. Moreover, the situation was incongruous: the full Appeal *document* had to be submitted within 7 days, but Silas would then have to arrange a date when the Appeal *Hearing* would take place, which would necessarily be beyond 7 days. In fact, judging by the way things had gone so far, it could take months to organise. So what did it matter if it took Dan a couple of weeks to write his Appeal? Tony Rice rang Silas to work things out, and it was agreed that Dan would have more time to set out his Appeal.

*****

Dan requested an electronic copy of Aileen's Report, lifted it into a new Word document, saved it as 'Appeal' and began to address each point carefully. Every insinuation, unfair comment and lie was deconstructed and laid bare. Night and day he worked on it until it was done: Aileen's sentences in

Barsteadworth College

Times New Roman interspersed with his deconstructing commentary in Arial. But that was only part of it. His main grounds for appeal had to be set out to give a context to the now annotated Report.

The clear bias in Aileen's thinking was palpable, but things went further: to any reasonable person the whole report had become a carefully choreographed piece of character assassination, created by the course team with substantial input from Aileen herself, but it was also vital to recognise that there was important material missing from the report; the very material that made Dan's case. In short, the most breathtaking distortion in a wholly skewed report was nothing less than the complete omission of Dan's evidence. His bullying diary and the evidence of his only witness – Phil Flanagan – were missing. Aileen had turned what should have been an investigation of a complaint into a trial of the complainant. And at this trial, she had set herself up as the prosecution and the judge, and in the latter role had decided that any evidence in favour of the defendant was to be ruled inadmissible.

Thus, the key points in Dan's Appeal document were, firstly, that at the meeting of 21 February, he had read page after page from his bullying diary, which he had kept since things started to go awry nearly 3 years ago, giving a detailed account of events – and Nerys Crimp had minuted this – and yet, anyone reading Aileen Dimley's Report would have no inkling that the diary and its evidence ever existed. And secondly, Phil Flanagan, though interviewed with the rest, was excluded from the list and his deposition was simply erased from the record. Meanwhile, Aileen took everything that Stella and the team said as unquestionably true, and went on to add her own elements of character assassination on the basis of 'information' provided not only by those who would have liked to have hanged Dan, but also on that contrived and insinuated by herself.

Dan submitted his Appeal in the form of grounds for appeal and Aileen's Final 24-page Report, annotated with his own commentary. This made it 60 pages long. The full grounds for appeal were that the Report contained:

- disparaging comments made about Dan that were unsupportable and had nothing to do with his Grievance;
- evidence given by those who claimed not to remember the event on which they were giving evidence;
- evidence given by those who were not employees of Barts when the event on which they were giving evidence was alleged to have taken place;
- evidence given by those who were not present when the event on which they were giving evidence took place;
- the use of hearsay, sometimes from individuals several times removed from the investigation;

that Aileen had completely failed to examine the following:

- Dan's bullying diary; his detailed, diarised account of bullying and other malpractices in the department;
- that Stella had been working towards constructively dismissing Dan (as well as Phil and Mervin);
- Phil Flanagan's deposition;
- Stella's deliberate imposition on Dan of an unmanageable workload;
- the expunging of inconvenient minutes (dealt with instead as a 'failure to record');
- the unfair delegation of Course Leader duties to lecturers by Stella to reduce her own workload;
- breaching by Stella of SDR confidence;

that the following were reported as acceptable by Aileen, but she had used flawed or non-existent information to justify that acceptability:

- the unofficial promotion of Linda Froggatt to Acting Course Leader;
- unsanctioned leave taken by Sky Gelding and Stella Jobby;
- Tim Small's casting workshops deemed as lecturer work rather than tutor-technician demonstrations;

- Patricia Kleb's duplication of Dan's and Phil's teaching;
- Stella Jobby's connivance with the all of this;

and also, that Aileen had challenged Dan to give evidence that the Gelding-Froggatts and the Small-Jobbys were close friends, as they had denied it, but this issue had vanished once he had given his response. Dan had given in evidence that they kissed on parting, looked after each others' children and so on. Why was this answer not disclosed in the Report when Aileen had seen fit for it to be a question? Could it be that it was an inconvenient truth?

As Dan put the finishing touches to his Appeal, he was distracted by the metallic clap of the letterbox. Between two unbeatable offers of cheap finance and a chirpy postcard from Siobhan and Steve in Crete was a letter from the bank. He opened it. The computer-generated letter said that the bank was concerned that no money had been paid into his account for some time and he had exceeded his overdraft limit, and they would be pleased if he'd do something about this. He checked his account on the internet. He had not been paid since the end of March. He rang Barts and asked to speak to Nerys Crimp in Personnel. She was not available to come to the phone, nor was Perdita Box, or anyone else in authority. The temp who answered tried to deal with the enquiry. She could not; at least not straight away.

She rang back later. His pay had been stopped because the Report had been issued and the Grievance Procedure was therefore over... *hadn't he received the letter they had sent to say this was going to happen?* He hadn't. He never did.

Dan stapled a short covering letter to his Appeal and put it in an envelope, which he addressed to Silas Beasley. He then took the short walk up to the crusty brick post box on Tennyson Road. The letter explained how he'd structured the Appeal and said that he would not be able to present it in person: he was in no fit mental state to undergo another inquisition and, in any case, the text said everything he needed to say. The written Appeal *was* the Appeal.

What was also bearing on Dan's mind was that it been made clear that Treetops Hotel would not be on offer this time. The Appeal hearing would take place in Silas Beasley's office. *Not negotiable.* Dan had been unable to go anywhere near Barts since he'd first collapsed, and these recent events had thrown his recovery violently into reverse. This was not going to happen.

*****

June. Dan got his reply: a terse missive 'From the desk of Silas Beasley'. In an uncompromising tone it said that unless he appeared in person to present the Appeal, there would be no Appeal. Silas reckoned that according to the Grievance Procedure he could not *read* an Appeal sent to him in writing, he could only *listen* to one given in person. Dan close-read the Grievance Procedure once again, but could not see anything in its wording that made such a pedantic interpretation necessary. Such a debate was academic anyway: there was no way Dan could comply with the demand. Perhaps that was the point: make the Appeal go away by forcing Dan to default. But Dan couldn't compromise on this. He was borderline agoraphobic again. The doctor had had to increase his Citalopram dose to try and bring it under control. And that was making him woolly-headed again. And the cockroaches were back. He rang Tony Rice for help.

*****

"It took a long time to get hold of Beasley", said Tony. "We kept missing each other. He's been abroad or something."

Dan sat by the glass-topped dining table, silver Panasonic handset pressed to his ear, and gazed disconnectedly at the garden.

"We had quite a long conversation," continued Tony. "A lot of it you wouldn't want to hear."

"How do you mean?" said Dan.

"I mean, if what you've heard so far has got you into a state, you wouldn't want to hear all this."

"Such as?"

"I'm not telling you. It's just destructive. More of the same. There's no point. Let me put it this way, Silas said he wanted you to come in because there are serious questions you need to answer."

"WHAT?" Dan leapt up sharply from his chair and paced to and fro on the laminate flooring. "What have they come up with now? Am I murderer? A rapist? Don't tell me they've found the 'weapons of mass destruction'."

"Like I said, there's no point…"

"Well, he can fuck off. I had no 'serious questions' to answer before I complained. I was the model employee. Fuck him. That's the limit. Even if I'd felt like going in before, I wouldn't now. He's just confirmed it, hasn't he? It was supposed to be my Appeal – and *I've* got 'serious questions' to answer? Why should I be answering questions? Why should I be answering anything? It's my Appeal. It's he and his staff and his despicable management team who should be answering questions. The investigation process was turned into ritualised bullying and he wants to do more of the same with the Appeal. A show trial for defying the Fuhrer! That's what happens in fascist regimes, isn't it? Book-burning, guilt-by-association and now a show trial! Is none of this ringing a bell? Tell him to shove it."

"Right, well, if you've done: I did, in the end, manage to get him to change his mind. I quoted Equal Opportunities legislation. It says that allowances have to be made for those who are hindered by health issues, and since your mental health problems prevent you from going to Barts and making your presentation, he had to agree to accept a written Appeal."

After hanging up the phone Dan wondered what would happen next. There was no way Silas would back Dan against one of his Directors, but how could he dismiss an Appeal predicated on the fact that the appellant's evidence was excluded and Silas himself had never actually seen it?

*****

Dan opened the Barts-franked envelope and unfolded the contents onto the glass dining table. He'd been expecting this for a couple of weeks now. He knew exactly what it was when it arrived, and he knew pretty much what it would say. Silas' letter was short and not to the point. It simply failed to engage with anything Dan had said and went onto support Aileen wholeheartedly. The closest it came to acknowledging Dan's complaints was to say that Aileen had carried out a thorough investigation into them. However, she had found nothing to support his allegations, and this being the case, Silas could only agree with her findings. *Interesting logic: he can't support the Appeal because it disagrees with what the Report says.* So why bother to have Appeals? The fundamental point, that vital evidence had been withheld and therefore Silas was not in a position to arrive at a valid conclusion was disregarded. Even without seeing the evidence, Silas was clear in his mind that nothing had happened, and by implication, Dan had imagined it all.

*****

Dan replied to Silas to say that he found his response unsatisfactory and would appeal to the Board of Governors. It was, by now, September.

It was inconceivable, of course, that the Board of Governors would fail to support the Principal. But the whole thing had become a game by now: a meaningless paper-chase that had been flawed from the outset by its basic structure. Barts' management as a corporate body had been told it had done something wrong by one of its powerless underlings. It had then set itself the task of investigating itself. And guess what? It had found that it was perfectly all right after all, and that the complainant was in fact an evil little shit ever to have suggested otherwise. But he might as well see the dance through to the end, though, once again, he would be submitting his Appeal in writing. Apart from his psychiatric issues, there was another reason not to go: he had no desire to dignify proceedings. His presence would only serve to give validity to something that it was now clear would be rigged and meaningless.

Dan wanted to know who the Governors were and he imagined that such information would be public. It was, after all, the public's money of which they oversaw the spending. But he couldn't find this out from Barts' website or from the net in general, and Personnel wouldn't tell him: *Data Protection and all that*. But whatever the case, a Board of Governors was likely to be a varied group of people – some of them might even be open-minded – and at the very least Dan felt that if he could present his material to them it would embarrass Silas and his senior managers and might begin to change things at Barts.

Dan's Appeal to the Board of Governors was basically the same as the one he had sent to Silas, plus the evidence provided by Silas' letter, that Silas had effectively ignored the content of the first Appeal.

*****

The 'Board' of Governors, as such, never saw the Appeal. The Grievance Procedure allowed for a 'panel' from the Board to hear (or rather, *read*, in this case) the Appeal, but it did not define the term 'panel'. Thus, instead of the Appeal document being read by sixteen potentially concerned individuals, it was given to just three: the Secretary, Norman Swivel; a new Board member, Scott Sowerbutts, who was just feeling his way; and Chair of the Board of Governors, Neal Biffcock; local businessman, pie magnate, and close personal friend of Silas Beasley. Dan wasn't even sure if this number made it quorate.

*****

It was almost winter again by the time the Appeal took place. Dan received the deliberations of the panel from the Board of Governors' in a two-line letter. An Appeal meeting had taken place. The Appeal had not been supported. There was nothing in this to indicate that Dan's Appeal had even been considered. Dan suspected that because he hadn't been there, the panel had simply rubber-stamped Silas' decision and gone home. Dan wrote to Norman Swivel and asked for minutes.

*****

After some weeks the minutes had failed to arrive, so Dan wrote again.

Eventually, a reply came from Norman Swivel, written on Silas Beasley-headed paper. It said that the minutes had not yet been prepared. Evidently these would be the sort of minutes that were compiled some months after the meeting to which they pertained. Dan replied to say he looked forward with interest to reading them, once someone had written them.

Chapter Ten
This Year

New Year. Dan was back in his study once more, computer screen in front of him, piles of Barts headed paper scattered on all sides. Dealing with the successive layers of his Grievance Procedure had become his employment, and with Christmas done he was back at 'work', whatever that now meant. Like Kafka's *Josef K.*, his case had taken over his life.

The minutes of his Board of Governors Appeal had still not arrived. *Surely someone must have thought them up by now.* Dan typed out another reminder for Norman Swivel, though he didn't really expect a reply. He could imagine what was going on: there had been no evaluation of his Appeal and therefore nothing to minute, and they were all now scratching their heads, wondering how they could make the whole thing go away.

It was nearly two years since Dan's breakdown (and nearly one since Phil's – he was still off work and also going through Barts' pointless, tokenistic Grievance Procedure). Something had to give. Dan had exhausted the system and himself. The only thing left for him now was to take his case outside of Barts and go to a tribunal. However, Tony Rice advised him that if he had found the past few years emotionally exhausting, that was nothing to what would happen next, if he followed that course of action. And, ultimately, he couldn't win anyway. Things would roll on for years and the bottom line was that it was his word against theirs, and for everything he said, they could wheel in four or five people who would say the opposite, and they had already shown themselves as being quite prepared to lie. There was no chance of proving anything. The only glimmer of hope was that the union's solicitors had said that Aileen Dimley's Report had been so extreme in its bias and so bewilderingly brainless in the quality of its arguments – the worst they had ever seen – that it might undermine Barts' case. But this was a long shot, and Tony's advice was that Dan should either go back to work or seek a Compromise Agreement.

Dan could not go back to work in this situation. Apart from the fact that he was still far from well – the stress of running his case had done severe damage to his recovery – he simply could not go back into the circumstances that he would now have to face. His case had been overturned and the workplace bullies had been exonerated and praised by the Investigating Officer. Not only would this be yet more humiliation, it would give carte blanche to the bullies to pick up where they had left off, knowing that they would have the full support of Barts' senior management, in the event that they needed it again. That made leaving the only viable option. But he was still ill, there were no jobs to apply for and he didn't have the confidence to apply for anything anyway. Nevertheless, leaving was the only route left open. He asked Tony Rice to negotiate a Compromise Agreement.

*****

By the time the Compromise Agreement document arrived, Dan was resigned to his fate and felt strangely relaxed about it all. At least things were clear now. It was over. He'd lost his job, but with what he now knew he wouldn't want to work in that shit-hole anyway. It was time for a new start, whatever that would be. He extracted the Agreement from its windowed A4 envelope, flicked back the covering letter and read. It was a truly astonishing document. Tony had warned him that it would be. There was always a 'gagging clause', Tony had told him. Organisations don't like things like this going public. Dan could understand that a private company might want to keep things under wraps because of commercial sensitivities, even though from other perspectives, shutting up an aggrieved employee was to say the least morally dubious. Indeed, what was actually taking place could be seen as a form of bribery or blackmail: *you're losing your job, your income and quite possibly your career; if you want anything out of this at all, you keep quiet, ok*. But what struck him as odd in his case was that Barts was a publicly-funded teaching establishment, which should be transparent and publicly accountable in its dealings. Moreover, its senior management – the Principal and Board of Governors indeed – had forcefully made the case through the Report and the rejection of Dan's two

Appeals, that it had nothing to answer for, so why the coyness? Why not tell Dan to publish and be damned? And what did all this mean in times when transparency, accountability and freedom of information are supposed to be so important?

Dan studied the document. It was in very carefully worded legalese and its clear priorities were that nothing of what had taken place should ever be made public and that there should be no possibility of any later claim, should fresh evidence come to light or new, but related, health problems develop. Dan could not tell anyone what had happened to him at Barts or why he left; he could not tell anyone what the content of the Compromise Agreement was; he could not say anything, ever, that might damage Barts' reputation; he had to stop asking for minutes of the Governors' Appeal meeting; he could never make any kind of claim now or in the future against Barts for injury; and he could not tell anyone what the level of compensation was.

He got £6,767 in compensation for loss of office and £2,116 in lieu of missed holidays. After tax it came to just over eight grand. He took it to the Mazda garage, traded in the Rover and bought a little blue sports car.

www.ingramcontent.com/pod-product-compliance
Lightning Source LLC
Chambersburg PA
CBHW030407020726
47493CB00003B/977